AND BABY MAKES THREE

Before seeking his own room, Trevor decided to look in on Ashley. As he opened the door to her room, he saw the glow of a candle. Beside the bed, Caitlyn looked up as he entered.

They stood in companionable silence gazing at the angelic countenance of their child asleep. Trevor could not resist reaching to touch an errant blonde curl.

"She is so beautiful," he whispered. Profoundly moved, he turned to Caitlyn and made no effort to hide his emotions. "Thank you. Thank you for giving me this child."

Her response was a soft, nervous laugh. "Perhaps I should thank you. Ashley is quite simply the best thing that ever happened to me." Her eyes shone brightly in the candlelight.

Not knowing what to say, he reached for her hand and locked his fingers tightly with hers. They stood in quietness for a few moments, each lost in thought; then she gently disengaged her hand. She extinguished the candle as they left Ashley's room and descended the stairs to their own chambers. Reacting to the shared moment, Trevor felt a wave of desire, not just to possess Caitlyn's body, but to erase her concern, to protect and cherish . . .

Books by Wilma Counts

WILLED TO WED

MY LADY GOVERNESS

THE WILLFUL MISS WINTHROP

THE WAGERED WIFE

Published by Zebra Books

THE
WAGERED
WIFE

Wilma Counts

ZEBRA BOOKS
Kensington Publishing Corp.
http://www.zebrabooks.com

This one is for Joyce—and for Nick and Linda

*Who says once bratty siblings
cannot become treasured friends?*

One

May, 1808

"How long do you intend to continue burying yourself in debauchery, little brother?" The Honorable Marcus Jeffries addressed what might have been a younger version of himself—had he been suffering the aftereffects of a night of pursuing the bottom of a bottle.

Trevor lifted his aching head from the pillow and squinted against the light when Marcus flung open the drapes. "As long as it takes. What are *you* doing here? Did Hansen not tell you I am not in?"

"He told me. My God, Trevor, how can you live like this? This room reeks." Marcus pushed the window open to let in fresh spring air.

"Go away, Marcus. It will do no good for *you* to ring a peal over my head. Our estimable father—the ever-so-worthy Earl of Wyndham—*and* his heir were here before you last week."

"I know. They told me. Thought you might listen to me."

"Oh, I'll listen. Not much choice, eh? I'll even *want* to do as you wish. But always it comes back. I keep seeing that damned carriage and Terrence and Jason just lying there . . ."

"Trev—it was not your fault—"

"Yes! It was! If I had not pushed the idea of the race . . . They did not even want to buy that team, you know."

"It was an accident. No one blames you."

"Well, they should." Trevor ran a hand through his dark-brown hair. "*I* should have been driving."

Marcus snorted derisively. "With a broken hand? I doubt it."

"Could we talk about something else? Maybe say goodbye as you leave?"

"I'm not leaving. Now get yourself out of that bed. Robbins is preparing a bath for you, and Mrs. Simpson is sending up some coffee and food."

Trevor groaned and pulled himself to a sitting position. He knew his brother well enough to know that Marcus would not give up. And perhaps—just perhaps—talking with Marcus would keep the memories at bay.

But as he settled into the tub, they returned. Everything reminded him of Terrence—even the smell of his bath soap. And why should it be otherwise? After all, he and Terrence had shared everything all their lives—even the womb before they saw light of day.

And now Terrence was gone. Along with quiet, amiable Jason Garret with whom the twins had shared so many schoolboy escapades.

And Melanie. Do not forget Melanie. You ruined her life, too, he told himself. *She and Jason might have made a match of it but for your selfish need to see what a pair of prime goers could do.*

He would give anything—anything—to undo that day. He had talked Terrence and Jason into joining him in the purchase of a racing curricle and a splendid team of grays. Despite the others' reservations, the three of them had felt like real men of the town—cocky, sure of themselves, reveling in a marked degree of popularity. He knew how they were viewed—those handsome Jeffries twins and their friend Jason. An inseparable threesome. Invited everywhere.

"Trevor! Are you going to take all day?" Marcus called through the open dressing room door, interrupting the reverie.

"I'm coming." Trevor grabbed at the dressing gown Robbins held out to him.

Soon he was seated at a small table devouring poached eggs and toast that had been sent up on a tray. Marcus sat across from him, sipping a cup of coffee.

Finally, Trevor sat back and eyed his brother. At nine-and-twenty, Marcus was eight years older than Trevor. His hair was slightly darker, but the blue-gray eyes were a mirror of Trevor's own. Trevor had only to regard Marcus to see himself a few years hence. The mature body of his older brother was fuller, more muscular than Trevor's slim, wiry physique, but they both had large, well-shaped hands.

"Well? Out with it," Trevor demanded. "I suppose Father and Gerald sent you."

"As a matter of fact, they did not. However, you must know we all care about your welfare. Melanie is beside herself with worry."

"Rubbish. Father and Gerald care only for their precious earldom and their standing with the *ton*. Melanie *might* care—"

"Of course she does. Good grief, Trevor, Terrence was our brother, too. This wallowing in self-pity has to stop. It has been four months since the accident."

"Self-pity? Is that how you see it?"

"For the most part, yes. All right—it was an accident. An unfortunate accident. And if there is any blame to be laid at a doorstep, there seem to be candidates enough."

Trevor gestured dismissively. "You just do not seem to understand—"

"I know there was more than your vehicle out there racing on a public thoroughfare. What were there—five? Six?"

"Five."

"All right. Five. And the race was not your idea, was it? I understand it was Fitzwilliam who suggested it. True?"

"Yes. But what does it matter now?"

Marcus stood and began pacing. "*He* should have known

better than to issue such a challenge to a bunch of greenlings—young bucks like you."

"Now see here." Trevor straightened up, taking umbrage at his brother's condescending tone. "We knew what we were about."

"Sure you did. But it was Fitzwilliam who collected on all those bets, was it not?"

"Fitz won the race. He even offered to forgive my loss, but as it was a debt of honor—"

Marcus snorted. "More like dishonor, I should say."

"Look. I know you have no great liking for Fitz, but he is our—my—friend. 'Twasn't *his* fault that farmer's cart pulled out in front of Terrence and Jason."

"Perhaps not, but Fitzwilliam was in the class ahead of me at school. Always instigating things that made him look good—and left him free of blame."

"Be that as it may—"

"Trevor, do you not wonder why a fellow well into his thirties seeks the association of men so much younger than himself?"

"Maybe because we ain't into our dotage yet?" Trevor raised an eyebrow in sarcasm.

"And maybe," Marcus said grimly, "he finds preying on green boys extremely profitable."

"Having reached my majority, I am hardly what you would term 'a green boy.' " Trevor knew his voice had become haughty and defensive. "Did you come here this morning—sorry—this afternoon—to choose my friends for me?"

"No. I came to discuss the Bennington Trust with you."

"What about it?" Trevor vaguely recalled his maternal grandmother having left funds for her daughter's younger children.

"With Terrence gone, the trust is to be divided between you and me and Melanie. As the eldest—that is, the eldest of the younger sons—I, along with the solicitors, control the distribution of the trust."

"So? We knew that. Grandmother Bennington was such an old pinchpenny there cannot be a great deal of money involved. Remember that ancient carriage she went around in? Her clothing was always woefully outdated, and her drawing room carpet was positively threadbare."

"She was a frugal soul."

"So just give me my twenty guineas and I shall use it to start tonight's game."

"That is what I feared." Marcus resumed his seat. "It is considerably more than twenty guineas, Trevor." He named a sum that Trevor found hard to fathom at first.

"Wha-a-t? You cannot be serious."

"Yes." Marcus repeated the amount. "However, there is a catch—"

"Why does that not surprise me?"

"Apparently, our grandmother was more astute than any of us gave her credit as being. Your share of the fortune is the Atherton estate in Suffolk. Properly managed, it could produce a tidy income, but it cannot be sold—only passed on to your heir."

"Are you saying there is no money in hand now?"

"That is precisely what I am telling you."

"What about you? And where would Terrence have fit in all this?"

"Terrence and I were to share the investments on the 'Change, from which part of Melanie's dowry is to come as well. I shall continue to manage the investments and will share with the two of you Terrence's portion of the profits as they accrue. *When* they accrue."

"There are none now?"

"No. Napoleon's blockade of British shipping has hit us rather severely."

Trevor recognized his brother's propensity for understatement.

"Hell! Damn! Blast!"

"Just so, little brother. You must curb your profligate ways.

Father has reached the end of his patience with you. There will be no increase in your allowance from him."

"Hah! When did Father ever show patience with any of us but Gerald—and you on occasion?"

"You may have a point. Well . . ." Marcus set his hands on his knees and rose. "I must be off."

While he did not do so intentionally, in the weeks that followed, Trevor nevertheless dismissed from his mind the interview with Marcus. There was too much of his father's and Gerald's stodginess in the second brother, Trevor told himself. True, Marcus was not nearly so pompous as Gerald—and had always been more understanding of the younger siblings than either the earl or his heir. Still, the age difference was such that the twins had never had much in common with either of the two older boys.

Trevor was sure Gerald had been born with a middle-aged mind-set. And he thought Marcus had long since forgotten how to have fun. Terrence would have understood. And Melanie seemed to.

In this, her second season, Melanie was well received. She had gone into mourning for their brother and had only recently gone into half-mourning. Trevor knew she had had more than one offer of marriage.

One afternoon he called at the Wyndham townhouse primarily to see Melanie, though his mother was in the drawing room when he arrived and deigned to acknowledge her son. The townhouse was his mother's residence, since the earl rarely came to town—except when he wanted to dress down an errant child, Trevor thought sourly.

"Oh, Trevor, you are just in time to drive me in the park," Melanie said as she bade one of her suitors goodbye.

"You failed to talk Thornton into doing so?" He gestured to the closing door.

"He offered. I want to spend time with you," she said brightly.

Instantly he was on his guard. "I do hope *you* are not going to join the rest of the family in haranguing me about how I spend my time and the company I keep," he said, sounding defensive even to his own ears.

"I am sure you deserve such—but no, that is not my intention. So will you drive me?"

"No. I will gladly walk with you, but you know very well I do not drive or ride for any but the most necessary purposes anymore."

"I forgot," she said contritely and placed a hand on his arm. "I heard Bellson bought the grays."

"And my hunter."

"I'm sorry, Trev. Surely you do not blame the animals for what happened."

"No, of course not. Just my insane interest in them. I shall never again allow myself to become involved with horses for sport or pleasure."

"But, Trev, you love them so. Even when we were small children, you loved them far more than Terrence and I did. We feared them at first. You never did."

"And look what disaster my obsession wrought . . ."

She had started up the stairs to the bedchambers above. She paused on the first step, turned, and took his face in both her hands, forcing him to hold her gaze.

"Trevor, it was an accident." She clipped each word off precisely. "It was not your fault. You must stop this."

He held her gaze a moment, then looked away. "Hurry on up and get your cloak," he said.

As they walked along toward a small park a few minutes later, he turned to his sister.

"Out with it, Mel. What is it you wanted to tell me without the countess hearing?" The twins and Melanie had always referred to their mother in this impersonal fashion. Early on they had realized that the position of countess was infinitely more important to her than the role of mother.

"Um . . . you know Sir Andrew Sheffield, do you not?"

"Drew? Of course. We were in school together, though he was two classes ahead of Terrence and me."

"Wh-what do you think of him?"

"Nice enough fellow. Why?" He paused and turned to her.

She colored up. "Well . . . he and I . . . we . . . he has called several times," she ended lamely.

"I see. I always thought you and Jason . . ."

"I know," she said gently, "but that was a young girl's infatuation. Perhaps it would have eventually progressed to something more, but . . ." She paused. "Andrew is . . . Oh, Trev, I truly do care for him."

"So what is the problem?"

"The countess, of course. Andrew is a younger son. His father is a mere baron."

"I see. This *is* an obstacle—for her."

"How do I get round her?"

"Hmm. Enlist the aid of Marcus, to start with. She usually attends what *he* says."

"What about Aunt Gertrude? She is acquainted with Andrew's family."

"Good Lord, no! The countess detests Aunt Gertrude. Wait. If Aunt Gertrude were to *oppose* such a match, our esteemed mother would automatically approve it."

Melanie laughed. "Yes, but Andrew says Aunt Gertrude is quite fond of him."

"Well, if it would put a stick in our mother's wheel, I am sure Aunt Gertrude could be persuaded to dissemble. Would you like me to speak to her?"

"Oh, Trev, would you? Please?"

He patted her hand. "You are sure this is what you want?"

She was sure. They spent a pleasant hour sharing bits of gossip and irreverent observations on the antics of various members of the *ton's* elite.

Later, however, Trevor admitted to himself he had been taken aback by his sister's *tendre* for Andrew Sheffield. Not that there was anything wrong with Sheffield. Fine fellow. A rising star in diplomatic circles, if rumor was to be credited.

It was just that . . . well . . . Melanie seemed to be getting on with her life so easily. Was *he* the only one who treasured the memory of Terrence and Jason? Was he alone in continuing to mourn them?

God! How he missed them. He wished Terrence were with him tonight. He could always count on Terrence to say "Enough" without getting his—Trevor's—back up.

And play was likely to be deep this night.

He shrugged. His luck was due to change. . . .

It was late. Very late, Trevor thought, judging by the level of liquid in the brandy bottle at Lord Fitzwilliam's elbow. Fitz still sat at the table, though he had ceased playing some time ago. Others who had also played earlier stood around the table idly watching the play. Only two players remained— Trevor and Baron Fiske, a balding man of middle years with small, pale-blue eyes in a round, too-soft face. There was nothing soft about his hard look of triumph as he raked in his winnings.

"Another hand, sir?" he asked invitingly.

"I should dearly love to accommodate you, my good man," Trevor said a trifle too expansively, "but I fear you have reduced me to penury."

"Oh, come now. Not as bad as all that."

"No, but uncomfortable all the same. Tonight's losses along with the vowels you already hold put me sadly in your debt, sir." It occurred to Trevor that, had he not imbibed from the bottle quite so freely, he might be less frank about the state of his finances.

Fiske gave him a speculative look. "Sure you will not go one more hand?"

"Sir, I've nothing of value left to wager."

"Oh, I would not say that," Fiske suggested in soft innuendo.

"I shall redeem those when I have my quarterly allowance." Trevor pointed at an appalling stack of IOUs. *Though how on earth I will meet any other obligations is beyond me,* he thought. *How on earth—or why—had he allowed himself to get in so deep? Oh, God, Terrence, I needed you this night.* He looked over at Fitz, who seemed to give him a look of sympathy.

"I should be glad to give you a chance to redeem them now, Jeffries." Fiske calmly shuffled and reshuffled the cards.

"You do not understand. My pockets are to let. I have nothing left to wager."

"Oh, but you have."

Trevor gave a short, scornful laugh. "I have no idea what it would be."

"You. Or more to the point, your name."

"What do you mean?" Trevor looked from the baron's beady eyes to Fitz, who shrugged and looked away. Others seemed to tense with anticipation.

"It is my intent, young man, to make you a wager you cannot refuse," Fiske said.

"You are free to try." Trevor was both curious and disinterested. He knew he should get up and leave, but he sat and took yet another sip of brandy.

"I propose we play one more hand," the older man said. "If you win, I will turn over all your vowels of indebtedness to you."

"Go for it, Jeffries," a voice on the sidelines said. "You've had three devilish bad hands in a row. Next one has to be a winner."

"Easy for you to say," another voice said, but Trevor was looking at Baron Fiske.

"And if I lose?"

"If you lose," the baron replied, "I will still turn them

THE WAGERED WIFE 17

over to you." He paused as others leaned in closer. "But—you will marry my ward—my wife's niece—before the week is out."

There were several gasps, but no one said anything, waiting for Trevor's response.

"Ridiculous. Impossible." Trevor started to rise.

"Now just hold on, son. I think tonight's losses along with those from previous sessions amount to a good deal more than a quarter's allowance—even for one of Wyndham's sons."

"So? You know I will honor my debts."

"But I should like them settled sooner than later, you see." Fiske squinted his little pig eyes at Trevor in a cold look. "I should hate to have to approach your father . . ."

Trevor felt his stomach knot up. The last time his father had bailed him and Terrence out of a scrape, the earl had cast him a glare that made the baron's frigid look seem positively tropical by comparison. And then had come the humiliating lecture, telling them precisely how worthless his younger sons were. And this situation was worse by far.

He returned the baron's stare. "Win or lose, the debts are cleared, right?"

Fiske smiled mechanically. "Right."

"Don't do it, Trev," someone said.

The baron turned a malevolent eye on the speaker. "This is none of your concern, young man."

"At least get a new deck," another voice said. "For luck."

"An' let Fitz deal," the same voice added.

"All right by me," the baron said. "You?" he asked. Trevor shrugged his acquiescence.

The new deck was called for, and silence weighed heavily until it arrived. Lord Fitzwilliam shuffled the cards thoroughly and offered them to Trevor to cut. He dealt the two hands and waited. There was none of the usual betting—after all, there was only one wager on the table. *My life,* Trevor thought ruefully.

Trevor exchanged two cards. The baron exchanged three, and the dealer turned up the trump card. The baron took the first trick. They seesawed back and forth. The tension in the room mounted. The players were even when it came to the last trick. Trevor's last card was a king, giving him great hope. He laid it on the table.

Only to have the baron trump it.

For a moment, Trevor thought he might be violently ill. He closed his eyes and took a deep breath.

"Well, son, you are about to join the ranks of married men." The baron fairly chortled as he handed over the stack of IOUs. "We shall set the ceremony for Saturday morning. Perhaps you will call tomorrow to meet your bride."

"Saturday will be soon enough," Trevor said.

"As you wish."

Two

"You wished to see me, ma'am?" Miss Caitlyn Maria Woodbridge entered her aunt's sitting room feeling both curious and apprehensive. In general, Aunt Sylvia ignored her niece's presence in the household.

"Yes, my dear. Do come in and close that door so we may be private. Sit there." Sylvia Fiske pointed to a particular chair, and Caitlyn felt her inner tension grow. She sat and began nervously pleating and repleating her skirt.

"I have great news for you, Caitlyn."

"You—you have?" Caitlyn's experience was that, when Aunt Sylvia broached a topic with such patently artificial enthusiasm, the news did not bode well for others.

"Your uncle has arranged a splendid match for you, darling." Aunt Sylvia clasped her hands together in a show of delight.

"Oh." A tremor of fear assailed Caitlyn; then she relaxed. "Oh. Bertie did persuade his father to relent."

"Bertie? Oh, you mean that Latham boy. No, my dear. Hubert Latham is the son of a mere viscount. Fiske has arranged your marriage to the son of an earl. Is that not wonderful?"

Caitlyn was struck speechless. No. This could not be happening to her. And Aunt Sylvia expected her to believe such a disaster to be "wonderful"?

"But . . . but I do not know any earls—or their sons."

Caitlyn focused on the obvious to try to think as she absorbed this news.

Her aunt ignored Caitlyn's comment. "You are a very lucky girl. You will be connected with one of the finest families in England."

Caitlyn had thought the Lathams quite a fine family. After all, was her aunt not always bragging of her own association with Lady Latham, lioness of society in their parish? Caitlyn knew Lord Latham wielded a good deal of power as the largest landowner in the area. The Latham estate ran parallel with her uncle's. That was how she and Bertie had become acquainted—how long ago? Ah, seventeen months, two weeks and three days ago. Dear, sweet Bertie.

"There must be some mistake, Aunt. Bertie—"

"Forget Bertie. The Lathams would never countenance such a match for their son."

"No, not now, perhaps. I—we—know we are very young. Bertie has not quite eighteen years—but in a few years—"

"And you are nearly seventeen. But it matters not. Latham has made it quite clear you would never be suitable. Not that your uncle and I ever had such presumption as to think otherwise."

"I—I do not understand." Caitlyn fought to quell threatening tears. "Lord Latham was always very kind to me when we chanced to meet."

"You mistook mere courtesy for approval. I am sorry, my dear." The baroness sounded neither sorry nor affectionate. "You will simply have to put the Latham lad out of your mind."

"But . . . but I love Bertie. And he loves me."

"Love! What does a green girl like you know of love? Now you listen to me, young lady." Her voice turned hard and her dark eyes glared. "The marriage is arranged. And a very fortunate one it is. After all, you have no dowry, you come from a family of nobodies, and you are certainly not a 'diamond of the first water' as far as looks go."

Her aunt's cruel words released the tears Caitlyn had held back. "My . . . my parents were perfectly acceptable," she insisted.

"Barely. Your father was a country vicar—hardly a member of the *ton*. And your mother certainly improved her social standing when she became my stepsister—only to throw it all away by marrying a clergyman."

"My parents loved each other." Caitlyn stifled a sob.

"And look where it got them. And you."

"I do not want to marry this stranger."

"You have no choice," her aunt said coldly. "Fiske cannot be responsible for you forever. You are far too young to become a governess—and you look much younger—even had you the education for such."

Caitlyn stifled another sob. She knew that her aunt spoke only the truth. Spoken brutally, but the truth all the same.

"How long . . . when . . . how many weeks until . . . ?"

"The wedding will take place Saturday."

"Saturday! But that is only three days away. But—the banns. What about banns?"

"Not necessary. A special license is being obtained. Now run along, Caitlyn, and wash your face. Fiske will not be pressed for a season for you after all, so he has agreed to a new gown for you to be married in."

"How very generous of him." Caitlyn was sure the irony in her tone was lost on her aunt.

Back in her own chamber, she flung herself on her bed and sobbed aloud. "Oh, Bertie. Bertie. All our plans, our dreams . . ." If only they were older. If only they had control of their own lives. . . . When she had cried herself out, it finally occurred to her that her aunt had not mentioned, and she herself had not asked, the name of her betrothed.

In another neighborhood, that young man's despair matched her own. His eyes held a bleak, trapped expression as he welcomed a visit from his longtime friend Theo Ruskin, a captain in His Majesty's Army.

"I heard about what happened," Ruskin said. "God! I'm sorry I was not there."

"You missed quite a show."

"No. I meant I might have been able to help avoid this disaster."

"I doubt it. I have fairly done it this time."

"Can you not go to your father and explain?"

"Good God, no. He would have a fit of apoplexy. You know how he is."

"What about Lord Gerald? Or Marcus?"

"No, Theo. I cannot do that. I got myself into this."

"I doubt you could be held to this affair legally."

"Look. I *am* of age. It is a debt of honor, after all. Worse things have happened to stupid young men."

"Have you even met the girl?"

"No."

"Perhaps she will cry off."

"Not likely. Denton knows the family. Her father was a churchman. Good connections, but no blunt. The girl's been living on Fiske's charity since her father died."

"And friend Fiske is not noted for his charity," Theo said.

Trevor merely grunted in response.

"Don't you even *want* to meet her?" Theo was plainly curious.

"Saturday is soon enough. I shall have a whole lifetime to know her."

"You seem extraordinarily complacent about this, Trevor."

"It is merely a matter of accepting the inevitable. Either that—or go insane. Come, let us make the most of the time I have left."

The two young men planned to spend the next two days in a continuous round of high living. First, however, Trevor had to take time out to pay a morning call on his aunt, Lady Gertrude Hermiston. Aunt Gertrude, a sister-in-law to Lydia,

Countess of Wyndham, was a widow, having lost her husband in "that unfortunate war with the colonies." She was a woman of independent means—and an even more independent demeanor.

As a new widow, she had been subjected to innumerable lectures from the countess—for whom Gertrude had no great liking. Lydia had assumed that Gertrude would turn over her affairs to Wyndham to handle. When Gertrude refused to do so, both the countess and the earl were quite put out with her. Then Gertrude compounded the "error."

Once she came out of mourning, she found her dead husband's sister determined to play matchmaker. The trouble was, Gertrude had no interest whatsoever in the useless fribbles Lydia found so fascinating. Trevor recalled vividly his mother's complaints of being embarrassed by her ties to such a "bluestocking." Nor did his father have much time for his wife's in-law relative. Gertrude made no secret of the fact that she found the Earl of Wyndham to be singularly boring, pompous, and prosy. Thus it was that the elder Jeffries and Lady Gertrude seldom sought each other's company.

When her husband's title passed to a distant relative, Lady Gertrude had chosen to reside in town, for, as she put it, the new viscount and his family did not need her around to supervise them. Besides, she had dozens of pursuits in town that commanded her attention. She lived modestly on her dowager's pension, and moved in several worlds of *ton* society. These included political circles, her precious literary society, and a social reform group whose current interests focused on rescuing children sold to chimney sweeps and country girls lured to London's streets.

While their parents had little to do with the eccentric Gertrude, Wyndham's younger children had always adored her. She made children feel important. She took them fishing and on picnics. In town, she did not shrink from visiting the menagerie at the Tower with them, nor the "horrors" of the wax museum—though she steadfastly refused to allow them to see a hanging or a flogging. When they were old enough to see such things on their own, the twins had fully understood her reasoning.

"Trevor! Dear boy." His aunt turned up her cheek for his obligatory kiss when he was shown into her private sitting room. She gave him a keen look and then said, "It must be something important for you to seek the company of an old crone like me."

"Now. Now. No fishing for compliments. You know very well you put many younger women to shame—and Lord knows, you are infinitely more interesting!"

"So—I get compliments anyway. But what is it—really?"

"You mean besides merely enjoying your company?"

"Yes, besides that." He caught the rich irony in her tone.

"Well, it is Melanie. She needs your help."

"And why does she not simply ask me herself? Not like her to resort to roundaboutation."

"She—we—thought it best if the countess did not know— and Melanie visiting you would surely get back to our dear mother."

Lady Gertrude sighed. "I gather Lydia is on her high horse about something?"

"Not yet. But she is likely to be." Trevor explained about Melanie's attachment to Andrew Sheffield and the proposed role for their Aunt Gertrude. "So—will you help?"

"There is nothing untoward about the Sheffield lad. Fine boy. Of course I will help. Let me see . . ." She tapped her nails on the arm of her chair. "It should not be difficult. Lydia and I do often go about in the same circles. I shall just quietly warn her away at some tea or musicale. That should do it."

Trevor chuckled. "I am sure it will. If you determine a thing to be black, the countess is sure to label it white."

"Now." Lady Gertrude looked her nephew directly in the eye. "What about you? How are *you* doing? I keep hearing disturbing things."

Good God, Trevor thought. *Had word of that blasted card game already reached the* ton's *drawing rooms?* "Such as?" he asked, stalling.

"Well, I am told you sold your cattle."

"True. I did."

"Was that wise?"

"I think so." He knew his tone sounded bleak. "They no longer held my interest."

"I see . . ." Her tone suggested she would not press him on that subject. "I also hear you spend a good deal of time in the company of Dexter Fitzwilliam."

Trevor shifted uneasily. "He is a friend, yes."

"Well, take care, my son. I am sure you know what you are about, but I do hear disquieting rumors about that man."

"I will." He rose to take his leave. "And—thank you."

He wanted to pour out this latest trouble of his own to her sympathetic ears. But no. That would not be the manly thing to do. He would just have to muddle through this on his own.

On the eve of the wedding, Trevor and Theo spent the entire night on the town, returning to Trevor's quarters only in time to freshen up and change for the event. Arriving at the church—actually a small chapel—they found the Fiskes there before them. *Oh, my God,* Trevor thought on seeing his bride for the first time.

He had hoped—dreamed—that one day he would marry a beautiful woman of sophistication and poise. He had always leaned toward tall, ultra-slim blondes with style and flair. The female clearly needing to be prodded in his direction was not quite of medium height. Her head *might* be even with his shoulder. She had light brown hair and eyes that reminded him of the sea, despite their being red-rimmed and filled with despair. She seemed inordinately pale, causing a profusion of freckles to stand out across her nose. She was rather plump and wore a pink gown with far too many flounces for a woman of her proportions.

"I thought you said she was nearly seventeen," Theo whispered.

"She is. But she looks about fourteen, eh?" Trevor whispered back.

"Ah, Mr. Jeffries." Fiske greeted them affably. "I see you brought your own witness. Good. Good."

Introductions were made all around, and Trevor tried to smile encouragingly when he caught the girl studying him. It felt more like a grimace than a smile. She looked away without returning his gesture of goodwill.

"Well, shall we get this over with?" Fiske asked, leading the way to the front of the chapel.

"Trevor." Theo put a hand on his friend's shoulder. "You can still back out."

Trevor returned Theo's sincere gaze and merely shook his head.

Caitlyn stumbled through the ceremony as in a trance. Two days ago she had received a note from Bertie, smuggled to her through a kitchen maid. She imagined a tearful Bertie writing it secretly. She was especially touched by his quoting from Shakespeare's *Romeo and Juliet*. Caitlyn would always have his heart, he told her.

As she stood to repeat her vows, she stole another peep at this stranger who would be her life's mate. She had not expected him to be so tall. Nor so handsome. No, that was not right. He was not precisely handsome, was he? Attractive. That was it. He *seemed* amiable enough.

When the minister pronounced them man and wife, her new husband leaned to kiss her on the cheek. She smelled a mixture of shaving soap and spirits on him. Had he had to fortify himself for the ordeal? Was he as willing a party to this affair as she?

The necessary documents signed, he took her by the elbow and propelled her toward the door and a waiting carriage that would take them to his estate in Suffolk. Her aunt and uncle stood beside the carriage as she was handed in.

"Do let us hear from you, dear," her Aunt Sylvia said with a great show of affectionate cheer.

Caitlyn stared at them, marveling inwardly at the hypocrisy. The previous day she had gone to the library to try once more to persuade her uncle to change his mind. The door was ajar and her aunt was with him. Aware that they were discussing her, she did not knock. Instead, she deliberately listened. She remembered later her mother's oft-repeated adage about eavesdroppers never hearing good of themselves.

"—never would have taken her in in the first place," her uncle had been saying.

"It was our *duty* to do so. Caitlyn is family."

"Not really. There are no blood ties with a *step*sister."

"Well, then, there was a moral obligation, and we have fulfilled it—thanks to you, my clever love." Aunt Sylvia was doing it a bit brown, Caitlyn thought.

"It cost me a bundle, but we shall be free of her."

" 'Tis not like it was money out of hand, though, love," his wife replied.

"No. And it ended by being much less than it would have cost to sponsor her for a season. Don't know why you insisted on a season for her."

"My dear sir," her aunt said playfully, "you know very well it would have taken that and more to find that girl a husband. I truly dreaded the prospect."

"But I saved you the trouble."

"Yes. Not to mention saving yourself the expense."

"Wyndham will not be thanking me, I'm thinking."

"What can he do?" Sylvia Fiske asked, her scorn sounding clearly in her voice. "The boy is of age, after all."

"Yes, he is. But Wyndham and his heir are said to be rather high sticklers. I cannot think they will welcome a little country nobody into their family."

"Unfortunate, but not our concern after tomorrow."

Caitlyn had turned away, knowing there was, indeed, no hope now.

She did not have even the comfort of running to the stables here in town, for her uncle kept no carriage or cattle here, preferring to save himself that expense. In the country she had had the freedom of the stables. That freedom and access to his rather limited library had been her only comforts after losing her father and being taken in by Baron and Baroness Fiske nearly two years ago.

That is, until she had made the acquaintance of the shy, sensitive son of the neighboring viscount. She and Hubert had been immediately drawn to each other. Hubert seemed as neglected by the adults in his household as she was, for the two of them spent hours together riding across the countryside.

Often dear Bertie would bring a book of poetry to read to her. Once, he wrote a poem of his own praising her eyes and rosebud lips. She knew her mouth was far too wide to be described so, but the thought was so sweet. . . . There were even a few chaste, but awkward, kisses.

She stared out the carriage window and refused to look at her relatives. Her aunt gave a haughty sniff and turned away. Caitlyn's husband—his name was Trevor, was it not?—took the opposite seat, and they were off.

Reluctant to look at the man across from her, and panicked at being alone with him, she continued to stare out the window. A movement caught her attention. Bertie! Bertie had come to bid her a silent farewell. There he stood, looking so woebegone her heart fairly ached for him. She raised her hand briefly as the tears threatened to well over. She caught herself and glanced at her husband.

He gave her a tentative smile. "A friend?" he asked.

She nodded and looked away. She heard him heave a sigh.

It was going to be a long journey to Suffolk, Trevor thought. Well, at least she was not a chatterbox. He leaned back and feigned sleep as he studied his wife through half-closed eyelids.

She was a dumpy little thing. Pretty hair, though—the sunlight picked out red and gold highlights. Tied back with a pink ribbon to match her dress, it hung loose around her shoulders; she looked like the schoolgirl she probably was. He found himself wondering how she would look in a dress that matched the aquamarine of her eyes.

He felt distinctly sorry for her. That clutch-fisted uncle of hers did not even provide her a proper wedding breakfast. He wondered briefly why her family was so eager to be free of her. What if she were a bit mad—not playing with a full deck—or possessed of an unstable disposition? This was a fine time to think of *that,* he told himself.

The Atherton estate to which Trevor was taking his bride was located in East Anglia. He remembered visiting his grandmother there and being disappointed that, in the heart of England's horse country, the various farms associated with the property dealt largely in sheep and the production of wool.

Well, that suited him just fine now. He knew little of sheep, but surely there was a competent steward and Trevor considered himself a "quick learn."

Soon, the swaying carriage and his sleepless night combined to make his dozing off no longer feigned.

When they stopped for a change of horses and the midday meal, Caitlyn shook herself out of the sense of melancholy that had settled on her after that brief glimpse of Bertie.

She had always been a cheerful child, accepting what fate sent her way, dealing with it, and getting on with her life. Had she not lived in relative harmony with the Fiskes? She could surely deal with one young man.

The innkeeper had shown her to a room where she could freshen up. When she came into the parlor, Trevor stood to assist her to the table where a modest meal was laid out.

"How is it that you travel without a maid to assist you?" Trevor asked. His tone indicated only conversational curiosity.

"A maid?" She was surprised. "I have never had a maid, sir. My father had only the housekeeper and a handyman. My aunt and uncle have their own dressers, but I could hardly expect to have a maid assigned to me."

"Hmm. That will have to be remedied. I shall not have my wife going about unattended." He poured himself another glass of wine.

She was pleased that he wanted her to have the privileges of any young matron. She was emboldened to ask, "May I . . . uh . . . may I know where we are going, sir? And when we expect to arrive?"

"Oh, I am sorry. I just assumed you knew—though why you should is a mystery." He smiled, and it occurred to her that that smile had probably caused many a heart to flutter in London drawing rooms. Why, look what it was doing to hers already. "We shall arrive at our destination sometime late tomorrow afternoon, I hope."

"And that is . . . ?"

"Atherton. Near Lavenham and Newmarket." He explained how he had come by the estate and told her as much as he remembered of it.

"It sounds wonderful, sir," said she who had lived in a modest vicarage most of her life.

"Do not allow your expectations to get too high," he warned. Then he added, "You must call me Trevor, for that *is* my name. And I shall call you Caitlyn. I believe first names are customary between married people." His tone had a teasing note.

"Trevor. Trevor. . . . Yes, I like it." She smiled. "It seems to suit you."

"Thank you, kind lady." He gave her a mocking little bow, and they continued the rest of the meal talking of innocuous subjects and generally getting to know each other.

Caitlyn noticed that Trevor drank rather more wine with

the meal than she had ever seen her father imbibe in the middle of the day. But he seemed in control of himself, and, after all, what did *she* know of the habits of a gentleman?

Back in the carriage, they continued to chat amiably until each lapsed into silence. Caitlyn thought he might have dozed off again.

She tried to keep her mind on other matters, but she could not help wondering what this night would bring. In truth, she had no idea what to expect.

She recalled overhearing her father's housekeeper and her friend talking one time. What was it they had said? Something about the marriage bed being the price women had to pay for a roof over their heads.

That sounded a bit coarse to Caitlyn. Slightly sordid, actually. But with fewer than seventeen years to her credit, what could *she* say?

Aunt Sylvia had called Caitlyn in the day before to discuss her duties as a married woman. Caitlyn had actually anticipated this discussion—eager to know what she should expect. In the event, however, Aunt Sylvia had been so imprecise that Caitlyn had been more confused than enlightened.

As a girl who had spent so much of her time in the stables, she felt she had *some* idea of what to expect. However, it surely would have been nice to be better informed than her aunt's vague "You must strive to please your husband."

Three

That evening they stopped at an inn where Trevor arranged for a bedroom, a small dressing room, and a private parlor for himself and his bride.

During dinner Caitlyn seemed extremely nervous. Her tenseness increased, though he tried to keep up a patter of conversation. She seemed to be trying gamely to match his efforts. He had asked for a bottle of champagne as well as a bottle of brandy to accompany their meal, and now urged a second glass of champagne on her as a toast to their future. She had downed the first glass like a desert nomad at an oasis. With a giggle, she raised her glass to his.

Trevor's more intimate experiences with women had been with members of the demimonde, women far more experienced than he. Actually, there had been rather few of those encounters. He had never bedded a woman with whom he would be required to spend the following day. And he certainly had never taken a virgin to his bed before. He had some idea of the situation, but, in truth, he knew himself to be sadly limited in both knowledge and experience.

Moreover, his previous encounters had been with women he found distinctly more enticing than this shy little frump who was his wife. Still, she was not repulsive in any way, and he found his body responding to the mere idea of having sex. He moved over to the settee to sit next to her and slid his arm around her shoulder. She stiffened.

"Relax," he said softly as he kissed her on the neck just beneath her ear.

She turned toward him slightly. "I . . . I . . . uh . . . you will have to teach me what to do," she said shyly.

No man could resist such a request, Trevor thought, his chest fairly expanding in male pride. He touched his lips to hers, and she returned the pressure. He showered little kisses on her closed eyes, her nose, the base of her throat. He returned his mouth to hers and flicked his tongue against her lips. Which remained firmly sealed.

"Open for me, Caitlyn," he whispered, his hand caressing her breast.

She drew back. "My mouth? You want me to open my mouth? Whatever for?" It was sheer curiosity in her tone.

"I want to taste you. All of you," he said in what he fancied to be a seductive whisper.

"Really? Well—all right." Her tone was doubtful, but she settled back into his arms. The kiss was deep, exploring. At first she was passive, apparently absorbing the idea of such a kiss. Then, very tentatively, she began to explore on her own.

Trevor was amazed at his response to this. He pulled back and took a deep breath. "Oh, Lord," he moaned softly.

"Did I not do it correctly?" she asked, worried.

"No . . . I mean, yes. You were fine," he reassured her. He took a large gulp from his glass and handed hers to her.

"The bubbles tickle my nose." She giggled again. "I never had champagne before. I like it."

He grinned and gave her a light kiss, which she willingly—eagerly?—returned. "You go on and prepare for bed," he whispered. "I shall join you when you are ready."

As she retreated into the bedroom, he reached for the brandy bottle. Downing a quick glass, he savored the warmth of the alcohol—along with a sense of well-being—then removed his coat and his cravat. He cursed himself for having dismissed Robbins before he removed his boots, but finally managed to get them off.

He waited for her to call, but there was no sound from the other room. He sipped at another glass of brandy and waited some more, increasingly impatient. Finally, he went to the bedroom door and gently pushed it open. She sat on the edge of the bed staring blindly at the floor. She was dressed in a cotton nightrail more suitable to a schoolgirl than a bride. Strangely enough, he found her garb appealing.

"Caitlyn? Are you all right?"

"Y-yes." She turned large questioning eyes toward him.

He sat beside her and put his arm around her. "It will be all right. I promise."

"I-I'm sorry to be so henwitted. It is just that I . . ." She buried her face in her hands.

He gently pulled them away. "I know. Neither of us has been married before." He stood, pulling her up with him. He kissed her, hugging her to him, aroused by the pressure of firm young breasts against his chest. He caressed her back and deepened the kiss. She put her arms around his neck and responded warmly.

Part of him knew he should be taking this much more slowly, but another part of him—a throbbingly eager part— wanted her now—right now. Still holding her with one arm, he reached over to toss back the covers on the bed and nudged her into it.

He quickly divested himself of the rest of his clothing and crawled in beside her, sliding his arm under her to pull her close. He groped for the edge of her nightrail and pushed it up, caressing her thigh as he did so.

"T-Trevor? What are you doing?"

"Ssh. It's all right," he whispered as he felt for the most intimate part of her body.

"I do not think so," she said aloud, her doubt quite clear. She pushed at his hand and tried to pull the hem of her gown back down.

"You are my wife. And I want you," he said. Oh, Lord, *how* he wanted this. He knew he could not wait much longer. "Relax, sweetheart. Let me in."

"I do not understand. What is it you want me to do?"

He told her, and she did as he said, but she did so mechanically. The shy warmth she had shown earlier was gone, but he was beyond thinking of anything but his own desperate need.

"Ow!" she cried. "You're hurting me."

He put a hand over her mouth. "Be quiet. Do you want the whole inn in here?"

"No," she whispered, "but that hurts."

"It always does the first time," he said, sounding at least to his own ears as though he knew what he was talking about. "It will get better."

He tried to kiss away her fear. She lay quietly for a few moments.

"It is not getting better," she announced. She pushed at him. "I want you to get off me."

"I . . . I can't," he gasped as his body seemed to be acting independently of any conscious direction. She pummeled his back with her fists.

Finally, when he rolled off her body, she tossed the blanket aside and leaped from the bed.

"Oh, my heavens! There's blood!" she cried. "You have injured me something dreadful."

"Keep your voice down," he said fiercely. "That is perfectly normal. Good God. Did that aunt of yours tell you nothing of the marriage bed? Can you truly be so ignorant?"

She sniffed, looking down at him. "Can you truly be so selfish and unfeeling?" She ran into the dressing room, and he heard water splashing.

He rose and put his trousers and shirt back on. He went to the other room to retrieve his boots. He had to get out of here. Take a walk. Or something.

He suspected he had not handled this well.

* * *

Caitlyn heard her husband moving around in the bedroom. She also heard the bedroom door and then the outer door open and close. *Good riddance,* she thought petulantly. Then she had a moment of panic. What if he drove off and just left her to fend for herself among strangers?

When she had determined that she was not going to bleed to death—that, in fact, there had been very little blood—Caitlyn calmed down enough to consider the situation rationally. So *that* was the big secret of the marriage bed. No wonder women hated it so.

Still, she had rather enjoyed the kissing and cuddling. She blushed to think how she had responded to Trevor's kiss and pressed her own body so close to his. She had even felt the beginning of something wonderful when he touched her— there. But then suddenly he was *in* her and there was the pain—and, good grief, would *this* be a nightly occurrence for the rest of her life?

Perhaps not. She knew many married people had separate bedchambers. Surely they had *some* totally peaceful nights. In any event, what choice did she have? She knew very well that a wife was her husband's property to do with as he wished. Discovering what gentlemen wished had been a revelation.

Perhaps there *were* compensations. She would have a home of her own. Eventually there would be children—not soon, though, she hoped. By the time she had cleaned herself and removed the soiled sheet from the bed, she had talked herself into a modicum of complacency about the whole matter. Surely he would come back. Would he not?

She had just settled herself back into bed when she heard the outer door open and close. There was some slight movement in the other room, the clink of glass, then—nothing. She waited. Still, nothing. She rose quietly and opened the door a crack. Trevor sat staring into the dying fire, a glass of brandy in his hand.

Well, if he wished to drink himself into a stupor, that was just fine with her. She flounced back to the bed.

Trevor spent what was left of the night on the uncomfortable settee. He woke in the morning with a stiff neck, a rotten taste in his mouth, and in a foul mood. The very thought of food made him feel queasy, so he sipped coffee and watched, faintly resentful, as his bride devoured a hearty breakfast.

"Are you sure you will not have something?" she asked yet again.

"No. No, thank you." He took another sip of coffee and lowered the cup carefully. "Uh . . . Caitlyn?"

"Yes?"

"I want to apologize for last night. I . . . I am sorry it did not go well."

"Well, I supposed it did not," she said matter-of-factly, "but as I have no experience by which to judge . . ." Her voice trailed off, and she blushed.

Trevor was not about to admit that his own experience was nearly as limited as hers. Instead he said lamely, "It will go better next time."

"Oh?" She sounded rather doubtful. Then she shrugged and looked away. "All right."

And that night it did go better.

They had traveled all day and arrived rather late to find the household understaffed and not fully prepared for them. However, the master's bedchamber had been aired and a fire laid. A light supper was brought up, and Trevor deliberately exercised greater self-discipline on the wine this night.

He made a concerted effort to engage his wife in entertaining conversation, much of it involving childhood adventures he and Terrence had engaged in. For the first time since

Terrence's death, he was able to recall amusing incidents without choking up.

"It must be wonderful to grow up with brothers and sisters," Caitlyn said longingly.

"Usually," he agreed. "With Terrence and Melanie anyway. You have no brother or sister?"

"None that survived. There were four babies after me, but I remember only the last two. One of those—a baby boy—lived for only a week. The other was stillborn, and Mama died the next day. It was very sad. I was nine."

"But you still had your father," Trevor noted.

"Not really. Oh, he tried. Truly he did. But I think he simply could not go on without Mama. I am convinced that he died of a broken heart, not influenza."

She told him of her father's losing his parish and being sent as a curate in a poorer district. Trevor, who had never in his life had to deal firsthand with deprivation, was astonished at her simple acceptance of the reduced circumstances she had endured. When her father died, she had gone to live as the proverbial "poor relation" in her uncle's household.

He expressed sympathy for her.

"Oh, you must not feel sorry for me," she assured him. "I have not been trained to run a fine household, but I promise I can learn. I shall try to be a good wife to you."

Was this what had occupied her mind most of the day? She had been remarkably quiet during the journey.

"I am sure it will work out fine," he said with far more confidence than he felt.

She was apparently determined to start her "good wife" project that very evening. She made no demur at sharing his bed—and in the next few days she willingly let him "have his way with her." However, despite the release he found in her body, he came away from their encounters with a vague feeling of disappointment.

Perhaps if he loved her, it would be different. But he knew

he would never love her. He felt sorry for her and rather liked her, but, after all, she was not his type.

The day after their arrival at Atherton, Trevor planned to spend the morning examining the property with the steward, Mr. Felkins. After he left the breakfast table, Caitlyn asked the footman who had served them to send the housekeeper to her. It took some time, but eventually the woman, whom Caitlyn had met only briefly the night before, arrived.

The housekeeper was a very plump female of indeterminate years with iron gray hair and dark eyes. She wore a dark dress and had a ring of keys hanging conspicuously at her belt.

"You wanted me, Mrs. Jeffries?"

It was the first time Caitlyn had been addressed by her married name. She found herself inordinately pleased.

"Yes. It is Mrs. Bassett, is it not?" The woman nodded, eyed the new mistress, and then looked at nothing above Caitlyn's head and waited. "I should like you to show me through the house. My husband tells me he, too, is unfamiliar with it."

"Right now?" Mrs. Bassett's tone was slightly challenging. "I was just finishing me breakfast."

"Oh. Well, then . . . in—say—fifteen minutes?" Caitlyn tried to sound firm.

"Very well." The woman turned to leave, the keys jangling as she waddled back to the kitchen.

Twenty minutes later, Caitlyn glanced again at the mantel clock. The door opened and Mrs. Bassett came in, wiping her mouth with her bare hand.

"Oh, there you are," Caitlyn said brightly. "I should like to begin with the kitchen, if you please."

The housekeeper shrugged. "Makes me no never-mind, but Perkins might not take too kindly to it."

"Why?"

"She don't like being interrupted when she's baking, and Monday is her baking day."

"I see." Caitlyn considered this for a moment. "Well. She will have to tolerate it today, will she not?"

"If you say so."

Even to Caitlyn's unpracticed eye, the kitchen seemed to be run in a rather slipshod manner. True, the supper served the night before had been acceptable and this morning's breakfast had been edible, if a bit spare in terms of variety. But she observed that pots piled in a tub to be washed seemed encrusted with long-dried food. Ashes from the hearth spilled over to the surrounding floor. Elsewhere there were dried splashes of Lord-knew-what on the slate slabs that made up the kitchen floor.

The cook, Perkins, started to growl at their entrance, but on being introduced to the new mistress, merely scowled instead. Caitlyn surmised the woman had worn the same apron for a week.

"Where does that door lead?" Caitlyn asked, pointing to one of the four besides the one through which she had just entered.

"That one goes to Cook's quarters," Bassett said. "They are private quarters, of course." Again there seemed a slight challenge in her tone.

"Of course," Caitlyn agreed with a glance at the still scowling Perkins.

"That one is the pantry. Silver is stored there. And that one"—Bassett pointed at each—"goes down to the cellar. The other opens to the back garden and out to the stables."

"I shall see the pantry and the cellar," Caitlyn said firmly.

The housekeeper made a production of unlocking each of the doors. Caitlyn knew when she saw it that the disordered mess of the pantry should not be surprising after the slovenly care of the kitchen, but it was. The cellar was filthy and smelled of stale wine and rodent droppings.

"Good heavens. When was this cellar cleaned last?"

"All cellars gather dust, miss—uh, ma'am." The house-keeper sounded both condescending and defensive.

Caitlyn said nothing, but vowed that *this* cellar would have a thorough cleaning in the very near future. Before she gave such an order, though, she wanted to see more of her new home.

By the time she had been through the rest of the house—and it took the whole morning, with the housekeeper ostentatiously rattling keys as she unlocked and relocked each door—Caitlyn was overwhelmed by what it would take to set it to rights. Even the master suite, which last night had seemed passable, was in dire need of a thorough cleaning.

A thick coating of dust rested on furniture in rarely used rooms, and one could see exactly which corridors were used most by the trails through dust in halls and on stairs.

Mrs. Bassett became more quietly defensive in her attitude as the inspection progressed. "As you can see, ma'am, we have not enough help for this big house."

"Hmm," was Caitlyn's noncommittal response.

"There has not been a proper mistress here since Lady Bennington passed on—more than three years gone now. She was ill a long, long time before that, you see."

Caitlyn was of the opinion that there had not been a proper housekeeper in all that time, either, but she kept this thought to herself. No sense in alienating members of the staff just yet.

"Where are the household ledgers?" she asked when the tour was finished.

"I . . . uh . . . they are in my quarters." Bassett sounded a bit hesitant, but her voice was more firm as she added, "I take care of the books."

Caitlyn was suddenly aware of her extreme youth. And she knew the fact that she appeared even younger than she was often misled others into underestimating her. She suspected that was the case with the housekeeper.

"Mrs. Bassett."

"Yes, ma'am?"

"You will bring those ledgers to me in the library after lunch. You will also see that I have a set of those keys with each of them properly labeled."

"Well, now. That might take some time, Mrs. Jeffries."

Caitlyn merely raised an eyebrow at the slighting intonation the other woman put on her name. "After our luncheon," she said firmly.

"Yes, ma'am."

That evening Caitlyn shared her concerns about the state of the household with Trevor.

"Somehow your report does not surprise me," he told her, "for, indeed, the whole place is in need of attention."

"This is such a lovely area." Caitlyn's voice was almost plaintive.

"Aye. It is. East Anglia is said to have some of the most productive land in all of England. But this place has been let go to ruin. It will take a better man than I to put it to rights. And a lot more money than I have."

"You think it hopeless, then?"

"That I do. Everywhere one looks there is something in need of repair or attention. I am sure Marcus was mistaken in saying Atherton could ever become a profitable endeavor as it now stands."

"So what are we to do?"

"Muddle through, I suppose. Or find some funding to begin to set things aright."

She thought he sounded totally overwhelmed.

Four

Ten days later, it was apparent that there would be no funds forthcoming. A hastily drafted appeal had produced the not surprising information that older brother Marcus had no access to ready cash, though Marcus was quick to add that he admired Trevor's willingness to persevere at Atherton.

Trevor's quarterly allowance was nearly exhausted, but the home farm on the property was productive. They would not starve, at any rate, Trevor thought as he earnestly considered his options. It was time he took responsibility for his actions. Unanticipated and unwanted as it was, perhaps this marriage would put him on the right track.

True, she was not the wife he had dreamed of. Nor had she brought anything to the marriage in terms of the material settlements usual to a marriage in his class. But she was an amiable sort and willing to work; had he not caught her on her hands and knees scrubbing at the hearth in the drawing room? She had organized such maids and footmen as they had into a cleaning team despite the housekeeper's superior reluctance.

If their personal relationship had not quite the thrill and passion he had once dreamed of—so what? Other couples managed to go along all right. Look at his parents. Why, they did not even *like* each other. Of course, his father had had a string of mistresses—and perhaps he would one day, as well.

Trevor knew his mother had also had discreet affairs. Would Caitlyn do so? Now, why on earth should that idea be so unsettling? And this brought to mind that puppy who had been hanging around the street as he and Caitlyn were married. Who was that fellow? He shrugged. Perhaps, in due time, she would tell him. His musings were interrupted by Merrill, the middle-aged butler.

"Sir? There is a courier here to see you."

"A courier? Send him in." Trevor experienced a moment of panic. A message so urgent it could not be conveyed by ordinary post?

"Mr. Trevor Jeffries?" the courier asked.

"Yes." He stood behind his desk.

"I have a message from your father." The fellow handed over a thin missive with a wax seal which Trevor quickly opened.

"Oh, good Lord," he muttered, abruptly taking his seat again.

"Will there be an answer, sir? I was told to wait for an answer."

Trevor ran his hand through his hair. "No. I shall answer this summons myself."

Instructing Merrill to find the man some refreshment, Trevor went in search of his wife. He found her in the kitchen garden—on her hands and knees again.

"What are you doing?" he asked, seeing only her well-rounded bottom at first.

"Oh. Hello, Trevor. You startled me." Her eyes seemed darker today, more teal-colored. "I am—to answer your question—trying to distinguish between bona fide herbs and weeds." She plucked a leaf, rubbed it between her thumb and fingers, and handed it to him. "Here. Smell this. Is it not glorious? Lemon mint," she said as he inhaled.

"Nice. But come. I need to talk with you." He extended a hand to pull her to her feet and guided her to a nearby bench.

"What is it?" she asked, concerned.

"I have had what amounts to a royal summons—"

"A summons?"

"From my father, demanding I come to London. He must be in a rare taking."

"Why do you say that?"

"It takes something of earthshaking proportions to get him to leave Timberly. He hates going to town."

"You believe he is angry with you?"

"Oh, yes," he said in ironic understatement.

"About what?"

"Any number of things—but mostly this marriage, I am sure."

"He did not know?"

"He does now."

"I must admit I did wonder that none of your family saw you wed. I assumed my uncle had negotiated . . ." Her voice trailed off.

"Negotiated?" The single word conveyed surprise and scorn. "Caitlyn, are you telling me you do not know how this union came about?"

"Aunt Sylvia said only that Uncle Fiske had arranged a match." Then she said, in apparent reaction to his scornful tone, "Without considering my wishes, I might add."

Already upset over his father's barely concealed fury in the letter, Trevor found his hackles rising at her tone. "Well, you did not do so badly, did you?"

She lifted her chin. "I suppose that depends on one's point of view."

"What an interesting observation—from someone who was the subject of a miserable wager."

He knew he had gone too far when he saw shocked outrage in her expression, but his pride would not allow him to back down now.

"What, precisely, do you mean?" she demanded.

He told her the whole despicable tale of drinking, gambling, and that final hand of cards with her uncle.

"A wager? You won me in a wager?" Humiliation and despair had replaced the hauteur.

"Actually, I lost the wager," he said glumly, then suddenly realized how that bit of stark honesty must sound to her.

She jumped up and put the back of her hand to her mouth, stifling a sob.

"Caitlyn, I did not mean . . ."

But she was gone, fairly running into the house. He followed her, but she had locked herself in her dressing room.

"Caitlyn, please," he called through the closed door.

"Go away. I never want to see you again."

"Now, you know that is ridiculous."

"Just go away," she wailed.

"As you wish," he said, having the last word.

Within the hour he was en route to London.

Hearing the carriage leave, Caitlyn went from the dressing room to the bed, where she lay staring at the ceiling through what she knew to be red-rimmed eyes. But why should she care about her appearance?

The only person ever to find her attractive had been Bertie. And now he was totally out of her reach—thanks to the machinations of her self-serving uncle and the dissolute gambler to whom she was married. At this moment, she hated them both. And Bertie, too, for that matter. After all, if he had only asserted himself . . .

She did not understand fully what had happened, but she surmised that Bertie's father—whose forceful personality was complemented by very real power in his district—had some hold over her uncle. Uncle Fiske had merely found a convenient patsy in one Trevor Allen Jeffries.

And where did that leave Caitlyn Maria Woodbridge Jeffries?

She asked herself this question repeatedly in the next few days. No answer was forthcoming. She felt she was in a state of limbo. She knew of instances where wives had been turned out for the shabbiest of reasons—left with nothing, not even a modicum of decency. Meanwhile, her work—and that of directionless servants—came to a standstill.

Hurt and humiliated by the truth about her marriage, Caitlyn desperately wanted to be the driving force in her own life. She felt so manipulated, so out of control. There was something sordid about this—demeaning. It was rather like the wife-selling that was not unknown among the lower, poorer ranks of society. She tried to see some clear course of action.

Pain and embarrassment were accompanied by anger, which was focused largely on her uncle, but also on Trevor. Common sense told her if it had not been Trevor, it would have been someone else. Under the circumstances, Trevor was right in saying she had not fared so badly. Still, he was a party to her ignominy.

Common sense also kept nagging at her that Trevor, too, had been a victim of circumstances. Yes, but—her anger and hurt responded—he had been instrumental in creating his circumstances, while she had done nothing—nothing—to deserve what had happened to her.

So? Whoever said life had to be fair? Surely she knew by now that it was not, that no one was free of "the slings and arrows of outrageous fortune." By sheer will, she forced herself out of this labyrinth of self-pity and took up her duties.

She also spent hours wandering over the estate, sometimes on foot, but more often she rode. Atherton's stables offered little in the way of quality horseflesh, but "beggars are not allowed to be choosers" she told herself. She became acquainted with workers on the home farm and the tenants on other farms that made up the whole of Atherton. Many of the people were poor, but she thought they still showed spirit and ambition. If only there were some way to direct that energy.

She would discuss it with Trevor when he returned.

* * *

Trevor had given up his quarters in London as an expense he could ill afford. However, he refused to lodge at the Wyndham town house, knowing something of the reception he was about to have there. He would stay with Theo for the short time he intended to be in town.

It was with a great deal of trepidation that he climbed the stairs to Wyndham House. As he entered, Heston, the butler who had known him in short coats, gave him a sympathetic look and directed him to the drawing room above.

"Psst. Trevor." Melanie gestured from the doorway of a reception room off the foyer.

"Mel. Were you waiting for me? Why are you not with the rest of the inquisition?"

"Oh, Trevor, that is the exact word for it. They are in rare form. Why, Papa and Mama have actually joined forces for once. And Gerald is being even more pompous than usual."

"And Marcus?"

"He is here, too. Papa insisted on a united front, you see."

"Oh, Lord." Trevor felt his heart sink. "Well, come along. I guess you will be my only ally."

"I cannot. Papa has forbidden my presence. Oh, Trevor, I am so worried. Truly, I have never seen both our parents in such a rare taking—together!" She hugged him. He hugged her back and released her.

"Thanks for the warning. —Oh! By the bye, how did it go with Sheffield?"

A soft light came into her eyes. "Wonderfully. Aunt Gertrude was absolutely brilliant. Now Mama is championing Drew as exactly the sort of young man I should encourage."

"Good. I want to hear all about it, but first . . ." He gestured above.

"Good luck, Trev." She kissed him on the cheek.

He squared his shoulders and climbed the stairs to find his parents and two older brothers in the drawing room.

"There you are, at last," the earl growled. "Close the door. We do not need the servants hearing any more of this sordid affair than they already have."

Trevor noted that his mother, fashionably dressed in her favorite shade of blue, shared a settee with the rigid, superior Gerald. Marcus, leaning casually against the mantel, gave him a friendly nod which might have been intended to be sympathetic. His father sat in a wing chair and directed him to its mate placed to face the three family members already seated. An inquisition, all right, Trevor thought.

"Now. Suppose you start explaining yourself, young man." His father's black, unrelenting gaze bore into him from beneath heavy brows.

Trevor was glad he could return his father's gaze. A younger Trevor had invariably found that cold stare most intimidating. "Exactly what is it you would like me to explain, my lord?"

Gerald snorted impatiently. The countess dropped her demeanor of fashionable ennui to say, "Trevor, darling, it is all over town. The subject of every drawing room that matters. I cannot go anywhere . . ."

"So? Is it true? Did you indeed marry the indigent ward of some hanger-on?" Gerald asked, drumming his fingertips on the arm of the settee.

"I married Miss Woodbridge." Trevor intended to minimize explanation.

"And you did so after a night of drinking and gambling?" his father asked.

"Actually, it was a few days later, Father."

"Stop mincing words with me," his father ordered. "Did you or did you not marry this chit as the result of a wager in a card game?"

"Yes, sir. I did."

"Oh, Trevor, no-o," his mother wailed.

"What possessed you to do such a truly stupid thing?" Gerald demanded, his tone increasingly belligerent. "Had you no thought at all of the family name? You have made us the butt of laughter throughout the *ton*. The Mortons are deeply shocked."

"I doubt my indiscretions—whatever they may be—could seriously damage the staid, upright view the *ton* holds of the noble heir to the Earl of Wyndham." Trevor felt the same embarrassed resentment he had felt as a youngster when taken to task by the more autocratic of his older brothers. "Nor is Miranda Morton likely to refuse your suit on *my* account."

"Nevertheless, you had done much better to have considered your own position as a son of the Wyndham peerage," Gerald retorted.

"Stop this bickering." The earl slashed his hand in a cutting motion. "The first question is—is the marriage legal? Trevor?"

"Yes, I believe it is. Special license. Properly ordained clergy. Witnesses. I *am* of age. Of course it is."

"I just do not understand how this could have happened," his mother said with a dramatic sigh.

"I—it was a debt of honor." Trevor was embarrassed by the inadequacy of this explanation.

"Honor!" his father raged. "There was a great deal of *dis*honor in this affair. You, son, were the veriest gull—duped by that conniving Fiske and his pal Latham. And aided by the very questionable Fitzwilliam."

"You walked right into it," Gerald sneered.

"And now we Jeffries are the subject of such talk. And—and—even *cartoons* in the newspaper!" His mother put a handkerchief to her eyes.

"Is this true, Marcus?" Trevor turned to the one from whom he felt at least some empathy.

"I am afraid so, Trev."

"Show him," Gerald said without an ounce of compassion.

Marcus lifted a clipping from a table and handed it to Trevor. The cartoon was a vicious piece of work depicting a card table with caricatures of three players—unmistakably

Fiske, Fitzwilliam, and himself. The figure meant to be Trevor was clearly intoxicated. Behind the figure of Fiske was a buxom lass spilling over the top of her dress. She leered at the drunk young man. But what was really shocking was that the artist had depicted the woman as obviously pregnant. A balloon caption had her saying, "But, Uncle, I must have a husband—any husband." The uncle responded, "Coming right up, my child." The only comment of the young drunk with Trevor's features was "Hic!" The cartoon was labeled "The Wager."

Staring at this hideous distortion, Trevor felt bile rise in the back of his throat. He swallowed hard and glanced around to see harsh, accusing glares from three members of his family. "I . . . I . . . it was not . . ."

Marcus squeezed Trevor's shoulder. "Cartoonists sell only if they exaggerate, but—"

"But," Gerald cut in curtly, "this is essentially true, is it not?"

"Yes . . ." Trevor's voice was small. Then he jerked upright. "No. No, it is not. It is a malicious libel of Caitlyn."

"How so?" Gerald sneered.

"Caitlyn is—she—uh—she was—a virgin." He felt himself actually blushing. "I apologize for such plain speaking, my lady."

"And how do you know this?" his father demanded.

"Perhaps I should leave the rest of this discussion to you gentlemen." As the countess rose, those seated rose as well to bow her out. "I am most disappointed in you, Trevor," was her parting comment.

"How do you know?" his father repeated when she was gone and they sat again.

Trevor felt his blush deepening. "Surely everyone in this room knows the answer to that question."

Gerald gave another derisive snort. "What everyone in this room knows—with the possible exception of you, Trevor—is that women have been faking virginity since time began."

Trevor glared at him. As they were growing up, Trevor had always hated the way Gerald delighted in declaring some treasured belief of the younger children to be false or silly.

"All it takes," Gerald went on, "is a little pig's blood or chicken blood in a vial—easily secreted in the bedclothes. That, and a bit of clever acting."

Their father shook his head. "I cannot believe a son of mine could be quite so damned naive."

"But Caitlyn is not like that. She is sweet . . ." Trevor not only felt it a duty to defend her, he truly believed her to be sweet and chaste.

"Is it true that you never actually met the girl before the wedding?" his father asked in a calmer tone.

"Well, yes, but—"

"So you have even now known her for how long? Ten days? A fortnight?"

"About that."

"So you do not *really* know her at all well, do you?"

"No."

Could it be true? *Could* Caitlyn have manufactured that scene at the inn? He did not want to believe it of her. But what did he truly know? And had he not been in an alcoholic haze for two days by then? How observant could he have been?

"Perhaps you do not know much about your bride at all." Gerald picked up another paper from the table. "Her father was a country vicar in the Lake District. Lost his post and became a curate up north—near Durham—Monksford, actually. Our Uncle Hermiston's chief property was there." Aunt Gertrude, Trevor thought, as Gerald pressed on. "When her father died, the girl went to live with the Fiskes, where she ran wild over the countryside. She set her sights on Viscount Latham's son, but Latham put a damper on that. Apparently not soon enough—as you can see from that cartoon."

"Where do you come by this information?" Trevor asked, truly angry now. Most of his anger centered on Gerald as the bearer of such tidings, but in truth, he did not know precisely where his fury should be directed.

"I merely asked around," Gerald said with an airy wave of his well-manicured hand. "It is common knowledge."

"Common. Yes," Trevor said. But he recognized the basic facts of Caitlyn's background. Had she taken the Latham heir as a lover? Had he been the "puppy" outside the church that day?

"There is more," Gerald said. "Marcus, you tell him about his good friend Fitzwilliam."

Marcus shifted uneasily. "I am sorry, Trevor. Fitzwilliam has been suspected for some time of having lucky streaks at the table that were a bit too convenient."

"Suspicions are not proof." Trevor felt compelled to defend one he had considered a friend.

"He and a confederate were caught the other night. There was no doubt. No equivocation. He fled the country."

"I cannot believe . . ."

"It is true, though," Marcus said softly. "The pattern of their cheating was consistent with what witnesses reported of your game with Fiske."

"Oh, God." Despair washing over him, Trevor buried his face in his hands.

"After that racing fiasco, I assumed you had learned your lesson." The Earl of Wyndham sounded thoroughly disgusted with his youngest son. Trevor maintained a stoic expression, not wanting his father to know he had struck home. "Obviously, I was mistaken, for this latest escapade truly is beyond enough."

"Something must be done to quell the gossip," Gerald said.

"I have left town. What more can you want of me?"

"Frankly, I would have you out of the country," Gerald replied.

"Father? Marcus? Do you feel as he does?"

"Trevor, I am that far"—the earl held his thumb and forefinger in an extremely small measure—"from disowning you entirely."

Marcus shook his head. "I just do not know, Trev. Perhaps it would help if you were out of the country while we try to sort this out."

"But . . . that smacks of running away. Whatever else I may be, I am no coward."

"No one accused you of being a coward," Gerald said dismissively, "just a fool. Getting you away will allow more level heads to handle the situation."

"Handle—how?"

"You need not be concerned with the details." Gerald sounded as he might in speaking to a small child.

"I damned well do need to be concerned." Trevor felt long-suppressed anger rise at Gerald's supercilious attitude.

"All right. Hold on," his father said with a calming gesture. "How would you feel about traveling on the Continent? Italy and Greece are safe enough, despite Bonaparte's ambitions."

"I don't know . . ." Trevor tried to sort out his jumbled thoughts. He was being hit with too much at once.

"Perhaps Russia? Or the colonies?" Marcus suggested.

"I do not know. I need time to think." He was over-whelmed by their suggestions—and even more by their united wish to be rid of him. Never in his life had he suffered such total rejection. "What . . . what is to happen to Caitlyn?"

His father snorted with disdain. "No doubt that bit of baggage will be glad to accept a munificent offer to free you."

"A bribe? I do not think Caitlyn would readily accept a bribe." Trevor recalled a certain degree of pride in his young bride.

"Oh, come now. That was undoubtedly the plan all along. Why else would she be party to such a sordid affair?" Gerald asked.

"What do you mean by 'free' me?"

"Marcus? You are the law expert in the family," Gerald said.

Trevor knew that Marcus had studied law at the Inns of Court after leaving university.

"Well . . ." Marcus began hesitantly, "an annulment is probably out of the question. Trevor has admitted the marriage was consummated."

Trevor felt himself blushing again.

"So what about a divorce?" Gerald demanded.

Marcus shook his head thoughtfully. "That could be very complicated—especially if she should object."

"I doubt she has funds of her own, and God knows Fiske would never part with the blunt to fight us in a court battle," Gerald observed.

"True. But it could get very messy anyway. Of course, it is easy enough to buy necessary witnesses to prove 'criminal conversation.' " His tone suggested Marcus found this idea distasteful.

"Crim . . . con . . . ? You want to accuse Caitlyn of adultery?" Trevor found this idea appalling.

"What does it matter if you were cuckolded before or after the vows?" His father's blunt question set Trevor aback.

Marcus cleared his throat. "Hmm. There are other considerations . . ."

"What?" The earl obviously wanted a solution, not "considerations."

"All court proceedings would be published—and probably reprinted in penny pamphlets. The scandal would explode instead of dying down."

"And what else?" Gerald persisted.

"And, assuming she is with child, the babe would be born within Trevor's marriage. The child would, as far as the law is concerned, be *his* legitimate offspring. Fiske wins that one."

"It would not be the first time in our family history that a Jeffries man has had to deal with a bastard in his nursery," the earl declared in what Trevor thought to be an especially bitter tone.

"My lord?" Trevor's gaze engaged both his father and Gerald. "I do not mean to be disrespectful, but I would ask that you temper your language. Both of you. Caitlyn is, after all, my wife—"

Gerald gave a derisive "Hmmph" but was otherwise silent.

"Quite right," his father said, looking a bit chagrined. "However, we are trying to solve a *family* crisis here. And, I might add, it is a crisis of *your* making."

"Yes, sir."

"So—Marcus—have you a recommendation?" the earl asked.

"If Trevor agrees"—Marcus looked at his younger brother—"he could absent himself. A legally valid marriage may be easily—and I might add quietly—dissolved if it is not consummated for two years or more."

"Two years?" Trevor groaned.

"If you are out of the country, who could possibly say you had been in her bed?" Gerald was apparently striving for a reasonable tone.

"I . . . I . . . will need to think about this," Trevor murmured.

"Well, as you do so," his father said sternly, "think also on this: If you choose to remain in England, your allowance stops as of now. If you go, you may continue to enjoy the benefits of your current allowance abroad."

"What about . . . about my wife?"

"What about her? She may fend for herself. You may leave her at Atherton if you so choose. That property is yours, after all. I would guess a clever lass like that will move on soon enough." The earl reached for his brandy glass.

"As soon as she is aware that there will be no access to the Wyndham fortune, you may be sure she will be gone." Gerald sounded ridiculously smug.

Trevor rose, feeling thoroughly beaten. "I shall give you my answer tomorrow."

Five

On leaving Wyndham House, Trevor initially wandered the streets, caught up in thought. He wanted to reject the notion that Caitlyn had been a party to what amounted to a conspiracy against him, but his father was right. He did not know her—had never met her until that meeting on the church steps.

Yes, it was possible that ridiculous scene on their wedding night had been contrived by a clever actress. Would a clever actress not have handled things with a deal more sophistication, though? Or was that part of the cleverness?

Most of Gerald's information corresponded with what Caitlyn herself had told him. Logical reasoning would indicate that the rest was true, too. Damn her! Innate honesty, however, forced him to admit to his own role in the affair. Her uncle's success had been ensured by Trevor's gullibility.

Finally arriving on Theo's doorstep, he surprised even himself by refusing his friend's offer to share a bottle of brandy. Instead he accepted a glass of sherry, which he sipped absentmindedly as he related the newest developments to Captain Ruskin.

"So what will you do?" Theo asked.

"Go to the colonies, I suppose. My father has a cousin in Philadelphia. Should be able to occupy myself for a couple of years." But his lack of enthusiasm was clear even to his own ears.

"What about your property here?"

"Two more years of neglect will not make that much difference. There is a steward. He has little imagination, but he is adequate."

"What about your . . . uh . . . your wife?"

"I honestly do not know what to do, Theo. I feel *some* responsibility for her. I doubt her family will do anything to help her. You saw how eager Fiske was to be rid of her."

"Yes, I did."

"After today, I have some idea of what that was like for her," Trevor added, the bitter memory of his father's disgust and Gerald's contempt fresh in his mind. "Told you what my father said."

"Yes. That was cold of him, was it not?"

"True. But if she has saddled me with another man's brat . . ."

"You know that for sure?"

"No. But all indications are—"

"Trevor, you cannot just desert her. She bears your name, after all."

"I know. I have no intention of just walking away from my responsibilities. Not my style, you know."

"I do know."

"I guess . . ." Trevor said slowly, working it out even as he spoke, "I could see that she has a portion of my allowance until such time as she can decide for herself what she will do. She can stay at Atherton as long as she needs to."

"You cannot leave a young girl out there in the country alone." Theo was aghast.

"Well, I cannot afford to hire a companion for her."

"Perhaps she has some cousin—or a maiden aunt—or *someone.*"

"If she does, she has not mentioned such. But, wait—Aunt Gertrude knows the area in which Caitlyn's father had his last post. I shall check with her tomorrow." He felt better for having even this much of a plan.

"Philadelphia, hmm?"

"I think so."

"Your enthusiasm is overwhelming."

"Well, for God's sake, Theo, what is there for me in the colonies? I want to do something worthwhile. I know that has a hollow sound to it, given my recent past. . . ."

"Something—like what?"

"I do not know. . . . I actually thought with some help I might make a going concern of Atherton—but that's out for the present."

"There are a couple of lieutenants' commissions available in my regiment," Theo said.

"Go for a soldier? Do you think I could?"

"Don't see why not. Just a matter of purchasing the commission."

"So long as it is not a cavalry regiment. No horses, please."

"You know very well my regiment is the 96th Foot."

"Yes-s-s. That might answer. Wyndham would probably agree to part with the ready to buy colors for me."

"You will need to decide soon. We leave for the Peninsula to join Wellington in a matter of days."

"But I have no training," Trevor said, coming to his senses.

"Never mind. 'Tis not unknown for an officer to buy into a position with no military training. You do know how to ride and shoot, and you are in good physical condition. I shall help you as much as I can."

"Hmm. I must say, this idea has far more appeal than going off to Phila-damn-delphia!"

In a matter of days, it was all arranged and Trevor was on board a troopship sailing from Plymouth harbor. Prior to that, however, had come calls on Lady Gertrude and Lord Wyndham. And he had written a rather stiff letter to Caitlyn.

Aunt Gertrude had welcomed him with sadness in her eyes. She directed him to a settee and took a seat beside him.

"You should have told me, dear," she said. "I might have been able to help."

"I doubt anyone could have done much. But perhaps you can help me resolve part of the problem now."

"I shall try."

"Did you know of a curate named Woodbridge when you lived in Monksford? Came originally from the Lake District."

"I knew him quite well," she said with surprise. "His daughter Caitlyn was a student in my dame school."

"Caitlyn is my wife."

"Caitlyn? *Caitlyn* is the girl in that dreadful cartoon? It cannot be." Shock and disbelief registered in her tone and countenance.

"Believe it, Aunt."

"How? Why? I cannot comprehend this. I had heard she was summarily shipped off to some relative when her father died, but I had no idea to whom she had gone. I was here in town by then, of course."

Trevor gave her as much information as he knew about Caitlyn, including the knowledge that Gerald had supplied.

"It is not true," his aunt said emphatically. "The girl I knew would never be a party to such a nefarious scheme."

"Perhaps she changed, for it certainly appears that she was."

"Oh, dear. . . . Well, what is it that I can do to help?"

He explained his plan to take a commission and leave the country as his father had ordered. "But I cannot just go off and leave her alone at Atherton," he finished. "I thought perhaps you would know of a female relative she might call upon to stay with her until this mess is all sorted out."

She appeared to consider this request for some time. Finally, she said, "I am sorry, Trevor. I can think of absolutely no one. I seem to remember her father's brother emigrated to Canada years and years ago. I really think the Fiske connection was the only one she had. The poor dear."

"I just do not know what to do," Trevor said. "I know

this is probably as much my fault as hers, but my father refuses to budge from his decision."

"Encouraged, no doubt, by his precious Gerald," Lady Gertrude said, her voice harsh. Then it softened as she asked, "Have you no feeling for Caitlyn, then?"

Trevor shifted uncomfortably. "I . . . I hardly know her. She is pleasant enough. I even *liked* her, I think. But she . . . well . . . she is not . . . I don't . . ."

"You do not find her attractive? Is that it?"

"Well, yes—rather. It is just that I never would have been drawn to such a girl, you see. And now that I know . . . I just cannot deal with her—at least not now." He knew this sounded lame.

"But you do care enough to want to provide for her properly?"

"Well—yes. She bears the Jeffries name, after all. I cannot engender additional scandal. It would reflect on Melanie—and Marcus. They do not deserve that. And—in all honesty—Miranda Morton probably does not deserve it either."

"You *are* a good sort, Trevor. Oh, yes, misguided a bit, but basically good, I think." She patted his hand.

Trevor felt a warm glow at this rare praise from his opinionated relative. "Thank you, my lady."

"And I may be able to help you." She paused. "How would it suit you if *I* were to go and stay with your bride until such time as she finds a suitable relative of her own to join her? Or until matters are handled otherwise?"

"You would do that?" Trevor asked in wonder.

"Certainly. As I think on it, I like the idea even more. I have grown somewhat bored with life in town. Not that I would forgo it completely, you understand."

"Aunt Gertrude, I would be so grateful—"

"Never mind. I shall enjoy the country."

The visit with his father had had a much less amiable tone, especially as Gerald was a party to the interview. In the end, however, the earl agreed to the purchase of a commission.

He would also continue his son's allowance, half of which would go to the unwanted bride until Trevor's return and a divorce could be quietly effected. However, the earl wanted nothing to do with "that girl"—the business would be handled through a solicitor.

Trevor departed, saddened by what he perceived as the defection of his family. Offsetting this despondency, though, was a feeling of purpose and direction he had not felt since the deaths of Terrence and Jason. He was also heartened by another visit with his sister. Melanie would, in all probability, marry Sheffield and follow him to some foreign post with the diplomatic corps.

He knew that writing Caitlyn a letter was rather cowardly, but time was of the essence if he was to ship out with the regiment. Secretly, he was glad not to deal with her directly. Best not to encounter pain in those aquamarine, teal-colored eyes.

Caitlyn was furious—actually trembling with anger. In fact, she had been annoyed for several days at her husband's continued absence. Married less than a month, and her husband had been away for over half of that time! And there were estate matters he should be seeing to. Mr. Felkins, the steward, had brought them to her, but what did *she* know of running an estate?

Heavens. She barely knew anything of running a household. Had not Mrs. Bassett kept her keenly aware of *that* shortcoming?

But now—not only was her blackguard husband absent, he had no intention of returning! She reread the letter several times, her anger increasing with each reading.

Caitlyn,
 This will undoubtedly come as a surprise to you, but I shall not be returning to Atherton—at least not in the foreseeable future.

Having at last learned the details of the circumstances which led to our marriage, I have elected to abide by my father's wishes and leave England for an indeterminate period of time. As soon as may be appropriate, my family will take the necessary steps to procure the dissolution of our marriage.

Assuming you do not lodge an objection, a divorce can be handled discreetly, but it will take time and is somewhat dependent on your continuing to live quietly and avoid bringing notice to the Jeffries name. I am confident that you will agree to this course of action.

Trevor

"Details of the circumstances" indeed! And just what details were there that he did not know previously? After all, it was he, not she, who had been aware of—party to—that infamous wager.

And leave her to fend for herself, would he? Oh, yes, the letter had included a postscript with news of his providing for her from his allowance and that some aunt of his was coming to look after her. She did not need looking after and would soon enough send some meddling busybody on her way.

A *divorce?* He would have her tainted with such a smear for the rest of her life? True, divorce was not unknown, but only persons of the very highest echelons of society could weather the disgrace. Even then, it was rare for a woman to be accepted after such a scandalous action. And for a female of Caitlyn's status? Impossible.

When she finally calmed down enough to think about it rationally, she wondered what had precipitated Trevor's decision. There had to be something more than the wager—bad enough in itself, but Trevor knew of *that.* Then she had the answer.

Mrs. Bassett set a newspaper at Caitlyn's place at breakfast one morning. "Thought you might be interested in this, madam," she said with a rather peculiar twist on the term of respect.

Curious, Caitlyn leafed through the journal twice before the cartoon caught her attention. She drew in her breath. Yes, two of the card players were clearly meant to represent her uncle and Trevor. She did not recognize any of the other figures. The artist had apparently had no inkling of characteristics in *her* that would be clearly identifiable. But he did not need a personal trait to do his damage. One look at the female figure long gone with child was more than enough.

Now Trevor's behavior had an explanation, even if it did not excuse him. And Trevor actually believed . . . She had not felt much like breakfast this morning anyway, and this item sickened her. Idly, she wondered just what it was that Mrs. Bassett had intended by showing this to her.

Caitlyn spent the rest of the morning in her room—the one she shared with Trevor—pondering her options—or rather, the lack of them. In the end, she simply did not know what else to do but carry on as before.

Three days later Caitlyn was in the library, located in the front of the house on the ground floor, when she heard carriage wheels on the driveway. For an instant, she wondered if Trevor had changed his mind. She went to the window and peeped through the drapery. An older woman in a huge hat with fluttering ostrich feathers shielding her face was handed down from a smart traveling carriage. Another vehicle loaded with luggage drew up behind hers.

Caitlyn's first thought was a small prayer of thanks that at least one of the guest rooms had been prepared, for it looked at though this traveler planned a stay of some duration. It had to be Trevor's aunt. She waited for Merrill's announcement, which came immediately.

"Lady Gertrude Hermiston, madam."

"Lady Gertrude?" Caitlyn fairly squeaked in surprise and wonder. "Whatever are you doing here?"

"Did that infernal boy not tell you I was coming?"

"Infernal boy?" Caitlyn thought her wits were surely deserting her.

"Trevor. My scapegrace nephew."

"Oh. No. I mean—yes. He *did* write me that his aunt would come, but he neglected to tell me who she was. Oh, Lady Gertrude, I cannot tell you how glad I am to see a familiar face. I have dreaded meeting Trevor's aunt—and here it is *you*." She smiled and extended her hands in greeting, aware that she was babbling foolishly.

"Dreading me, were you?" Lady Gertrude smiled as she removed her cloak and handed it over to Merrill along with her oversized hat.

"No. Not you. Just an unknown aunt Trevor said would come." Caitlyn paused to ask Merrill to bring a tea tray and see to the disposition of Lady Gertrude's luggage, then went on, "Actually, I am extremely happy to see you. It has been a long time since I have seen a truly friendly face."

"But—I understood that Trevor left here only a fortnight ago."

Caitlyn felt herself blushing. "You must know that Trevor and I do not know each other well. . . ."

"And I gather he is not in your good graces now, either."

"No, he is not," Caitlyn said in a tone that she hoped would eliminate further discussion on this head.

"You and I will talk about it all later, my dear," her ladyship said as Merrill produced the tea tray. "I have brought you a small gift." She handed over a gaily wrapped packet.

"A gift? For me?" Caitlyn could not remember the last time anyone had given her a gift. She accepted it eagerly. "A book. Poetry! Oh, thank you so much."

"A slim volume by one of your former neighbors in the Lake District—Mr. Wordsworth."

"I remember seeing him a few times. Mama knew his sister. Oh, how exciting to have one of his books. Thank you again."

Eventually, they did turn to the topic of Lady Gertrude's

stay, and Caitlyn learned that Trevor had not been quite as impervious to his wife's needs in his absence as she had thought. Still, he *had* deserted her.

"I shall never forgive him," Caitlyn declared. "What is more, as I see it, the only reason to approve a divorce would be to remarry. I never want to marry again. So Trevor—and his family—can just wait until pigs compete with the birds for room in the sky before *I* shall agree to blacken my name so."

"You were sorely used," Lady Gertrude agreed. "But you may change your mind one day."

"Never."

"In any event, I am here until you no longer have need of me."

"Then you shall be here a very long time, I am thinking, my lady."

"Perhaps you could be persuaded to call me *Aunt Gertrude* as Trevor does."

"I should be most happy to do so."

In the next few days, Caitlyn could hardly believe her luck in discovering a relative who seemed so genuinely concerned about her welfare. She could not help drawing a comparison with the last woman she had addressed as "Aunt." Gertude Hermiston was a far cry from Sylvia Fiske.

Aunt Gertrude's presence brought an immediate change in the attitudes of certain members of the staff. Mrs. Bassett became positively obsequious, and it was apparent that Perkins took greater care in preparing meals.

Caitlyn and Aunt Gertrude actually reveled in each other's company. Gertrude confided that she had always wanted a daughter, and Caitlyn had missed much in losing her mother at such a young age. She became more and more fond of Lady Gertrude.

Then their happy amicability encountered a serious rupture.

Caitlyn was with child.

The two women discovered it almost simultaneously. Caitlyn had not felt well for several days. When she abruptly left the breakfast table two days in a row, Aunt Gertrude followed her to her bedchamber, where Caitlyn lay on the bed after losing her breakfast again.

Aunt Gertrude's expression was grim. "So. You *are* in an interesting condition. I did not believe those rumors, but it appears I was wrong."

"I . . . I do not know what you are talking about." Then Caitlyn remembered that cartoon. "Oh. Oh, no. You have it all wrong. I am not with child—I cannot be. Trevor and I . . . we . . . Well, we were only together for a week or so."

"And before that?" Aunt Gertrude's voice was distant, unrelenting.

"Before . . . ? There was no 'before,' " Caitlyn said. "Please. You must believe me. I just have a touch of the flu."

"The nine-months variety. I would stake my life on it."

"Oh, no. It cannot be." It came out as a wail of utter despair. Caitlyn, caught up in her own emotions, did not immediately notice Lady Gertrude's reaction. Later, when she considered the scene again, she thought there was a softening in the older woman's demeanor.

"Well, my girl, you must know it takes only once."

"Truly?"

Lady Gertrude looked at her in surprise. "Truly. When *was* your last monthly?"

Embarrassed, Caitlyn told her and watched as Aunt Gertrude's face registered the mental calculation she was doing.

"Well. If you are telling the truth—and I must say I am inclined to believe you—the babe must be Trevor's."

Caitlyn felt anger and indignation rise at this. "Of *course* it is Trevor's. I went to my marriage bed a virgin—and anyone who says otherwise is a liar."

"What about that Latham lad? Your name was linked to his in London gossip."

"Bertie? Bertie never touched me." Then she blushed and added, "That is, not beyond a few *very* innocent kisses. Even I know it takes more than a kiss to make a babe."

"Well, now. Calm down, my dear. Strong emotion is not good for the babe. This situation puts a new twist on matters."

Eight months later—give or take a few days—Caitlyn Maria Woodbridge Jeffries was delivered of a healthy baby girl whom she promptly christened Ashley Gertrude.

Six

May, 1814

In the aftermath of Wellington's successful campaign against French forces in the Iberian Peninsula, the British army was sent home. London's citizenry threw themselves into victory celebrations. Every ball or rout—the streets themselves—boasted a sprinkling of uniforms.

Among the soldiers returning to civilian life were Major Ruskin and his friend Captain Jeffries. Nearly five years of warfare had toughened them, turning naive youngsters into men, incompetent officers into seasoned leaders. Among Peninsula veterans Ruskin and Jeffries were quite well known—and respected—as a formidable team.

The journey from Portsmouth, where their ship had landed, had been long and tiring, but they had dropped into a gentlemen's club briefly. Prior to their Peninsula campaign, other club members had barely tolerated them as encroaching puppies. As returning veterans, they were accorded accolades, their company actively sought by others. Now, at the end of their first evening back in London, Theo and Trevor sat in Theo's father's study.

"Here's to us. We survived the misery, the rotten food, and enemy shot." Theo raised his glass.

Trevor returned the salute. "And to absent friends."

"And to absent friends."

As they sat in silence for a few moments, Trevor contrasted

the elegant luxury of the modest Ruskin town house to the hardships he and Theo had endured as the army fought its way through dust and heat in Spain, and mud and cold in the Pyrenees.

Theo broke into his reverie. "What will you do now that we are home, Trev?"

"I hardly know. For five years, I have thought about this—and suddenly I have no answer. How about you?"

"Derbyshire calls. My father wants me to take over running the textile mills and the pottery so he can devote himself to being a gentleman farmer."

"Going to turn you into a cit, is he?" Trevor grinned.

"Perhaps." Theo laughed and held up his hands. "But as the heir to a title, I have to keep these pristine hands above the stench of trade—"

"Even as you grow increasingly rich on the produce of such."

"Does not make much sense, does it?" Theo shrugged. "So—do you think you will return to Atherton?"

"Eventually, I expect to do so. Probably not while Caitlyn is still there."

"She *is* still there, then?"

Trevor looked up, mildly surprised. Theo had carefully refrained from probing into his friend's marital affairs in the years since the initial fiasco, but now Trevor himself had introduced the subject.

"Yes. She adamantly refused to go along with the divorce when my father's solicitor approached her—about two years ago, I believe."

"Why?"

"Sent him away with a flea in his ear about how such an action would be damaging for the child."

"Mothers in any species get mightily protective." Theo sounded deeply philosophical. "So what now? Will *you* pursue a divorce?"

"Perhaps—in time. No hurry for that. I have no desire to remarry any time soon."

The conversation then turned to other matters, chief of which was a huge celebration the Prince Regent was planning to honor Wellington. But later, Trevor lay awake a long while thinking of the wife he had known for less than two weeks over five years ago.

He had never heard from her. Now, *there* was proof—if any was wanting—of her supreme indifference. He had received rare bits of information *about* her—mostly afterthoughts and asides in very infrequent missives from his family.

Thus he had learned about three months after his departure that, yes indeed, the gossip had been true. The girl was definitely breeding. Then, several months later, his mother had added a postscript to a letter. "By the bye, I suppose you have heard your wife was delivered of a babe—a girl—several weeks ago."

Despite his determination to remain nonchalant about the whole affair, these bits of news came as blows. Somehow, he had been hoping it really was all a lie.

There had been little else—besides the news from the solicitor about her refusing either a divorce or legal separation. Well, eventually . . .

Eventually, he told himself firmly, he intended to resume living at Atherton. She would simply have to move to town— or wherever else she wanted to go. It made no difference to him.

Finally, he slept. And dreamed of aquamarine eyes that changed to teal. He arose early the next morning, shaking his head over that dream—one that had not troubled him for many, many months now. Why had it suddenly returned?

Theo had not risen yet, so Trevor decided to take a walk before breakfast. Ruskin House was located near Hyde Park. At this hour, there would be serious riders on Rotten Row— people whose interest in good horseflesh and skillful riding counted for more than the desire to see and be seen which motivated the *ton*'s elite dominating the park later in the day.

Despite his vow to give up owning, riding, or driving excellent horses for sport and pleasure, Trevor had never lost his interest in them. As an army officer, he had been mounted much of the time—soldiers needed to be able to *see* the men leading them. He had a reputation for knowing horses, and was often consulted about purchases or problems with the animals. Still, he adhered to that vow—and became something of an anomaly among his companions.

It was a fine morning. The sun had been up long enough to disperse the night's dew and promised a lovely day. War and death were a world away, and Trevor found himself happy just to be alive. There were a few people in the park, mostly grooms clearly charged with the duty of exercising blooded horses. Trevor watched idly, mentally weighing the merits of the animals paraded before him.

Then he saw her.

Actually, he noticed the horse first—a sleek black going at a hell-for-leather pace. Then his attention went to the rider, drawn there by the fluttering skirt on a riding habit. A woman. A very attractive woman—and in total control of her mount. She was dressed in a dark-blue habit designed in the popular military style. Her hat was a silk top hat with a blue veil, its ends fluttering behind her as she rode. Having let the horse run for some distance, she pulled it up, apparently waiting for someone. The horse was spirited, frisky, but the rider seemed to control it with ease. Finally, her companions caught up with her—a gentleman in the ultra-fashionable dress of a veritable "pink of the *ton*" and a man who could only be a groom.

Trevor was too far away to distinguish what she said to the fashionable one, but he heard clearly her throaty laughter. He caught a glimpse of shiny brown hair with a reddish glow and noted a proud, confident air about her. Unexpectedly, he found himself envying the gentleman. As they turned to leave the park, he noted again how in tune with her mount she seemed.

He stood aside as their horses trotted toward him. When they were almost upon him, the woman seemed to look at him directly, though he could not be sure that she did so because of the veil on her hat. Her mouth formed a round O. Then she was gone.

For a moment, he could have sworn she seemed to recognize him. Throughout the day, the image of the woman in the park stayed with him. That night he dreamed of her—only this time *he* accompanied her. The next morning he made sure he was in the park at the same time. However, she did not appear and he felt foolish for even anticipating she might present herself.

In the evening, he and Theo attended the opera, accompanied by two other officers with whom they had served in the Peninsula. From their box on the second level, they were able to observe a good deal of the audience as well as the stage. One of the other men had been jokingly checking out the women in the audience with his opera glasses.

"Ooh! Found one!" he said with a note of triumph. "How would you like to storm *that* fortress?"

Trevor and the others followed his gaze to a neighboring box occupied by three women and two men. Two of the women were young, as were the men. The other woman, older, was turned away from Trevor and his friends.

There was no doubt about which of the women had caught his friend's attention. Trevor drew in a breath. The beauty from the park! Instantly, he wondered how he could meet her—and just as instantly he told himself what a foolish notion that was.

A woman like that was probably married anyway—as was he, he reminded himself. There was something oddly familiar about her. Her head was uncovered tonight, and that glorious hair was arranged in a stylish manner that complemented her features. She was dressed in a gown of deep iridescent green of what he thought must be silk. He glanced at the other people in the box. He recognized none of them. Wait. The older woman was turning her head.

Aunt Gertrude? Could not be. But it was, indeed, Lady Gertrude Hermiston. He looked more closely at the beauty.

"Here, give me those," he said, grabbing the glasses, too agitated to be polite.

"Hey! I saw her first," the other fellow said.

Just as Trevor focused the glasses on the woman, she looked in his direction. He knew the instant she recognized him. Those distinctive eyes—aquamarine darkening to teal—registered surprise and shock.

He lowered the glasses and sat stunned as the orchestra stopped their discordant tuning noises and the conductor made his appearance.

No wonder she looked familiar. Caitlyn. A very different Caitlyn, but it had to be she with Aunt Gertrude. There was no mistaking those eyes.

Dumbly he handed the glasses back to their owner and sat unseeing and unhearing through the first act. At the interval, he and Theo rose at the same time. Theo gave him a questioning look.

"You all right, Trevor?"

"Yes, of course."

"Seem distracted—or something."

"I . . . uh . . . saw someone I know. Going to pay my respects." He walked away hurriedly to discourage Theo's following him.

When he reached the other box, it was occupied by only one of the gentlemen and the other young woman.

"I beg your pardon," he said. "I thought Lady Gertrude Hermiston was in this box. I intended to pay my respects."

"You just missed her. She and Latham left to take her niece home. Mrs. Jeffries was feeling unwell."

"Oh. Another time, then." He bowed and left without giving his name.

* * *

Caitlyn said barely a word on the return to their London residence and on arrival she bade Latham a hurried good night. When they had divested themselves of gloves and cloaks, Aunt Gertrude steered her into the drawing room.

"Now—would you mind telling me what, precisely, is going on?" the older woman said, taking a seat beside Caitlyn on a settee.

"N-nothing. I told you. I am not feeling well."

"You were fine earlier. Something has upset you. In fact—now that I think on it—you have not been your usual self for a couple of days. What is it, love? Perhaps I can help." Her companion squeezed Caitlyn's hand affectionately.

"Oh, Aunt Gertrude, I am so frightened."

"Of what? Or whom? Surely Lord Latham has not—"

"No. No. Bertie has been kindness itself." She took a deep breath. "Trevor is back."

"Trevor? But he has not called." Caitlyn thought this a foolish statement of the obvious, but surprise did that to people sometimes.

"I saw him in the park two days ago. Tonight he was there—at the opera."

"And he said nothing to you? Nor has he called. How strange. I have heard nothing of his being in town. And I saw Lydia only yesterday at the Seymours. Believe me, had she known he was about, she would have said something, hoping thereby to hurt you."

Caitlyn caught the hint of protectiveness and loved Aunt Gertrude all the more for it. "I—I do not think he recognized me until tonight."

"Well, you *are* much changed from the girl he married."

"I am—thanks to your efforts to turn an ugly duckling into a swan."

"And such a swan!" Aunt Gertrude smiled, then sobered. "But why are you afraid of Trevor?"

"I am afraid of what he might do."

"Do?"

"He may be angry that I refused to agree to the divorce."

"I am sure he will understand that you could not allow it because of Ashley. A divorce would label our darling a bastard—all of society would be assured she is not Trevor's—which she *is!*" This last was added in a most vehement tone.

Caitlyn smiled and kissed her companion's cheek. "Oh, Aunt Gertrude, you *are* a love. You are probably the only one in all of England who believes that."

"No. I hope *you* believe it," she said with a laugh. "And I am sure Melanie believes it, for when she visited prior to going to India, she noted that Ashley looked exactly as she herself did at that age."

"There was a striking resemblance. What a shame Melanie is not here now."

"Oh, but she will be. Did I not tell you? Sheffield is being posted to Vienna when the Congress convenes, but they will be here for a few weeks at any rate."

"Still, I do not know that her presence will make any difference. Trevor believed the lie. He did not respond to any of my letters."

"I know. That was not like the boy I once knew." Aunt Gertrude's voice held a curious blend of wonder and regret.

"People change," Caitlyn said abruptly. "I never knew him well. I can judge only by what he has done in regard to me—and Ashley. And now I am afraid . . ."

"But why? Surely you would like to be free of such uncertainty. You have lived in limbo for five years."

"I am afraid he will not recognize our child—and I fear he will."

"That does not make sense, dear."

"I know. But consider. If Trevor does not accept her—if he goes ahead with a divorce—he brands Ashley an outcast. A boy might have weathered such scandal, but a female cannot. And . . ." She breathed deeply.

"And . . . ?" Aunt Gertrude prompted.

"And if he does accept her, he could . . . he might keep her from me. Aunt Gertrude, I would simply die if I lost her." Caitlyn's voice caught on a sob.

"Now. Now." Gertrude opened her arms, and Caitlyn laid her head gratefully on the older woman's shoulder. "He was never so cruel. Why, he left you with Atherton, did he not? And part of his allowance?"

"That was to be a temporary arrangement only."

"You have done wonders with it."

Caitlyn straightened and wiped at her eyes. "But—but that, too, is frightening."

"I do not understand."

"Atherton belongs to Trevor. Everything I have achieved is *his* legally. I did it for Ashley, but I love Atherton. Now he can take everything. Good grief, he can dispose of *me*— and Ashley—just as he would a . . . a mare and her foal."

"I am sure Trevor would never—"

"How can you be so sure? Just look what happened before. He did exactly as his family demanded. And they hate me. They refused to acknowledge Ashley's birth."

"Still, I cannot believe . . ." Gertrude's voice trailed off.

Caitlyn stood and extended a hand to the other. "Come. Let us both retire. It is bound to look better in the morning."

But after a nearly sleepless night, the situation did not strike Caitlyn as significantly rosier. If anything, she was more frightened and more upset than she had been the evening before. She arose earlier than usual and went directly to the stables, where she found the black gelding to be extremely frisky.

"Ah, you need to work out some kinks, too, don't you, boy?" she murmured to the horse, which merely pricked its ears in response and swiveled its head for the lump of sugar or an apple she was sure to have. This brought a smile. "You are a spoiled child, are you not?"

She and Black Knight had soon left her groom far behind.

She allowed the horse to run at will for perhaps twenty minutes, then slowed him to a walk, waiting for the groom to catch up.

"He's lookin' real fine, ma'am," the groom said, a bit out of breath.

"Yes," she agreed, patting the animal's neck. "I think he is almost ready. Lord Carstairs will be pleased with our noble Knight."

"Ain't none of our horses but would please the most pa'tic'lar of gentlemen, I'm thinkin'."

"Your loyalty is most appreciated, Henry." She gave him a smile and glanced across the field over which she had just ridden. Yes. Over there—near the gate she usually used—was a figure she knew instinctively to be her husband.

"We shall use this gate to return," she said to the groom, gesturing to another entrance. Henry gave her a glance of curiosity, for they both knew this route would increase the horse's exposure to street activity and likely be unsettling for an animal of Black Knight's sensibility. "Knight must become accustomed to traffic," she explained.

"Yes, ma'am."

Seeing her departure, Trevor cursed his luck. Had she seen him, then, and deliberately avoided him? She must know they would eventually have to meet. He had thought to have their initial meeting in this relatively private location. Well, nothing for it but he would call on his wife and his aunt this afternoon, for he had learned that Caitlyn rented a house for the season.

Distracted during breakfast, Trevor gave a start when Theo called to him.

"I beg your pardon," Trevor said.

Theo laughed. "And well you might. I have spoken to you three times with no response. Where *were* you?"

Trevor shrugged and avoided the question. "I am here now. You were saying . . . ?"

"It occurs to me that I need a good mount. I plan to check out offerings at Tattersall's this morning. Would you care to come along?"

"No, I think not. I intend to see my solicitor and then pay a couple of calls." When Theo said nothing, merely raised an eyebrow, Trevor added, "I must begin to sort myself out sometime, you know."

"You have not forgot about tonight? Wilson is expecting us."

"I know. I shall be there."

Trevor did not elaborate on his plans. For some inexplicable reason, he had not shared with Theo the news of seeing Caitlyn. The *shock* of seeing her. Before discussing anything with his friend, he would see her—*after* calling on his solicitor and his mother. He was quite sure his father would not be in town. He would pen the earl a note later.

The visit to the solicitor, a man named Whitcomb, produced yet another shock. Far from being run-down and in need of large infusions of money, Atherton, it seemed, was now a going concern, producing profits that were, in turn, generating other funds.

"But how . . . ? I had not thought Felkins so capable," Trevor said, dazed. "Did my brother Marcus—"

" 'Twasn't Felkins. Nor your brother," Whitcomb interrupted. "It was her—Mrs. Jeffries."

"Mrs.—?"

"Your wife, Captain That little gel has a real head on her pretty shoulders."

"My wife?" Trevor repeated dumbly.

"She worked with Felkins and the tenants. Pestered anyone who would listen for books and treatises. Can't say I approve of a woman doing such, but she managed to turn that place around."

"She did?" Trevor simply could not digest all this.

"First thing she did was instruct me to inform Wyndham that henceforth your allowance would come from your own property. And so it has—for about three years now."

"You mean—?"

"Yes, Captain Jeffries. You have been a man of independent means for that long. But surely you knew. Surely your wife wrote you?" Whitcomb sounded confused and curious.

"Perhaps she did." Trevor was deliberately vague. "Things were a bit chaotic where I was."

Whitcomb gave a sympathetic chuckle. "As I say, I cannot condone a woman meddling in a man's business, but now that you are home . . ."

Later, Trevor thought he must have nodded agreement, for Whitcomb carried on in that vein for several more minutes. Finally, Trevor left the man's office carrying a packet of copies of reports on his estate and other financial affairs associated with it.

Back on the street, it struck him. He had not remembered to ask about dissolving the marriage. Well, perhaps he should talk with Caitlyn first. He owed her that much.

He called at Wyndham House to find his mother blessedly alone. In five years, the countess had aged only a little. A few pounds—not even a stone, he thought—and a few fine lines. His mother was fighting the battle against time with style and flair.

"Trevor, you naughty, naughty boy!" she simpered. "Why has your own mother learned of your return from common gossip?"

Trevor did not immediately respond, though he dutifully kissed the cheek she presented to him, and she went on, "I heard the news last night from Mrs. Drummond-Burrell who had it from her husband who saw you at some club."

"You must know, Mother, that I was unsure of my reception in this house." Something in his tone or demeanor seemed to register with his mother.

"Why, whatever do you mean?"

"I am sure you know that the wishes you and Father and Gerald expressed at our last family gathering have not been fulfilled."

"Yes. I do know, dear. That nasty bit of baggage managed to thwart our plans. But now that you are home, it will be sorted out, will it not?"

"That 'nasty bit of baggage' is still my wife." His voice carried a warning note that surprised him—and was apparently not lost on his mother.

"Oh, I did not mean . . . Well, you must know, Trevor, that she is received in some circles. Not the highest *ton,* of course."

"I know little of Caitlyn's activities," Trevor said, not wanting to admit he knew nothing. He really did not want to sit here discussing his wife, but he understood his mother well enough to know she would chew this bit of gossip to the very bone.

"She goes around in Gertrude's tiresome literary and political circles. Oh. And I understand she is seen frequently in company with the new Viscount Latham." The countess looked at him as though she were assessing how he would take this news.

"Latham." Trevor kept his voice carefully neutral. He was well aware that this was the name associated with his wife at the time of their marriage—and the name of the man last night.

"I must admit," his mother said grudgingly, "she has been discreet in this liaison. And," she ended airily, "it really will not matter once you are rid of her."

Trevor gritted his teeth and changed the subject to ask about his brothers and Melanie. He learned that Melanie was to arrive soon from India where she had gone after her marriage to Sheffield. Currently posted to Paris, Marcus, like Sheffield, was in the foreign service. And Gerald continued to school himself to become the fourteenth Earl of Wyndham.

Having stayed longer than he intended, he finally took his

leave when other guests were welcomed to his mother's drawing room.

His next stop was Caitlyn's town residence.

He told himself he probably should have gone here first, but he was reluctant to confront Caitlyn. He genuinely wanted to see the beautiful woman who had caught his eye first in the park, then at the opera. But he was apprehensive about all the unresolved issues between them—chief of which now loomed as the continuing presence of Latham in her life.

The butler was a superior sort who seemed not to recognize the significance of this visitor. "I am sorry, sir. Mrs. Jeffries is out and Her Ladyship is entertaining her Society for Saving the Overlooked Unfortunates of Our Nation. Should you care to join them?"

"No. No. I will not intrude." Trevor reached for a card and, taking a pen from a table in the foyer, scribbled a hasty note. "Please, give them this."

Seven

Caitlyn knew she was merely postponing the inevitable by avoiding Trevor. Twice now he had called to find her not at home. The first time had been purely chance, but the second incident was by her design. Time was no longer on her side, and she had to come to a decision. His presence in town and absence from his wife's home was rapidly becoming the latest *on dit* in *ton* gatherings.

Viscount Latham invited her for a drive in the afternoon of the day she had deliberately avoided Trevor. As soon as he had served a proper period of mourning for his father, the new viscount sought to renew his acquaintance with his adolescent love.

Flattered by his continued regard, Caitlyn could not bring herself to reject one of the few people in her own class to offer genuine friendship. Early on, she made it clear to him that she was not free to accept anything beyond mere friendship.

"I shall honor your wishes, Mrs. Jeffries," he had said stiffly, "though I would hope one day to change your mind."

"Bertie!" She did not bother to hide her impatience with him. "You need not poker up so. We were friends once. I hope we will remain so."

"As you wish, my dear Caitlyn, for I have ever thought of you so."

Now as he handed her into the carriage, he squeezed her hand and held it a shade longer than she found comfortable.

He took up the reins and seemed to devote himself to the business of driving, though she was aware of an occasional lingering look. She concentrated on enjoying the sunny afternoon and seeing the *ton* on parade in all their finery.

On entering the park, Latham slowed his horses and turned his attention directly to her. "Caitlyn, I . . . uh . . . I understand your husband is back in town."

"Yes, he is." She did not elaborate.

"Does that mean . . . that is . . . will he free you now that he has returned?"

"Free me?" She knew she sounded a bit haughty, but the question rankled.

He ran an index finger around his intricately tied neckcloth. "You must know there is talk of a divorce . . . I mean . . . well, 'tis well known his family does not receive you."

"Well known, is it?" She hoped her tone would deflect this topic, but Bertie seemed determined to state his view.

"Yes, it is." His voice was adamant, but he looked uncomfortable.

"You would do well, Bertie, not to allow yourself to be a party to common gossip."

His face reddened at this reprimand and he caught at her hand.

"Oh, Caitlyn, my own. I would never, ever myself be a party to hurting you." His tone fervent, he brought her gloved hand to his lips.

She extricated herself from his grip as adroitly as she could without drawing undue attention from passersby. "Please. Lord Latham, you forget yourself."

"You cannot say you care nothing for me. Have you forgot what we once meant to each other?"

"Bertie, we were children." Her tone deliberately suggested she was even now talking to a child.

"While my father lived and controlled my income, I could not approach you. And since we have become reacquainted,

I thought to allow you far more time, my darling, but now *his* reappearance causes me to act in a more precipitous manner than I intended."

"Bertie—Lord Latham—I hardly know what to say."

He had stopped the team entirely, motioned his tiger to hold their heads, and turned now on the seat toward her. He grasped her hands again. "When you are free, we can be together. I care not what society will say—nor my mother! I love you, Caitlyn, and I will wait for you forever."

His melodramatic tone struck her as funny, but she could not bring herself to crush him by openly laughing at him. "Please, Bertie. This is neither the time nor the place." Again she loosened herself from his grip. She could see that they were attracting attention. She pasted a carefree smile on her face and nodded to an acquaintance in a passing carriage.

She was relieved when Bertie seemed to do the same, but he continued in a low tone, "I have waited for you, wanted you all these years—"

"Please. You must stop this line of discussion immediately. It is most improper."

"My feelings are far too strong to regard empty rules of propriety," he said in the same melodramatic tone. Caitlyn wondered if part of him sat aside applauding his performance.

"Bertie!" Her tone was stern now. "I have, in the last few weeks, enjoyed a renewal of your friendship. But never—not once—have I intended to give you reason to think I would welcome such a declaration as this."

"But we loved each other—" he wailed.

"Whatever we may have felt for each other was over long, long ago. Over. Do you understand?"

"It was never over for me." He seemed to be pouting now.

"Well," she declared firmly, "I have a child whose welfare comes first for me." In truth, she was finding him tiresome and wondered how she had ever fancied herself in love with such a shallow coxcomb.

"Which makes me admire you all the more for being will-ing to sacrifice your own happiness for hers."

"Oh, good grief," she muttered under her breath. Aloud, she said, "This has gone quite far enough. I am no martyr. And I will thank you to take me home. Now."

Finally, her tone seemed to break through the scene he imagined himself playing. He gave her a reproachful look, but he signaled his tiger and they returned in relative silence.

"I hope I may be allowed to call again?" he asked as he accompanied her to the door.

"Of course." Her tone was distantly polite. "You are wel-come—as a friend."

He bowed and departed.

Viscount Latham's performance in the park served as a reminder to Caitlyn that her situation was delicate, to say the least. Five years since her marriage!—since her husband had deserted her—and her feelings were as ambivalent as ever.

She had been angry when Trevor left. Furious, in fact. It was his action that had trapped her in this marriage. And then the blackguard had not even stood by her as his family and the *ton* gossips tore her to shreds. She was his wife. Husbands were supposed to protect their wives, were they not?

He had left her to fend for herself. Honesty compelled her to remember that he had been responsible for his Aunt Ger-trude's coming to her. She knew it had been Lady Gertrude's own idea to come, but Trevor had not wanted her to be en-tirely alone, had he? Also, Caitlyn remembered the warmth they had begun to feel for each other—at least, she had thought they both felt it.

The man in the park and at the opera was not the callow youth who had left her. This man's physical presence—even from a distance—was more solid. His shoulders were broader, and he carried himself with self-assurance, none of the swag-ger of the young. That first recognition as he stood at the side of the bridle path had been a shock to her. She had accepted, however reluctantly, the idea of making a life with that youth of yesterday. Could she do the same with this man?

The idea of a divorce had been repugnant from the very beginning. To the daughter of a churchman, it was especially abhorrent. Then she had discovered herself with child. She remembered being sick at the very idea of bringing a babe into such a world. She hated the idea of bearing the child of a man who despised its mother. She even thought for a while she would never be able to love the child.

How preposterous that idea seemed now! And she knew exactly when her view had changed.

She had been about six months into her pregnancy when the Jeffries family had taken the first step to be rid of her. As heir to the Wyndham title, Trevor's brother Gerald had thought to lend his importance to the solicitor's presence when that gentleman called at Atherton.

Caitlyn and Lady Gertrude had received the two visitors together. After greetings, Gerald said, "Um . . . Mrs. Jeffries, I wonder if we may speak with you privately of a family matter?" Caitlyn could tell he hated according her the Jeffries name.

Apprehensive, she looked at Lady Gertrude, who shrugged and excused herself, giving Caitlyn an encouraging pat on the shoulder as she left, saying, "I shall be in the next room, my dear." Gerald nodded to the solicitor, a man of some fifty or sixty years, who was dressed soberly and seemed ingratiatingly eager to please his client.

The lawyer cleared his throat. "Hmm. Yes. Now—it is our belief that your . . . uh . . . husband informed you of his and his family's wishes?"

"Their wishes?" Caitlyn refused to make this easy for them.

"Regarding a divorce." The lawyer's tone was patient and condescending.

"Oh. A divorce is out of the question." Unconsciously, she placed her hand on her stomach. "I do not know the Jeffries family history well, but divorce is simply unknown in my family."

She saw a deep flush suffuse Gerald's features. "Now see here, madam. This so-called marriage is a ridiculous embarrassment to my family."

"The marriage was not of my making," she said, keeping her voice calm, "but I am assured it is perfectly legal."

"Well, yes," the lawyer said, "and as such may be legally— and I may say quietly—dissolved."

"It will be *quietly* dissolved only if I quietly agree. I do not agree." She enunciated each word very precisely.

The color deepened in Gerald's face as he asked, "How much?"

"I beg your pardon?"

"I said, 'How much?' My father and I are prepared to pay to have this problem go away. How much?"

"The 'problem,' as you put it, is not going to go away." Caitlyn felt the babe move as though to confirm its interest in the discussion. "I do not mean to be rude, sir, but I fail to see how you are concerned at all."

Gerald looked nearly apoplectic as he said stiffly, "I speak for the Earl of Wyndham in saying it is simply unacceptable that our name be involved in such a distasteful affair."

Not knowing quite how to respond to this, Caitlyn remained silent, so Gerald went on, "You may congratulate yourself that the scheme you and Fiske manufactured has proved so lucrative. I ask you again—how much?"

"You, sir, are insulting. I believe this interview is over." She tried to rise gracefully, but in her condition that proved impossible.

"Please. Just a moment, Mrs. Jeffries," the lawyer said in a conciliatory tone. "I would ask you to reconsider. The earl is prepared to give you enough to allow you to go to the American colonies, where you may begin your life all over. And to provide adequately for your child."

"Oh, I see." She could not quell the sarcasm. "All I have to do is hang a label of illegitimacy on my babe."

"No one need ever know." The lawyer looked at Gerald, who nodded, and the two of them rose. "We shall leave you now, madam. I would urge you to consider carefully the earl's generous offer. Next time he may not be so magnanimous."

When they had gone, Caitlyn railed against these two—as well as the earl and her uncle and, finally and most vehemently, against her absent husband.

"My dear, such strong emotion is not good for your babe," Aunt Gertrude cautioned.

"He—or she—may as well know right off its mama has a temper. The idea! 'Magnanimous,' indeed!" She spit out the word. "Declare your child a bastard and we will treat you well."

"Now, now, dear."

A year later the lawyer returned—without the odious Gerald this time. His message was essentially the same. And so was hers. She remained adamant about protecting the interests of her daughter. Gossip might question the child's parentage, but Caitlyn would never willingly acquiesce to a court's denying Ashley's legal rights.

By that time, however, Caitlyn's hard work on Atherton had already begun to pay off. That is, she could see that rewards would eventually materialize. She remembered well her sense of triumph when she had directed her own solicitor to inform Wyndham's agent that henceforth the family of Mr. Trevor Jeffries would not rely on Wyndham's largess.

Lady Gertrude had been invaluable, providing help wherever it was needed. Without asserting herself as an authority, that intrepid lady set about training her nephew's bride to command a large staff.

Having demanded that Mrs. Bassett turn over the ledgers of household accounts, Caitlyn read them with interest as a source of knowledge about her new home. Then she read them with a sense of puzzlement. Something was wrong, but Caitlyn could not put her finger on the problem. She asked Aunt Gertrude to examine the accounts. Immediately, the older woman pointed out precisely how the housekeeper had managed to juggle the books so as to double her salary.

"I knew there was *something* wrong," Caitlyn said.

"Had you more experience with the running of a household and keeping accounts yourself, I have no doubt you would have seen it, too," Aunt Gertrude assured her.

Caitlyn felt overwhelmed. "I have so much to learn—and not just about household matters."

"Motherhood is a lifelong school of learning."

"Oh, I am quite sure it is—and I shall certainly need a great deal of guidance there. But what I meant was I need to learn about managing the entire estate."

"The estate? A slip of a girl running a concern of hundreds of acres and dozens of tenant farms? You cannot be serious."

"I am serious, though."

"But there is a steward . . ."

"Mr. Felkins is a very amiable gentleman. Honest, too, I think. He performs adequately, but he has so little insight. He is a follower, not a leader."

"And you are thinking *you* will provide necessary leadership?" Aunt Gertrude's tone held more curiosity than challenge.

"Well—with your errant nephew off to the Peninsula, there seems no one else to do it."

"That would be a huge undertaking, my dear."

"I know. But I rather think I would enjoy the challenge."

"I fear it would be much more. You have two major obstacles to overcome—perhaps insurmountable obstacles."

"What?"

"Your sex and your youth. Not to mention inexperience there, too. The men you would have to work with—both here and elsewhere—would never welcome a woman in their midst—and certainly not one who looks like a mere girl."

"That is why I must continue to rely on Mr. Felkins. He shall convey my orders and conduct any negotiations. We will thus endeavor to protect delicate male sensibilities."

Lady Gertrude laughed. "Ah, Caitlyn, my love. You remind me of myself thirty years ago."

"I consider that a compliment of the highest order indeed, my lady."

"Back to the issue at hand. What is to be done about your Mrs. Bassett?"

"She will have to go," Caitlyn said without hesitation. "I could deal with incompetence, but not dishonesty."

"That would be my view, too. Would you like me to inform her?"

"No. I thank you for offering. I know all the staff respect you greatly, but I think this is something I must do."

"I agree." The older woman's tone was admiring.

The subsequent interview with Mrs. Bassett was as unpleasant as Caitlyn had feared. Confronted with evidence of her pilfering and altering the accounts, the surly housekeeper had little to offer in her own defense. She left Atherton muttering, "You'll be sorry about this."

Caitlyn knew she was in for another round of backbiting gossip, for Mrs. Bassett remained in the area, having gone to stay with her daughter in the village. It was common knowledge that the daughter—and, more particularly, the daughter's husband—did not welcome the woman with open arms.

The housekeeper's dismissal worked wonders with the remaining staff. Even the irascible cook became more tractable. So long as there were only Caitlyn and Lady Gertrude to provide for, the household would run smoothly without additional servants.

Her interview with Mr. Felkins in which she laid out some of her ideas for the estate went much more smoothly than the one with the housekeeper. Mr. Felkins proved to be every bit as amiable and helpful as Caitlyn had hoped. In his forties, Felkins was short and rotund. He reminded Caitlyn of pictures of a penguin. He had thinning dark hair and a double chin, but his brown eyes showed warmth and humor. Once he understood a given idea, he was able to come up with practical suggestions to implement it.

"Our biggest problem is lack of funds to make major changes," she said.

"Yes, ma'am," Felkins replied. "We are shorthanded because of the war. So many men gone for soldiers. Also, Boney's embargo of English goods has been disastrous for the wool trade."

"Do *all* our tenant farmers devote themselves exclusively to raising sheep?"

"Mostly. Some gardens, but generally for their own use. Some of the women sell some extra vegetables and eggs in the village."

"Would these families be amenable to making some changes?"

"Guess that would depend on what was in it for them." Felkins sounded hesitant.

"I want a meeting with all the tenant farmers—*and* their wives. Can you arrange it for, say, three days from now? We shall use the ballroom on the first floor. It is shabby, but freshly cleaned."

"Yes, ma'am. What shall I tell 'em it's about?"

"The future of Atherton."

Three days later, she welcomed an assortment of farmers and their wives, who had apparently decked themselves out in such finery as was available to them. The ballroom was set up with a buffet table of refreshments. Caitlyn had learned from her father's dealings with parishioners that people were more receptive to new ideas if they were plied with food and drink. Still, these were conservative farm people, suspicious of change. Moreover, most of them were ten, twenty, or even thirty years older than she. Caitlyn knew them all by name, for she had made a point of learning as much as she could about them in the last few weeks. She recognized curiosity in many, and apprehension on the faces of some.

"This isn't about an increase in the rents, is it, missus?" one grizzled old fellow asked, his voice showing a conflict between assertiveness and deference. He was obviously one whom others looked to as a leader.

"No, Mr. Hawkins, it is not." She heard a collective sigh, especially from the women. She took a seat at a table that had been set in the front of the room. Mr. Felkins also sat at the table, and Aunt Gertrude occupied a chair unobtrusively in the back row. Caitlyn was grateful for her moral support. "It is about making Atherton more profitable. And since you folks *are* Atherton, Mr. Felkins and I thought to get your views."

There were some general murmurs of approval at this.

"Let's hear what the gel has in mind," an older woman called out.

"Thank you, Mrs. Porter." Caitlyn waited for attention and went on, "Mr. Felkins and I are agreed that we seem far too dependent on one thing—sheep. Perhaps if we were to diversify—that is, include other activities as well—we could weather setbacks more easily."

She paused to let this sink in.

"Makes sense to me," someone said.

"Other activities? Such as *what?*" someone else asked.

"That is the matter we are here to explore," she said. That was another thing she had learned as a child at parish meetings: let people come up with ideas of their own—or at least *think* they were their own. "We are sitting on some of the richest land in all of England. Surely we can come up with some ideas in addition to our sheep—and perhaps not be so dependent on foreign markets."

And indeed they did come up with ideas. A variety of crops were suggested, and aspects of dairy farming came under discussion. Enthusiasm spread as they began to entertain the idea that, by working together and sharing, they could not only make Atherton entirely self-sufficient, but turn a profit as well. Finally, Caitlyn offered her own idea, carefully couching it as a question to these older—and, of course, wiser—men.

"Horses?" It was more of a snort than a question from Hawkins. "You want to raise horses?"

"It . . . it was just a thought." She pretended hesitance. "I mean . . . we are so close to Newmarket . . . and there are other stud farms here in East Anglia . . ." She allowed her voice to trail off.

"Might could be a good idea," someone said.

"Why not?" another asked.

"Because gettin' started takes a bloody damned lot of the ready," another man replied, then turned bright red and added, "Beggin' your pardon, ladies."

Caitlyn ignored his unseemly language. "I suppose you are right, Mr. Watson. Still—it gives us something to think about. However," she said to the room at large, "Mr. Watson does bring up a serious issue, and that is capital—the 'ready,' if you will—to get started. Mr. Felkins will tell you about that."

Actually, it had been Caitlyn's plan, but she wanted the men in the room to think that most of the idea came from another man, one of their own. Time enough to tell them differently when it succeeded—or failed. But she could not think of failure. The very idea was terrifying, and if she thought about it, she might do nothing. "Nothing" was equally terrifying.

From that day forward, Atherton—and, later, baby Ashley—became the center of her life. Now, with Trevor's return, everything had gone topsy-turvy. Had she made a serious error in focusing her whole being in such a manner?

Eight

Trevor was angry. Well—annoyed, anyway. He had called twice at the London house his wife rented, but she had been "out" both times. At least that was what that infernal butler told him. Moreover, Aunt Gertrude was unavailable both times as well.

He descended the steps the second time in a thoughtful mood. Were *both* of them trying to avoid him? He could perhaps understand Caitlyn's desire to do so. But Aunt Gertrude? Such behavior did not seem at all in character for her. Should he wait around, hoping one or both of them would return shortly?

While the house did not boast an address in the most elite neighborhood, it was located in a very respectable residential area. Houses here all faced a small park with a high iron fence around it. The park was obviously for the exclusive use of the surrounding houses, for it was accessible only through a locked gate. Trevor could see benches scattered here and there, a sand pile, and what appeared to be a small shallow pool in which some little boys were eagerly sailing toy boats.

He smiled to himself, recalling fond memories of doing the same thing with Terrence. And Melanie usually on the sidelines, cheering them on in impromptu races. At this thought, his attention was caught by a little girl with golden blond curls enviously watching the little boys and their boats. Someone apparently called her name, for the little girl turned, answered, and with seeming reluctance left the pond. As she turned, she faced him fully, and Trevor thought again of the young Melanie of yesteryear.

Melanie.

His mother had told him Melanie would return to England soon. How he looked forward to seeing her!

He wandered slowly around the outside of the park twice, but in that time only one carriage entered the area and those who were afoot were mostly nursery maids out taking the air with their charges. When he had encountered the same middle-aged maid twice and she cast him a suspicious glance, he decided to leave.

That night he and Theo sat sipping port in the lounge of the gentlemen's club where they had just had dinner. Trevor had finally told Theo of seeing his wife and of his attempts to call on her.

"Do you think she deliberately avoids you, then?" Theo asked.

"Possibly."

"I suppose you could disguise yourself as a highwayman and waylay her carriage some evening." Theo grinned.

"Do be serious."

"Well . . . hmm. Maybe she goes to the assemblies at Almack's."

"I . . . uh . . . I doubt it. The patronesses are said to be high sticklers. My mother informs me that Caitlyn is received, but not among the highest *ton*."

"Oh." Theo seemed embarrassed at having mentioned it, then added, "You know, we both have invitations to the Bathmoreson ball. I hear the marchioness fancies herself outdoing the prince himself—she has invited everyone with even the slightest claim to society's recognition."

"I should much prefer seeing my estranged wife privately."

"But if she will not see you . . . ?"

"You are right. It is an idea. She could hardly make a scene in such a public arena."

Just then their attention was diverted by a rather loud discussion nearby. The chairs in the lounge—big, overstuffed, comfortable pieces of furniture—were arranged in conversational groups. In one group there were three young men whose talk was louder than it should be. They seemed to revel in the attention they were drawing, unaware that it was censorious.

"Lord! Were *we* ever so young and stupid?" Theo asked softly.

Trevor nodded. "Yesterday."

"Must have been the day before yesterday. Yesterday was the Peninsula."

"Right." They were both quiet for a moment, remembering.

"What are they talking about anyway?" Theo asked.

"Horses."

"Reminds me. I still want you to look over a purchase I am considering."

Before Trevor could respond, two other young men in high spirits joined those in the neighboring chairs.

"Atkins!" one of the newcomers called. "Did you buy that pair Severson was selling?"

"I surely did." Atkins's voice had a note of smug triumph.

"Good show." the newcomer replied.

"Wish I could have bid on those," the other newcomer said.

"You do?" someone else asked.

"Yes. Severson got 'em from the Jeffries farms."

Hearing his own surname, Trevor suddenly took real interest in the neighboring conversation.

"No, he didn't," another said. "Those animals came from the Ratcliff stables."

"Oh." The voice sounded deflated, and their talk turned to some pugilistic contest. Suddenly there were as many experts on the art of boxing as there had been on horses a few moments before.

"Jeffries farms?" Trevor asked. "You ever hear of them?"

"No," Theo said, "I have not. Your brother? A cousin maybe?"

"Could be, I suppose. Marcus has quite an eye for horse-flesh. Might be Cousin Algernon. The whole Jeffries clan is enamored of our equine friends." Trevor shrugged and dismissed the idea from his mind.

Caitlyn dressed for the Bathmoreson ball with special care. The gown, teal-colored silk with silver trim, made her eyes seem darker. Her up-to-date hair style set off the clean lines of her face and neck. Her only jewelry, besides her wedding band worn under her glove, was a simple diamond necklace and diamond drops at her ears.

"You look lovely, my dear," Aunt Gertrude said as the two of them donned cloaks to set off for the ball.

"This neckline is not too *décolleté,* then?"

"No. One sees much more daring lines on even women my age, I am sure."

Caitlyn fidgeted nervously. "It is just that I am sure the countess will be there tonight and I do not want her to have anything in me to criticize." There was no need to explain to Aunt Gertrude precisely which countess Caitlyn had in mind.

"Lydia would find *something* to criticize if you appeared in a costume identical to the queen's. But no one else will do aught but admire you."

"Thank you, Aunt Gertrude." Caitlyn kissed the older woman's cheek. "What would I ever have done without you?" It was a sincere tribute.

Aunt Gertrude's eyes looked suspiciously watery at this. "We are quite a team, you and I. Now, come. Let us prepare to meet the *ton* in their own arena."

Caitlyn and Aunt Gertrude had been coming to town for the season for three years now. Caitlyn knew Aunt Gertrude had missed her sojourns in town before that. True, Aunt Gertrude loved their life in the country, where she was very active in helping to run the now expanded household. A few months after joining Caitlyn in East Anglia, Aunt Gertrude had given up her own house in London and brought her housekeeper and two maids to Atherton. Her other servants had chosen to find new positions in the city.

However, Aunt Gertrude had never given up her love of town—nor her interest in various "projects." Caitlyn thought coming to the city for a few weeks of the year was little enough she could do for this wonderful woman who had done so much for her. Therefore, she willingly indulged Aunt Gertrude in this. They lived modestly—and happily—on the fringes of society. Tonight marked their first real venture into the heart of the *ton*. Thank goodness, it was a huge affair—where one might become lost in the crowd.

"Caitlyn." Aunt Gertrude broke into her musings as the carriage made its slow way to the entrance of the Bathmoreson mansion. "Caitlyn, I had not wanted to bring this up, but I feel I should."

"What? What is it?" Caitlyn reacted to the concern in her companion's voice.

"Well, you know Trevor has called two—or is it three?—times. And we have been out."

"Yes. And of course I shall not again endeavor to avoid him. It was foolish to do so, and I do regret it."

"Your chance to live up to that intention may come sooner than later."

"Tonight? Here? Oh, surely not." She could not control a note of apprehension.

"Probably not. Trevor was never fond of such affairs before. But I thought you should be prepared for the possibility."

"Thank you. It really had not entered my mind."

And now that it had, how did she feel about it? Well—she mentally squared her shoulders—why should she fear a meeting? After all, is was not *she* who had run off to the Peninsula, shirking all responsibilities at home. Then their carriage was at the entrance and a footman was available to hand them down.

Caitlyn felt a frisson of trepidation as she went through the receiving line, but the marquis and his wife were both cordial and hospitable. Soon she and Aunt Gertrude passed into the ballroom, which contained an overwhelming number of elegantly dressed men and women. She saw the countess of Wyndham go into one of the card rooms. Although Aunt Gertrude had pointed the countess out to Caitlyn on more than one occasion, she had never formally met her mother-in-law. Nor did she expect the woman to acknowledge her tonight.

Viscount Latham had apparently been waiting for her arrival. "Ah, Caitlyn, dear Caitlyn." He ostentatiously kissed the air above her gloved hand and bowed to Her Ladyship. "Lady Gertrude."

The two women murmured polite greetings to him.

"You must allow me to stand up with you, Caitlyn." Latham extended his hand for her dance card. "I must have this country dance," he said, scribbling his name, "and this waltz which is the supper dance. All right, my dear?"

"No," she said sharply, all but grabbing the card away from him. "It is not all right. Bertie, you know very well two dances would draw undue attention. You may have the country dance."

"I have no fear of undue attention where you are concerned, dear Caitlyn." He looked slightly fatuous, she thought.

"Well, *I* have," she snapped.

"As you will, my dear," he huffed, and then excused himself.

"Insufferable puppy," Aunt Gertrude said.

"Oh, he means well." Caitlyn sighed.

Her dance card was by no means filled, but neither was she the most ignored of wallflowers. She danced with a young man who belonged to the literary society and with a middle-aged and well-married friend of Aunt Gertrude's, before Bertie came to claim his dance.

"Hmmph," he sniffed. "You may as well have allowed me that second dance."

"Oh, Bertie, do behave." She smiled to take the sting out of her words.

It was one of those country dances that allowed a couple to alternately dance vigorously and then pause while others swung down the line. During one of their pauses, Bertie looked over Caitlyn's shoulder and said, "Don't look now, but some newcomers just entered. I do believe one of them is Jeffries."

Sheer panic drained the blood from her face. She caught her breath and gripped Bertie's hand far more tightly than she intended.

"Caitlyn? Are you all right?" Bertie asked.

"Yes. Yes . . . I am fine." But she knew she was not fine, even as she allowed him to swing her into the remaining steps of the dance.

When Bertie returned her to Aunt Gertrude's company, there was Trevor, talking with his aunt just as though this were not a momentous occasion in their lives. How dare he be so calm, so relaxed?

"I shall stand by you, my dear," Bertie said softly, sounding melodramatic again and keeping his hand on her elbow possessively.

Aware that their little tableau was attracting the attention of bystanders, Caitlyn deliberately forced a smile and greeted her long-absent husband with a great show of cordiality.

"Hello, Trevor." To her surprise, her voice did not tremble.

"Caitlyn." His eyes locked with hers, but she found his expression unreadable. Then he gave a little bow. "Uh . . . Latham, is it not? You will not think it amiss, I am sure, if I take my wife off your hands for the next dance?"

It was an order rather than a request, and Caitlyn was sure Bertie recognized it as such. There was a fraction of a moment when it seemed Bertie might protest. Trevor's expression was pleasant enough, but his eyes and voice held a hint of controlled power and determination. Caitlyn glanced at Aunt Gertrude and knew the other woman shared her fear of a scene. Caitlyn moved closer to her husband and took the arm he offered.

Latham nodded and said to Caitlyn, "I shall call upon you on the morrow." He left them, his head at a haughty angle.

The instant she touched him, Caitlyn felt a distinctly physical reaction to Trevor. None of the men she had known in the last few years had affected her so. Bertie, with whom she had thought herself in love at sixteen, had never elicited such a response. She recalled feeling a warm sense of welcome for the younger Trevor, but not this violent bolt of emotion.

And, oh, good heavens! The music was a waltz. She would be in his arms in a moment. Then she *was* in his arms, and intensely aware of every point at which their bodies connected—his hand at her waist, hers at his shoulder, and their other hands loosely clasped. She could feel her heart beating and her pulse pounding.

She caught a whiff of a faintly spicy smell about him—clean and crisp, totally unlike the overwhelming and cloying cologne of her previous partner. She wanted to lean in closer. Was it spice or sandalwood? Then she came to her senses. Good heavens. What could it possibly matter?

She could not bring herself to look at him directly. Despite her reaction to him, Caitlyn was angry. Angry at him for high-handedly maneuvering her into this dance. Angry at herself for allowing it—for being helpless to refuse it in this public forum. She hated feeling trapped.

They danced silently for a moment; then he said, "Have you been deliberately avoiding me?"

So. He was not going to bother with small talk. And she took immediate umbrage at his putting her on the defensive. She looked up into those blue-gray eyes, not bothering to hide her annoyance at the challenge in his question. "Yes."

He waited, apparently expecting her to explain. She did not do so.

"Why?" he asked.

"Why should I not do so?" she countered.

"Because," he said, his patience sounding extremely forced, "we are, it seems, still tied by the bonds of holy matrimony, my dear."

"Oh." Her voice held a false note of surprise, and she smiled at him with ultra sweetness. "Is this a matter that has only recently come to your attention?"

His hand tightened on hers and his voice was cold. "No. It is a matter of which I have long been painfully aware."

"You poor dear." Her voice dripped sarcasm, but inwardly she winced. *A hit. A palpable hit,* she thought, foolishly echoing a line from *Hamlet.*

"Look. This is neither the time nor place for this discussion. Do you think you might possibly manage to be at home if I call tomorrow to continue our conversation?"

"Of course. Your wish is my command, husband dear."

He compressed his lips, and his eyes snapped with anger at this sally, but he merely swung her smoothly through the remaining steps of the waltz.

Caitlyn chewed the inner part of her bottom lip. She did not know why she had responded as she had. Perhaps because he seemed so in control and she wanted to break through that protective facade. Perhaps because she had been harboring her resentment for nearly five years.

He returned her to Aunt Gertrude and bade them both good night. Then he was gone—having left as abruptly as he had arrived. Soon afterwards, Caitlyn and Aunt Gertrude made their excuses and left also.

"How did it go? Or should I ask?" Theo's tone was light as he and Trevor once again sat in the Ruskin library at the end of an evening.

"Not well, I fear."

"She is a beautiful woman," Theo opined in a neutral tone.

"And a very angry one." Trevor flinched inwardly as he recalled her sarcasm.

"*She* is angry? Why? Because you did not die in the Peninsula?"

"No, it is not that, I am sure."

"I may have a distorted view—you being my friend and all—but it does appear to me that *you* have been the aggrieved party in this. I mean, most women wait a few years before saddling their husbands with another man's brat."

"You are right. But—still—I did not handle the matter very well. Maybe tomorrow . . ."

"Good luck, my friend."

Later that night, Trevor found it hard to sleep. Theo was right. She was a beautiful woman and she felt so *right* in his arms—as though she simply belonged there. He had wanted to dance her out onto the terrace and kiss her senseless. Had she felt any of the excitement that having her so close had raised for him? Probably not.

This was certainly not the pudgy, shy, self-effacing girl Fiske had foisted on the naive young Trevor. But perhaps that girl had never truly existed at all. This woman knew who she was and would be stubborn in asserting what she wanted from life.

So why had she not accepted what he was sure would have been a generous offer from his family? Why had she not just gone on with her life? And why was Aunt Gertrude so protective of her?

He had barely greeted his aunt—*his* relative, not Caitlyn's—when Aunt Gertrude had said, "If you intend to hurt Caitlyn, you will answer to me, young man."

"I have no intention of hurting anyone," he had replied. "But she and I must set things aright."

"Well, I hope you will accept a bit of advice from an old woman who loves you both."

"Not such an 'old' woman, at all." He grinned at her. "And I know better than to try to avoid listening to you."

She tapped his arm lightly with her fan. "Take it slowly, son. And learn all the facts before you take any steps you might later regret."

"What is that supposed to mean?" he asked.

"It means that others have tended to act from ignorance—if we are being charitable—or malevolence if we are not."

"I am not sure I understand you."

"You will. But it is not my place to set you straight. Just do take care, dear boy."

And then what had he done? Immediately challenged Caitlyn and set her back up.

Nine

The next day, Caitlyn dressed with as much care as she had the night before. All the time she was doing so, she berated herself for being so concerned about such an inconsequential matter as her appearance. She was further annoyed with herself for caring even the least bit about how Trevor might see her. After all, had he not deserted her when she needed him most?

Nevertheless, she donned her favorite day dress, aquamarine muslin trimmed with just a touch of white lace here and there. Polly arranged her hair in a popular style with carefully casual curls. Looking in the glass, Caitlyn turned her head this way and that.

"Hmm. Yes. I like it," she told the maid.

Polly beamed. "You want I should add a touch of rouge to your cheeks, ma'am? You seems a mite pale."

"I think not," Caitlyn said, pinching those offending bits of her physiognomy.

"You look right pretty, ma'am, if I do say so." Polly bent to straighten the hem of the dress.

"Thank you, Polly. I need to *feel* pretty today."

A few minutes later, when she entered the drawing room, she was surprised to find Aunt Gertrude already entertaining guests, several of whom had attended the Bathmoreson ball the previous evening. Vultures sensing a kill, Caitlyn thought, but she smiled brightly and greeted each with some semblance of warmth.

Seeing Bertie among the guests, Caitlyn breathed a sigh of resignation. But the sight of two other male guests raised her spirits considerably, for their conversation was sure to prove diverting. Sir Willard Ratcliff, who would one day inherit the prestigious Ratcliff Farms, had made a name for himself among horse breeders and trainers. His animals were known for both speed and stamina. She also welcomed the presence of David Graham, whom she had met at a salon she attended with Aunt Gertrude. Mr. Graham was an intimate of William Wilberforce and had supported the older man's efforts to outlaw England's participation in the slave trade several years earlier. Both Ratcliff and Graham were rich landowners and, though neither had ever behaved in any but the most proper manner, both had engaged in mild flirtations with Caitlyn.

Bertie immediately, and with little regard for subtlety, established a position near Caitlyn as she stood talking with Graham and another couple. When these three moved off to visit with others, Bertie took Caitlyn's elbow and steered her to a window alcove.

"I promise not to desert you, my dear," he said softly.

She gently but firmly disengaged herself from his grip. "Bertie, you go too far. I never gave you leave . . ." She wanted to scream at him, but she kept her voice low and even managed to smile for the benefit of anyone who might be observing. Looking around, she caught Ratcliff's eye, and he strolled toward them.

"I say there, Latham. Never think you can steal Mrs. Jeffries away from the rest of us. You must share, you know."

"Thought nothing of the kind," Bertie muttered.

"Oh, Bertie," Caitlyn said. "I would dearly love a glass of lemonade."

Bertie was not best pleased at this request, but he had little choice but to fetch her the drink.

When he had gone, Ratcliff asked, "Was I correct, then, in thinking you were a damsel in need of rescue?"

"Actually—yes." Caitlyn smiled.

When Bertie returned with the lemonade, Ratcliff was deep into his favorite topic—his stable of race horses. Two other gentlemen had joined the discussion, and Bertie was no longer able to monopolize Caitlyn's attention. Which was just as well, for her attention kept wandering, though it focused on the drawing room door with each new arrival.

"—do they not, Mrs. Jeffries?" A man named Harrison, along with his wife, had joined the conversation.

"I . . . I beg your pardon?" Caitlyn felt slightly embarrassed. "I am afraid I was not attending."

"We were discussing the racing meet at Brighton later in the summer," Mrs. Harrison explained patiently.

"Oh—"

"Do the Jeffries Farms not have some three-year-olds that might be entered?" From Harrison's tone, she knew he had asked the question previously.

"Yes. Perhaps."

"Yes? Perhaps? Either they are or they are not ready. Will you be entering the race?"

"I . . . uh . . . That decision has not been made yet." Caitlyn hated sounding so vague. The Brighton Race Meet had long been a dream for her—but now that Trevor had returned, would he scotch their participation?

"What about the earlier meet at Newmarket?" Harrison persisted. "Surely you will show your stock there."

"Oh, yes, I am sure we will have teams to show at Newmarket. After all, we have done so for three years."

"And shown to good advantage every time," Ratcliff observed.

"Thank you, Sir Willard. How kind of you to say so."

Harrison cleared his throat noticeably. "You may find the competition a bit stiffer this year. I've a pair of chestnuts that are prime goers."

Caitlyn made an appropriately polite response, then excused herself to circulate among other guests. She was deep into discussing support for a local parish school when she felt rather than heard the room go silent. Even before she turned toward the door, she knew. Trevor had arrived. At least half the room had been awaiting his entrance.

"Oh, there you are, Trevor." Aunt Gertrude called to him discreetly just as though his appearance were the most natural thing in the world. His aunt took his arm and maneuvered him into her conversational group. "Margaret—Lady Thurston, that is—and I were just discussing the ball the Prince plans for the newest duke in the realm."

Bless Aunt Gertrude, Caitlyn thought, though she was aware of several sets of eyes shifting their gaze from her to her husband and back. Good manners reasserted themselves and the buzz of conversation resumed. Soon, guests began to drift away, though Caitlyn thought some did so reluctantly. *Well, they have new grist for the gossip mill,* she told herself.

Trevor had not expected to find his wife and his aunt entertaining such a number of callers. He was also surprised at the makeup of the group. True, there were several members of what he thought of as "Aunt Gertrude's reformers," but there were also members of the sporting crowd. Nor was Latham the only guest with pretensions to stylistic grandeur.

Carefully keeping up his end of conversations in the next half hour, he was nevertheless intensely aware of where Caitlyn was in the room and with whom she talked. More than once her throaty laugh caught his ear, producing twinges of annoyance at his being on the outside of her merriment. He was not pleased at seeing that she commanded so much male attention.

Well, what did you expect? he asked himself contemptuously. A beautiful woman draws men as flowers draw bees. He wondered how many bees had tasted the nectar of this flower. A blast of sheer rage assailed him at this thought. But why? Was that not what he had assumed during his absence? Had he not long ago resigned himself to the fact of Caitlyn's betrayal? All that remained was to extricate himself from this farce of a marriage. That *was* why he was here, was it not?

He tried not to be too obvious in observing which men commanded Caitlyn's attention. Viscount Latham hovered near her at all times. Trevor smiled grimly to himself at the glares young Latham sent his way. He was not surprised that Caitlyn seemed to welcome Latham's protectiveness. After all, Latham had been her first choice as a husband. Now that his father was dead, Latham might cast his lures into whatever waters appealed to him. However, Trevor *was* taken aback by the ease his wife enjoyed among the Ratcliff lot. Trevor knew Ratcliff well, the two of them having been drawn together in an earlier day by their mutual interest in horses. Ratcliff sought him out now.

He offered Trevor his hand. "Jeffries. Glad to see you back safe and sound."

"Thank you, Willard. I . . . uh, may I say how sorry I was to hear about your wife?" Trevor had attended the Ratcliff wedding some years before.

"Thank you. It has been over two years now, though. Childbirth is a hazardous bit of business for women. We thought the second time would be easier." He brightened as he added, "But Mary gave me a fine son earlier."

"Oh." Trevor's tone was polite approval, but he could not quell the unbidden thought that Caitlyn had faced that hazard alone.

"Quite a boy, my Robbie," Ratcliff went on. "He is not yet five, but sits a saddle better than many an adult."

"Is that so?" Trevor feigned interest. Was it their children that Caitlyn and Ratcliff had in common?

Ratcliff shifted the topic. "Don't suppose you saw much in the way of prime racing stock in the Peninsula?"

"Not much. There were occasional races. Impromptu affairs meant to relieve the boredom between battles."

"Ah, yes. Well, now that you have returned to home soil, I expect you will be giving me some real competition."

"Not on the racecourse." Trevor deliberately employed a note of finality.

"You must be joking."

Ratcliff's tone annoyed Trevor. "No, I am not."

Ratcliff gave him a penetrating look but said nothing more on the topic. Shortly he excused himself, took his leave of the hostesses, and departed. Others began to follow suit. Among the last to leave was Viscount Latham, who rather rudely engaged in a whispered colloquy with Caitlyn at the door.

Trevor heard her say, "I appreciate your concern, Bertie," as she ushered him out.

While other guests took their leave, Trevor wandered to a window. The house Caitlyn had rented was a modest one, rather narrow with four floors besides a basement and an attic. This much he had seen from the street on his previous attempts to visit. Now he saw that the drawing room covered the entire back of the first floor and looked down into a charming garden.

Seeing movement off to the side, he caught sight of a child playing. A child in this house had to be Caitlyn's—living proof of his wife's deception. A woman he presumed to be the nurse sat on a bench nearby. He smiled absently as the little girl carefully laid a doll in a miniature pram and tucked in the covers around it. Then she looked up at the window and waved.

Trevor drew in his breath. This was the child of the park. Until now, he had been able to think of the situation between him and Caitlyn in abstractions and legalities. Here, he beheld the face of another victim—indeed, the real victim—of that damned wager. Had Caitlyn never given a thought to what the child might suffer when she brazenly tried to pass off another man's by-blow as Trevor's?

He suddenly became aware of Aunt Gertrude standing next

to him returning the little girl's wave. The silence stretched out until Trevor finally spoke, keeping his voice carefully neutral and his eyes on the scene below. "Caitlyn's daughter, I presume."

When Aunt Gertrude did not immediately respond, Trevor turned to look at her. Her voice was gentle as she said, "And yours."

"She bears my name. I suppose that makes her mine in some eyes."

"Oh, Trevor. *Look* at her." Aunt Gertrude tapped the window, and the little girl looked up again with a happy smile.

"Oh, my God!" The words were wrenched from him.

"Yes. She is the very image of Melanie at that age. You cannot see it from here, but she even has that very slight overlap of one front tooth over the other that Melanie has. You recall that family portrait that hangs in Timberly's great hall?"

"Yes." His voice sounded bleak even to his own ears. An image of that portrait flashed across his mind. The child below might have posed for it. What Aunt Gertrude was suggesting, though, could not be true. He tried to recall what had been said about Caitlyn's child in the infrequent letters from his family. Nothing. After that terse postscript from his mother, the subject had never come up. There had to be some reasonable explanation.

"Yes," he repeated. "But surely you do not believe this child is mine. It is not unknown for entire strangers to look alike. Why, we had a fellow in our regiment looked exactly like Wellington. Caused no end of confusion."

"Trevor," his aunt said, and again her voice was very gentle, "I was there when the babe was born on a cold day in February."

"February?" He mentally ticked off the months. "Are you sure it was not January—or even December?"

"It was the seventeenth of February."

"I cannot believe—"

"Oh, Trevor. Think." Aunt Gertrude sounded impatient now. "Had things been as you were told, Caitlyn would have to have been gone with child six weeks and more when you married. The babe would have come much earlier. Surely young men of today know *that* much of the procreation process."

Before he could respond, Caitlyn returned, having seen the last of the guests on their way.

"And what do you two find so interesting in the garden?" she asked with what seemed to be forced gaiety. She came to look, and Trevor heard her sharp intake of breath. "Ashley." The color drained from her face and she turned fear-filled eyes to Trevor. Time—the world—seemed to stand still.

"I . . . uh . . . I believe I shall leave you two to sort this out between you," Aunt Gertrude said, gliding out the door and closing it softly behind her.

"Why?" he fairly croaked the word. "Why in bloody hell did you not tell me about this child—which Aunt Gertrude assures me is mine?"

She took a step backward from the fury he knew himself powerless to quell. "I—I—"

He ignored her squeak as he grasped her shoulders. "How *dare* you keep something like this from me?"

He could see the fear intensify in her eyes, but then he saw rising anger as well. She wrenched away from him.

"I *did* tell you." She fairly spit the words at him. "I wrote you as soon as I knew a babe was coming. When I had no response, I knew you believed the gossip about me and the babe. But despite nary a word from you, I also wrote you again of her arrival. How dare *you* come marching in at this late date laying accusations at *my* door?" She ended on a sob but quickly recovered herself, her hands clenched at her sides.

"You wrote me?" His disbelief was in itself challenging. "How? Where?"

"The only way I knew of contacting you was through your

father and that odious Gerald." She seemed to be recovering some of her spirit. "Had you bothered with me beyond that ever-so-tender note of farewell . . ." Her voice trailed off.

He ran his hand through his hair. "I cannot believe my family deliberately withheld such information from me." But he was beginning to think they might have.

"To their credit," she sounded grudging, "they may have seen themselves as protecting you."

"Perhaps." He thought it more likely that the precious Jeffries family name was their primary concern.

"Even now, they do not acknowledge me—or Ashley."

"Ashley? That's her name?"

"Ashley Gertrude." The look she gave him seemed to seek his approval, so he nodded. "Aunt Gertrude has tried to tell them. They refuse to hear her. I think Melanie knows the truth, but of course she and Marcus have been out of the country almost as long as you have."

"Still—I cannot believe you did not make more of an effort to inform me." He was reluctant to give up his anger.

"Would it have mattered? I doubt you would have been any more willing to believe me than members of your family were."

"It might have mattered," he said, hesitant.

"Oh, Trevor. Admit it. You would not even think of believing me now if Ashley did not bear such a strong resemblance to Melanie."

"Well . . ." He hated the defensive note.

"You still think I was party to some grotesque hoax." Her voice was laced with sadness and disgust.

"I just do not know." He ran his hand through his hair again. He was trying to be totally honest. He was surprised to find he truly wanted to believe her incapable of such a nasty trick, but he had long harbored another view.

Nearly five years ago, he had thought himself a gullible young fool, ripe for the plucking by a conniving female and her accomplices. His embarrassment had turned to anger. At

some point during those years, the anger had turned to—
what?—acceptance? Complacency? Whatever it was, on his
return to England, he had thought to put it all behind him.

Was he being gulled again? No. That could not be. Aunt
Gertrude would never be party to such a scheme.

Realizing that neither of them had spoken for a time, he
said slowly, "I find all this difficult to absorb at the moment.
No . . . no." He put up a hand in protest at the militant look
he saw in her eyes. "I am not denying what you say, but . . ."

"But you just do not believe it." There was a certain dead
neutrality to her voice.

"That is not what I said. I . . . I need time to think."

"All right, Trevor."

He sensed both resignation and apprehension in her.

"If I may, I shall call again tomorrow," he said, holding
himself stiffly.

"Of course."

As Trevor left the house, a maelstrom of emotions assailed
him. He was inclined to believe his wife and his aunt. Believing them, though, meant disbelieving both of his parents
and his eldest brother, people he had known far longer than
the wife he had truly known for only a few days five years
ago.

Moreover, these were people who professed to love him.
Surely they would not have withheld such vital information
from him. But he knew they had—however much he wanted
to believe otherwise. Anger and regret vied in his ponderings.

If Aunt Gertrude was right about those dates—and Trevor
saw no reason to doubt her—the child was very likely his.
His family had actively conspired to hide that possibility from
him. And just how hard had Caitlyn tried to get word to him?

Trevor wandered the streets for some time, unaware of his
surroundings. Finally, he came to a decision of sorts. He was
in an unfamiliar neighborhood, but he hailed a hackney cab
and gave the driver his mother's direction. He found the

countess in her private sitting room reclining lazily on a
chaise longue.

"Oh, Trevor, darling." His mother greeted him with a
falsely bright mixture of welcome and regret. "You catch me
at an inopportune time, my dear. I was just about to change
for a ride in the park with Lord Staunton."

"Have Heston tell Staunton you are indisposed. I have
something important to discuss with you."

The countess was obviously taken aback by his authoritative demand and grim expression. She gave him a questioning
look, but called in the butler and did as he said.

"All right. Now. What is it?" Only his mother could sound
simultaneously bored and curious.

"I visited Caitlyn and Aunt Gertrude today."

His mother lifted an elegant eyebrow. "I do hope that tiresome girl is not going to continue to be difficult."

Trevor ignored this comment and plunged in with his own
question. "Why were Caitlyn's letters not sent on to me?"

"Her letters?" His mother's evasiveness was telling.

"Letters. Caitlyn informs me that she wrote of the babe
before and after the birth. She sent them to my loving family
to be forwarded. I never received them."

"Well, of course you did not, darling. What possible interest would you have had in missives from a woman you
intend to divorce? One who carried another man's child?"

"So you *did* deliberately keep those messages from me."

"Your father and Gerald thought it wisest there be no communication between you. I merely agreed with them."

"Did you, indeed?" He could not hide his bitterness. "Did
it occur to none of you that *I* might have had some say in
that?"

His mother looked uncomfortable, but her tone was dismissive. "Well, darling, it is water under the bridge now, is
it not?"

"Not quite."

She seemed startled as she asked, "Whatever do you mean?"

Trevor did not respond directly. "Why have you never visited Caitlyn or seen the child?"

"Good heavens! Lend countenance to her false claims? I think not!"

"What if her claims are not false?"

"Oh, Trevor, what has that dreadful woman said to you? You cannot have changed your mind about being rid of her."

"I cannot turn my back on a child which is almost surely mine." Now *he* was being evasive. Was the child truly his only concern?

"What makes you suddenly believe that it is?"

"Her appearance. And Aunt Gertrude firmly believes it to be so."

"Gertrude!" His mother's contempt flashed in her eyes and tone. "Lady Gertrude has merely found a new cause. How wonderful for her that it proves an embarrassment for *me*."

He closed his eyes briefly, willing himself to be patient. "Mother, this is not about you."

"Well, it certainly concerns me. I will not have that . . . that woman—either of them—besmirching the Jeffries family name."

"I rather think we can manage that on our own."

His irony was not lost on his mother, for she gave him a look of annoyance.

"Trevor," she said sternly, "I hope this conversation does not suggest you are having second thoughts about freeing the family of ties to that—that—person."

"Perhaps I am really *thinking* for the first time."

"Hmmph!" She gave an unladylike snort of contempt. "Your thinking may be directed by some part of your anatomy other than your head."

"Mother!" Trevor was truly shocked at her coarseness.

"Well . . ." She colored up and became more conciliatory. "I only meant to say I have seen her, and she *is* a comely wench—if you like that unkempt, out-of-doors brassiness. And many men do, you know." This last was added as a snide afterthought.

He rose. "This conversation is going nowhere."

"You *are* going to convince her to agree to a quiet divorce, are you not?" The countess sounded worried.

"I do not know, Mother. I simply do not know at the moment."

"You owe it to the family."

"The family," he said blankly, thinking that his "family" obligations had lately taken a very different turn than his mother envisioned.

That night he slept intermittently, dozing off now and then, but by morning he had reached a decision. Come what may, Trevor Jeffries would assume control of his life. His carelessly following the Corinthian crowd had led to the death of his brother and their friend. His guilt had then made him vulnerable to the manipulations of Fiske and Fitzwilliam. A misplaced sense of family obligation had led him to desert his wife and child. He had been as a puppet whose strings others controlled.

But no more.

The next day when he presented himself, Caitlyn received him alone in her small but cozy library and study. She feared this encounter more than she had ever feared anything in her life before. She had not slept well and knew the strain showed in dark circles under her eyes. She had even resorted to a bit of rice powder to erase them.

Caitlyn had been standing, staring unseeingly through the window at traffic on the street when the butler announced Captain Jeffries. Taking a seat on one of two barrel-like chairs at a small table, she motioned him to the other one.

They stared at each other for a moment, and despite her fears for her child, she felt comforted by his gaze. She noted fine lines around his eyes—from squinting into Spanish suns, she thought incongruously. She abruptly turned her thoughts to the topic at hand.

"Have you . . . uh . . . come to a conclusion?" She had not intended to sound so tentative.

"Yes. Several, actually."

His tone, firm and commanding, increased her tension. "And . . . ?"

"I am willing to believe Ashley is my daughter."

Caitlyn breathed a sigh of relief, despite the reservation she heard in his voice. She could not help herself. She had to ask the next question.

"That is not precisely the same as saying you do believe it. You still think I wronged you, do you not?"

"Caitlyn, what I believe or think is irrelevant. What matters is the welfare of the—our—child."

"On that, at least, we can agree."

"I want to meet her. Now."

"I will not have you upset her."

"She should know her father," he asserted.

"Only if you intend to *be* a father to her."

"I can do that only if you allow it."

She looked at him questioningly; then comprehension dawned.

"Do you mean that? Do you really mean that?" she asked with growing wonder.

"Of course. What else—"

"Oh, Trevor. I was so very afraid . . ."

"Afraid? Of what?"

"That . . . that you would take her away from me if you believed she was yours."

Trevor seemed confused. "I . . . I suppose that makes sense to you, but I confess I do not understand what you mean."

"I . . . I feared you would take her and never allow me to see her."

"Good God, Caitlyn. It that what you think of me? That I would keep a child from its mother?"

She took a deep breath. Her words tumbled over each other. "Lord Lennington divorced his wife and took her children and never allows her to see them, and the poor woman cries for them all the time, and I would just die if I lost Ashley."

"I am not Lord Lennington."

"No, of course not." For the first time, she gave him a feeble smile.

"Well? Am I to be allowed a role in my daughter's life or not?"

Hearing the words "my daughter" on his lips sounded strange to her, but she felt a certain reassurance at his use of them. Her smile deepened.

Then she sobered. "Wha—what role do you visualize?"

"I . . . I am not sure. This is pretty new to me. I . . . I want to spend time with her, get to know her." His voice became increasingly assertive.

She took a deep breath. She was embarrassed, but determined. "You must know that there has always been a great deal of talk about Ashley's parentage," she began.

"Fueled, no doubt, by certain members of my family."

"Well . . . yes."

"My mother never had an idea in her head that did not pop out in company."

Caitlyn was briefly amused at this, but quickly turned her thoughts back to what was on her mind. "Since . . . since your return, the gossip has renewed."

"I see." He did not sound as though he did see, but he waited for her to go on.

"Because you . . . Well, because you are staying elsewhere."

"When I arrived back in England, I did not even know you were in town. Later, I had no idea of what my reception might be."

"Well—now you do."

There was a long pause during which she gazed into his eyes and felt warmth rising in her cheeks. She broke the eye contact and twisted her hands nervously in her lap.

"Let me understand this. Are you—are you inviting me to live here—with you?"

Her gaze shifted back to him. "Not . . . not with *me* precisely. Only as Ashley's father."

"Ah. I see." He looked into her eyes. She held his gaze, making no attempt to hide her apprehension and doubt. He nodded. "All right. That seems reasonable. It will establish Ashley's claim to the Jeffries name. Regardless of what might happen later."

"Thank you, Trevor." She reached out to touch his arm, and the brief physical contact sent a bolt of awareness through her. Did he feel it, too?

"Now. May I meet my daughter?"

Caitlyn went to the bellpull and spoke quietly to the servant who answered. A few minutes later, there was a gentle rap at the door and Ashley came in clutching her doll.

"Thank you, Adams," Caitlyn said to the nurse, dismissing her.

Ashley stared at this strange man and sidled nearer her mother, apparently sensing something extraordinary. Caitlyn knelt beside her, put her arm around the child, and spoke softly. "Ashley, love. You remember I told you your papa went to be a soldier?"

The little girl nodded knowingly. "Uh-huh." She looked at Trevor. "My papa is a brave soldier in the 'ninsula."

Caitlyn was disconcerted by Ashley's revelation, but Trevor would at least know the child had a positive view of her absent father. "Well, darling," Caitlyn said, "your papa has come home."

"Really and truly?" Ashley's eyes widened in delight.

"Really and truly," Caitlyn responded with this catch

phrase between the two of them. "This is your papa, darling. He has come especially to see you."

Trevor knelt before the little girl and opened his arms. He seemed surprised when Ashley came into them immediately and slid one small hand around his neck, the other still firmly clutching her doll. He hugged her little body to him and kissed the top of her head.

"Are you really and truly my papa?"

He gazed into eyes that were a mirror image of his own. "Yes, poppet, I am."

He hugged her even more tightly, and when his gaze met Caitlyn's over their daughter's head, she saw that she was not the only one whose vision was blurred by tears.

Ten

During each of their London seasons, Caitlyn had rented the same town house in Bedford Square. It belonged to a sea captain who planned eventually to retire to the city. In all that time, the master's bedchamber had been empty. Caitlyn had preferred the angle of the morning sun in the adjoining chamber which had a small sitting room attached. Aunt Gertrude preferred a chamber that was not subject to an early morning wake-up by the sun. Now Caitlyn thought it fortuitous that they had left the master chamber free. She dismissed entirely the fleeting notion that some supernatural hand of fate had prompted her to leave that other chamber empty to await just this turn of events.

"Fustian," she muttered and went about the business of having it aired and prepared and seeing to another room for Trevor's valet. A dressing room connecting the chambers of master and mistress would remain firmly closed.

With little ado, Trevor moved in the following morning, pronounced his quarters "quite comfortable," and promptly set off for the park with his daughter and a dog Ashley said was her "puppy"—a huge German shepherd blend standing as tall as the little girl.

Caitlyn laughed at seeing his reaction to the dog. "He *was* a puppy when Ashley found him. I intended to get rid of him, but she became so attached to him . . ."

"Does he have a name?" Trevor asked as the dog greeted its little mistress exuberantly.

"Little Bit." Seeing his disbelieving grin, she added, "He was such a little bit of a thing when he came to us."

"And he is all right with a child?" Trevor eyed the dog skeptically.

"Oh, yes. He is very patient and very protective. You should see him in the playroom. He will lie with Ashley's doll on his front paws and never move until she takes up the doll again. Once, she had done something rather naughty—I forget what. I grasped her shoulders and spoke to her quite sternly."

"What happened?"

"Little Bit began to growl—not viciously, just enough to let me know I was not to be unkind to his darling." Caitlyn chuckled ruefully. "Now, if I need to reprimand my daughter, I make sure the dog is in another room."

"Little Bit may come with us, may he not, Papa?" Ashley queried anxiously as she put her hand in her father's.

"Your mother says it is all right. Where is his leash?"

"Oh, you will not need a leash," Caitlyn said. "Little Bit will not leave Ashley's side as long as she is out."

Trevor had seemed a little dubious about this, but he accepted her word and set off for the park with his daughter and her "puppy."

Watching them leave, Caitlyn felt a twinge of sadness and—yes—jealousy. Well, resentment, at least. *She* had always been the central figure in her daughter's life. Now she would have to share that position with a man who had previously been but a distant shadow. Suddenly the shadow was disconcertingly real flesh-and-blood substance.

Aunt Gertrude looked up from a newspaper she was reading as Caitlyn returned to the glassed-in sunroom where they often spent their mornings.

"Caitlyn? Is something wrong?"

"Not really. I am merely trying to adjust to the idea of my daughter's having two parents."

"Ashley seems pleased at the idea."

"*Ashley* is ecstatic."

"But you are not?" Aunt Gertrude put down her newspaper as Caitlyn took a seat in a cushioned wicker chair.

"I do not know *what* to feel. I am, of course, happy that Trevor has acknowledged our child."

"But . . . ?" Aunt Gertrude left the word hanging.

"Since he has done so, he has the power—the authority—to take her from me."

"Improbable—though it is within the realm of *legal* possibility." Aunt Gertrude spoke slowly and deliberately. "We both know of women who have suffered so."

"Lady Lennington—"

"Is a complicated case. Her husband is a mean-spirited, vindictive man, using innocent children to avenge himself on a wife who cuckolded him."

"Still—"

"Still," Aunt Gertrude interrupted, "Trevor is not Lennington."

"That is precisely what Trevor said himself."

"Well? Believe him. I have known Trevor his whole life. Impetuous as a youngster. Sometimes gullible—because he always expected the best of everyone he met. But never mean-spirited or deliberately cruel."

"Perhaps he changed." Caitlyn thought of the way he had been so quick to believe the worst of her.

"Oh, he has changed, I think. I doubt this is still the boy who went to the Peninsula. The earl and Gerald will find this man much less malleable than that boy was." Obviously, Aunt Gertrude found such an idea immensely pleasing.

"Well . . ." Caitlyn hesitated, still uncertain.

"And you have changed also," Aunt Gertrude went on. "I doubt either of you will ever again be pawns in someone else's game as you once were."

"I surely hope not." Caitlyn then changed the subject as they made their plans for the day.

* * *

In a surprisingly short time, Trevor found his days settling into a routine. Rising early, he would take a brisk walk before returning to share the morning meal with Caitlyn and Aunt Gertrude. Once, Caitlyn had asked him if he would care to ride in the park with her. He was rather abrupt in telling her no. She did not ask again. Talk over breakfast was usually filled with polite nothings—as, indeed, most of their conversations were. Trevor thought none of them wished to be the one to introduce a discordant note.

Later in the morning, he would accompany Ashley on some excursion or another, usually to the park to feed the birds. Once, however, he took her to see the menagerie at the Tower of London. The tower housed a pathetic collection of animals, but Ashley was excited at seeing an elephant and a tiger.

Still later, he would visit Gentleman Jackson's establishment for a pugilistic workout, often accepting the great man's or another's offer of a sparring match. Trevor rarely won these matches, but he held his own and was regarded with increasing respect among that sporting crowd.

Despite his aversion to the *ton's* delight in making "morning" calls—which rarely occurred before two in the afternoon—Trevor made a few such calls, some of them with his wife. The recipients of these calls were chosen with care, for Trevor was determined—with Caitlyn's concurrence—that Mr. and Mrs. Trevor Jeffries should establish themselves in society for the sake of their child.

He spent other afternoons in more worthwhile endeavors—seeing to the welfare of men who had been in his command. Several were in hospital here in the city, and Trevor visited them regularly. He also made himself available to other men—or their widows, in some cases—as an advocate with the War Office. Now that the war was over, and even the action in the former colonies was winding down, England seemed all too ready to forget her debts to the common soldier. Trevor was quietly determined that this should not be allowed to happen.

"Jeffries, you are becoming a source of genuine irritation to us, my boy," said an older officer, whose entire experience of battle had been from the fortress of his London desk. The man's jovial tone was hard-edged.

"I am sorry to hear that, Colonel Blake."

Blake went on as though Trevor had not spoken. "Hard to ignore a man with your connections, though."

"My connections?" Trevor asked dumbly. Well, he supposed being related to an earl had *some* attractions, even if one were the proverbial black sheep of the family.

Blake lifted his brows. "Your father and that brother of yours. When Wyndham speaks, Parliament listens. And Wyndham has had much to say about the interests of this office."

"Oh, my father." Trevor shrugged. He had grown up only vaguely aware of his father's political power. Not vitally interested in politics himself, Trevor had assumed his father's power came largely from his great wealth. It had only lately occurred to him that he might subtly use his family connections to help the men of his regiment, though God knew he did not want to incur any debt to his father or Gerald on his own behalf. "My brother? You mean Gerald?"

Blake's response was emphatic. "No! Marcus. He is the one Wellington thinks is a miracle worker, and everyone knows Wellington has Prinny's ear."

Trevor was unaware of a connection between Marcus and the commander-in-chief of the Peninsula armies, but he was careful to hide his ignorance from Colonel Blake. "Hmm. Well, you will see that Sergeant Hillyard's pension goes to his widow, will you not?"

The other man gave an impatient sigh and shuffled some papers on his desk. "Yes, I will see to it."

In the evenings, Trevor and his wife only occasionally attended a social affair together. Caitlyn had made it clear that she welcomed his presence in her life only in his capacity as Ashley's father. In truth, Trevor was not sure that he even wanted another role in Caitlyn's life.

Yes, she was a remarkably attractive woman, and she stirred his senses whenever she was near. And yes, Ashley was surely his child. But, denied her own choice of husband, had Caitlyn not been a willing party to her uncle's duping a naive young man? And God knew both he and Caitlyn were truly locked into the trap now. However, Caitlyn seemed not to worry about the shackles overmuch, judging by the number of gentleman callers she entertained and by the floral offerings that arrived on a regular basis.

Her most persistent admirers were Ratcliff, Graham, and Latham, though there were others who gathered at every soiree, ball, or rout they attended. Trevor tried to adopt an indulgent, "modern" attitude to his wife's flirtations, but often found himself grinding his teeth. Nevertheless, he had to admit that if she *were* carrying on affairs with any of them, she was extremely discreet about it. Had his mother not said as much to him?

Initially, his days seemed quite full. But as he settled in more completely, he began to feel they were not so full at all—at least, not with anything of importance outside of his time with Ashley and his efforts on behalf of his regiment.

"I am beginning to feel decidedly useless," he confessed to Theo one evening. Trevor had met Theo at the club after seeing Caitlyn and Aunt Gertrude home from a musicale. He and his friend had intended to play a few hands of cards, but seeing the boisterous company at the tables, they had settled for quiet conversation in another room.

"The season will be over soon," Theo observed, "and you can get back into the harness at Atherton."

"What you mean to say is it *should* be over soon. The general euphoria over Boney's defeat has prolonged it this year."

" 'Tis absolute madness," Theo said. "Traffic had to be rerouted around Pulteney's Hotel because of the mob hanging about for a glimpse of the czar."

"Our prince must be in his element, what with entertaining

Say Yes to 4 Free Books!
Complete and return the order card to receive this
$19.96 value, _ABSOLUTELY FREE!_

If the certificate is missing below, write to:
Regency Romance Book Club
P.O. Box 5214, Clifton, New Jersey 07015-5214
or call TOLL-FREE 1-888-345-BOOK
Visit our website at www.kensingtonbooks.com.

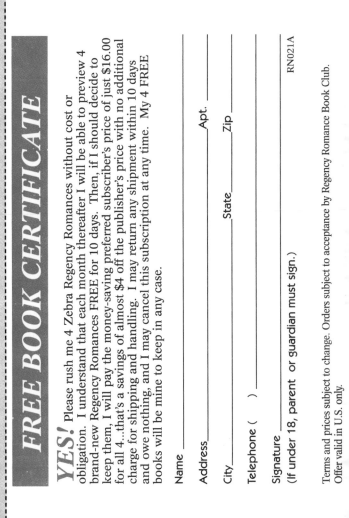

FREE BOOK CERTIFICATE

YES! Please rush me 4 Zebra Regency Romances without cost or obligation. I understand that each month thereafter I will be able to preview 4 brand-new Regency Romances FREE for 10 days. Then, if I should decide to keep them, I will pay the money-saving preferred subscriber's price of just $16.00 for all 4...that's a savings of almost $4 off the publisher's price with no additional charge for shipping and handling. I may return any shipment within 10 days and owe nothing, and I may cancel this subscription at any time. My 4 FREE books will be mine to keep in any case.

Name _____

Address _____ Apt. _____

City _____ State _____ Zip _____

Telephone ( ) _____

Signature _____
(If under 18, parent or guardian must sign.)

RN021A

Terms and prices subject to change. Orders subject to acceptance by Regency Romance Book Club.
Offer valid in U.S. only.

the Russian czar and the Prussian king at the same time to celebrate 'their' great victories over Napoleon."

"Not according to some accounts."

Trevor raised his eyebrows in question. "But he has all these elaborate doings planned."

"They do not always turn out as he would like them to." Theo's voice turned thoughtful. "I think Prinny may have seen this state visit as a means of recouping some of his lost regard with his own subjects, but the czar and the Prussian are getting far more attention than our regent. And—the star of his show is missing."

"Ah, yes. Wellington is still in Paris."

"And Prinny must make do with Blucher."

"The German general is very popular with the public."

Theo laughed. "Yes. Probably because he loves drink as much as they do—and holds it no better than most do. Blucher aside, Prinny's real problem remains."

"Princess Caroline."

"Princess Caroline. Despite our regent's aversion to his wife, she is extremely popular with the lower orders."

"Almost makes one feel sorry for the Prince of Wales." Trevor's tone was distinctly ironic.

"Actually, yes," Theo agreed. "He planned a fine evening at the theater for his exalted guests the other night, and she managed to upstage him."

"What happened?"

"The curtain had just gone up with the last chorus of 'God Save the King' when Caroline appeared in her box opposite his. She was resplendent in a black wig and many diamonds."

"You were there, I take it?"

"Oh, yes. A grand piece of theatrical timing. The audience went wild cheering her—with their backs to her husband, I might add. The Czar of All the Russias and the King of Prussia bowed to her, as did Prinny, but I daresay he was silently wishing her to perdition."

"Well, if he means to be rid of his wife, he should probably just get on with doing so." Trevor had spoken without thinking, and the words hovered in the air for a moment.

Then Theo cleared his throat. "I would guess there is more at stake than merely his freedom."

Trevor felt himself coloring. "Hmm. Well . . . yes. You are probably right."

Theo shifted the subject. "The *ton* seem as eager to see and be seen by the visiting royalty as ever the rabble have been."

Trevor seized on the diversion. "The Wallenfords's ball will bring them out in droves. My mother will be in alt."

"Will you go?"

"I rather think so."

"Meanwhile, my friend, if amidst all this glitz and glamour you have so little of substance to occupy your time in London, you might come round and lend me some of that expertise you expended on logistics and supplies in Spain."

"And what would *you* be needing help with?" Trevor asked skeptically.

"My father handed me a wagonload of information on our textile mills and that damned pottery. Said he thought I should 'study up on things' before taking over."

"Not rushing you at all, is he?"

"No-o-o. Nothing like that." Theo's sarcasm was clear. "But," he added more seriously, "he is anxious to turn over the reins. I think he wants to be sure I can handle them."

"So you are trading your regiment of soldiers for an army of workers, eh?"

"Something like that. Though a few of them will be the same people."

"Oh?"

"I have hired some of our men. The job situation out there is difficult, to put it mildly. Impossible if a man is lame at all."

"England does not seem to have been prepared for our return." Trevor thought his personal situation—feeling superfluous in his own household—was a reflection of the plight of the common run of former soldiers. At least, he had no worries about feeding himself or a family.

"No. And things are bound to get worse when the troops in America arrive back on home soil," Theo replied.

"Cheap labor for folks in your position."

Theo started, and his voice was cool. "I hope you do not harbor the view that I would take advantage of the less fortunate souls among us."

"No, of course not, Theo. *You* will not. But there are those who will."

"Right." Theo was mollified, but remained glum. "No wonder the Luddites go around smashing machinery they see as robbing them of the few jobs that *are* available."

"You have had troubles in that regard?"

"Not yet. But my father thinks it is a real danger. Be glad you do not own cotton mills, Trev."

"I say!" A merry voice broke in on them. "Why are you two old warhorses looking so blue-deviled?"

"Ah, Jenkins and Moore. Welcome. Thought you were still in the country at a race meet." Theo gestured to chairs and the nearly full brandy bottle.

"Returned this morning," Jenkins said.

As the newcomers helped themselves, Theo deepened his voice to a pompous tone. "We were discussing The Problems of Returning to Civilian Life After the Rigors of the Campaign Trail."

"Shouldn't think either of *you* have such great problems," Moore said. "I mean, Ruskin here is the heir of a viscount. And Jeffries's father is as rich as Croesus."

"Right," Jenkins said, falling in with Moore's teasing tone. "Now, we younger sons—we are the ones with genuine worries."

"Ha!" Theo and Trevor said in unison, for they both knew the other two to be very well positioned both financially and socially.

Trevor had no intention of discussing his private affairs with these two. Theo, yes; others, not at all. He turned the conversation by asking them about their activities of late. Jenkins and Moore had come just now from the opera again. This brought up the subject of a dancer who had caught Jenkins's eye.

"Our friend Harry here is fickle indeed." Moore gestured toward his companion. "He has already forgot about the beauty in the box the other night."

"I beg your pardon," Jenkins said in mock umbrage. "No man could forget such a delectable creature as that!"

Theo gave a bark of dry laughter. "Well, *you* had best do so, Harry. That 'delectable creature' is Trevor's wife."

"Wha—"

"Never say so!"

Jenkins and Moore were obviously stunned at this news.

"Thought I'd better stop you," Theo said, "before Trevor here was forced to invite you to grass for breakfast."

"Hmmph. Well. In such a case, I am sorely afraid you would all have discovered the ugly truth about me," Jenkins said, his voice a parody of sadness.

"And that is . . . ?" Theo prompted.

Jenkins lowered his voice to a loud whisper. "I am a coward at heart. I would never accept a challenge from Trevor. Why—he's a crack shot, don't you know?"

They all laughed at this and the tension was eased. Trevor tersely explained that he had not seen his family in five years and had not known his wife to be in town. He could tell the others were not completely satisfied, and he surmised that he and Caitlyn were sure to be a prime topic in at least two drawing rooms on the morrow.

As he took a hackney back to what he continued to think of as Caitlyn's house, he thought over the discussion he and Theo had had before the arrival of the other two. Theo's comments had triggered something. Ah, yes. Ledgers. Whitcomb, the solicitor, had pressed files and ledgers into his hands some time ago.

Perhaps he should have a look at them.

Caitlyn had tried to keep up a facade of normality about her life. Apart from inviting Trevor to ride with her once, she had made no personal overtures to him. She thought they had accepted enough invitations together to deflect the worst of gossip. These had been discreet affairs like that musicale the other evening.

She and Trevor were invariably polite to each other, but she thought they both studiously avoided being alone together. She had been unable to bring herself to remain with her husband one night when Aunt Gertrude rather pointedly excused herself. Pleading fatigue, Caitlyn too had retired early. She and Trevor did not live exactly as strangers, though—more like school acquaintances who did not much care for each other.

However, they both cared a great deal for Ashley. Caitlyn experienced sincere gladness—and growing apprehension—as she observed the developing affection between Trevor and his daughter. Already Ashley adored her papa and was in a fair way of wrapping him around her little finger.

Trevor had said he would not take her child away. Caitlyn would have to rely on that assurance for now. But what would he say later—when his family decided they opposed the uneasy truce between Trevor and his wife? He had bowed to their wishes readily in the past. She knew he had called on his mother, but he had not discussed the visit, nor did she feel free to ask about it. The crisis would come when his father and brother returned to town—as they were sure to do for the round of celebrations, which had already started, to mark the defeat of Napoleon.

The newspapers had babbled for months of the grand state visit of England's allies. The Prince Regent was sparing no expense in his plans to entertain Alexander, Czar of All the Russias, and Frederick, King of Prussia. The czar's sister, the Grand Duchess Oldenburg, had arrived as early as March to help smooth the way for her brother, though it was whispered she was also on a diplomatic mission to forestall any talk of marriage between the daughter of the Prince of Wales and a Dutch prince. Russia feared an alliance between the two great maritime powers of the day.

The society pages of every journal were filled with this soiree or that rout to honor the visitors. The grandest of these affairs, aside from a dinner and ball the Prince would host at Carlton House, was to be a ball staged by one of the *ton's* favorite hostesses, the Duchess of Wallenford.

Caitlyn had been surprised to find herself included in the Wallenfords's guest list. But then she supposed that it would have been "bad *ton*" even for the duchess to invite Trevor and exclude his wife, and Trevor's connection to the Earl of Wyndham insured his invitation. The gilt-edged vellum missive had put Caitlyn at sixes and sevens at first. Never in her wildest imaginings would Caitlyn Maria Woodbridge have dreamed of being in such exalted company. She had seen Trevor's mother on occasion, and, of course, had actually met the hateful Gerald, but she had never even seen her husband's father, let alone met the man.

Now she would be in the same room with her in-laws who despised her. Then she mentally raised her chin in characteristic stubbornness. Aunt Gertrude would be there. And surely Trevor would stand by her, figuratively and literally.

Eleven

Although he tried to immerse himself in his own affairs, Trevor found himself more and more interested in Caitlyn's activities. Not expecting anything for himself, he took little interest in the mail which Thompkins, the butler, set at Caitlyn's place each morning. She would sort through it, dividing the missives into piles of estate affairs and social doings. There were usually one or two of the latter addressed to Aunt Gertrude and, occasionally, one to him.

There would ensue brief discussions over acceptance of social invitations, which arrived at an increasing rate. Of course, the most significant of imminent events was the Wallenford ball. Breakfast over, Caitlyn would closet herself in the library while Trevor escorted Ashley on some excursion or another.

Trevor wondered about matters that required such concentrated attention, but Caitlyn had so far not volunteered any information, though he surmised she dealt with estate business that should probably be his. He was not yet ready to shake the fragile accord they had achieved by asking about those matters.

He was perplexed, intrigued—even overwhelmed—by his personal reaction to this woman who was, in fact, his wife. He came to savor the light floral scent when she was near. He listened for her throaty laugh in a room. His fingers itched to touch the warm brown softness of her hair. Her most arresting feature, of course, was her eyes. If he were not careful, he might lose himself in those eyes.

She seemed to avoid any physical proximity to him. If their hands happened to touch as she passed him a dish of tea, she would quickly draw away. It was usually a footman who handed her into or from a carriage, but if it chanced that her husband did so, she allowed only the briefest of contact. Yet she clearly was not a squeamish, "untouchable" sort. He had often seen her lay a hand on or touch a fan to the arm of a man or woman with whom she spoke. And she never failed to gather Ashley—or even Ashley's dog—into her arms, with little regard to mussing her gown.

Did she consider him so very repulsive, then? Even as he found himself responding to her more and more intensely? Her bare arms in the drawing room or at the dining table, the swell of breast at a low neckline, a glimpse of deeper cleavage as she knelt to hug Ashley—all would cause a catch in his breath, a tightening of his body.

He imagined his hands spanning her waist, caressing her body. He cursed himself for his fierce jealousy as she danced or laughed with other men—things she rarely did with him. Then he would shake himself with the reminder that he was still contemplating the dissolution of this marriage. Of course, that was not a matter of great urgency at the moment. . . .

One morning as Caitlyn sorted through the mail, she looked at a certain letter curiously.

"This one is for you, Trevor." She handed it across to him.

Trevor recognized the bold, heavy hand immediately. "My father." He opened it and scanned the brief contents. "A summons. The earl has returned to town and demands that I call immediately."

He looked up to see apprehension in Caitlyn's eyes. Such a summons no longer had the power to cause him any trepidation, but he well remembered how he had felt five years ago at the last such demand for him to present himself. He wanted to reassure Caitlyn, to erase that worried look he saw her exchange with Aunt Gertrude.

" 'Tis not a matter for worry, ladies. He is in town for the celebrations."

"Has Gerald come with him?" Aunt Gertrude asked in an apparent effort to discuss the matter normally.

Trevor glanced again at the letter. "Yes. Along with his bride. They all plan to stay through the celebrations."

"That should please Lydia," Aunt Gertrude observed. "She and Miranda get on quite well together."

"Being birds of a feather, you mean?" Trevor asked with a derisive but not malicious laugh.

Aunt Gertrude chuckled. "Well, there is that . . ."

Gerald had been married nearly four years. Trevor recalled his mother's letter and the clippings describing what had been one of the most lavish society weddings in a decade. He had noted at the time the pointed absence of his own wife, though Aunt Gertrude had been listed among the guests. So far, Gerald and his wife had failed to produce an heir.

"I shall go this afternoon," Trevor said. "I should, of course, have called upon them even without such a kind invitation."

Later, when he arrived at Wyndham House, he had a distinct feeling of *déjà vu*. Heston gave him a sympathetic look as he took Trevor's hat and gloves, but there was no Melanie to give him warning. In the drawing room, his father and his brother Gerald stood to offer their hands, but Trevor felt there was more courtesy than warmth in their greetings. Trevor kissed his mother's proffered cheek.

"You remember Miranda, of course," the countess said, gesturing to the woman next to her on the settee.

"Yes. How do you do?" Trevor took his sister-in-law's hand briefly. Miranda's severely styled, almost black hair failed to soften her sharp features and contrasted starkly against her very white skin. It was a warm summer afternoon, but this woman looked cold and forbidding. What had Gerald seen in her? Trevor wondered, and then answered his own unspoken question. The proper credentials, of course. A father who was a lord, a suitable dowry, all the "correct" accomplishments of a *ton* miss, and a firm sense of her own lofty place in the scheme of things. She returned his greeting condescendingly.

Salutations over, Trevor took a seat and waited. His father seemed to be silently assessing his younger son. Finally, the earl spoke.

"Your mother informs me that you have taken up residence in Bedford Square. Is this true?"

"Yes, sir, it is."

The earl seemed to be waiting for Trevor to say more, but he did not elaborate.

"With that . . . that connection of Fiske?" Lord Wyndham asked, hesitating when Trevor directed a hard, questioning glare his way.

"With my wife and daughter, yes. And Aunt Gertrude."

"*Your* daughter?" Miranda's innuendo was clear.

"Yes, my lady. *My* daughter." Trevor experienced a fleeting triumph when Miranda could not hold his gaze.

His mother sniffed. "No one in society believes that."

"They will." Trevor's tone was flat, matter-of-fact.

"You are still the veriest gull," Gerald sneered. "Five years seem to have taught you nothing. Nothing at all."

"On the contrary. I learned a great many things. Foremost among them is that I need not sit here and endure your insults. If you will excuse me . . ." Trevor rose, bowed curtly, and turned toward the door.

"Now see here," Gerald sputtered.

"Oh, Trevor, please—" his mother implored.

Miranda sat looking pinched, but said nothing.

"There is no need to fly into the boughs," the earl said. "Gerald, hold your tongue. This will get us nowhere. Please sit down, Trevor."

Trevor, surprised at the strength of his own fury, reluctantly resumed his seat.

"Now," the earl continued, "we should like to know why you are pursuing a course of action that will merely make an unpleasant situation worse."

"Sir, with all due respect, the 'situation,' as you put it, is mine, and the course of action will be mine as well."

Gerald gave an audible snort. "Are you daring to tell us that you will make this family the laughingstock of the *ton—again?*"

"Oh, my heavens!" Miranda sounded appalled.

"You cannot allow that bit of baggage to subject us to yet further shame," his mother said, her eyes flashing in rage.

"I will not sit here and have you insult Caitlyn, either." Trevor rose again.

"Sit down, son, please," his father said. "Lydia, you are not helping."

Trevor sat again, surprised by his father's reasonable tone with him, and even more surprised at the earl's mild reprimand of his heir and his countess.

"Oh, Alfred." Lady Wyndham seemed to be fighting tears. "I simply cannot bear the thought of more scandal in our family."

Trevor might have felt sorry for her had he not been wondering how much of this was show.

Ignoring his wife's outburst, the earl said, "Trevor, I thought you had agreed with the rest of us that this affair was best put behind us."

"That was before—"

"Before what?" Gerald demanded.

Trevor looked directly at his brother. "Before I knew my own family had deliberately deceived me. Before I knew Ashley to be my child."

None of them would meet his gaze.

"We acted from the best of intentions, darling," his mother said as though she were addressing a child.

"But you had no right to withhold Caitlyn's letters from me. You hid the truth from me."

"And just what 'truth' would that be, little brother?" Gerald employed a demeaning tone that Trevor had always hated.

"You knew very well that the child was mine, but you chose to keep me uninformed."

"We *knew* nothing of the kind," Gerald declared flatly. "Nor do *we* know it now. That woman may have successfully fooled *you*, but it takes more than a passably pretty face and some clever playing with the calendar to fool the rest of us."

"We cannot allow this, Trevor," his father said quietly. "There is no need to continue this charade. You must convince the chit to accept our offer."

"And if I cannot do so?"

"We shall cross that bridge only if we must," the earl replied.

"Well," the countess interjected in an adamant tone, "I can tell you right now I shall never recognize that . . . that woman—or her child."

"If one could truly believe the child was a Jeffries, that would shed a different light on the matter." Miranda's disbelief was clear.

"As it is, there will always be doubt, you know." The countess was placating now.

"When Gerald and I married, the initial scandal had died down." Miranda glanced at her husband. "Now it will be all stirred up again—and just as the whole country has come to London. It is too much. Really. Simply too much." She, too, sounded as if she would burst into tears, but her eyes were wondrously dry.

"Cannot you do something to spare the family further scandal, Trevor, darling?" his mother wheedled.

Trevor stood to lean against the mantel of the fireless hearth. "Look," he said. "I accept fully my role in the original contretemps. And I apologize—again—for any embarrassment I caused you five years ago."

Gerald interrupted. "That hardly excuses the situation now."

Trevor raised his hand as a signal for him to halt. "However," he went on, "the scandal was prolonged and has been kept alive all these years through *you.*"

"Wha-a-at?" His mother fairly choked on the word.

"Preposterous!" Miranda said.

Trevor held his hand in that silencing gesture again. "Had you listened to Aunt Gertrude—had you quietly accepted Caitlyn and the child, the gossip would have proved a nine days' wonder—and not worthy of renewed attention now."

"Well, I never." Miranda snapped her thin lips closed.

"Allow that blackguard Fiske to foist some unknown by-blow off on us? Unthinkable," the earl said, showing his strongest emotion yet.

Trevor glanced at his father and wondered at an enigmatic look he saw pass between his parents. He stood straighter and clasped his hands behind his back.

"Father," he said gravely, "I have no idea what the quarrel once was—or is—between you and the Baron Fiske. However, it has nothing to do with either my wife or my daughter."

"Your wife, yes. Unfortunately. *Your* daughter? Not likely." Gerald's sneer had not diminished.

"Gerald." Trevor's tone was deadly, and threatening in its quietness. "If you venture one more slur against Caitlyn or Ashley, I shall be forced to call you out, brother or no. Now, *there* would be a genuine scandal for you."

"You would not," Gerald said, but his voice indicated he believed otherwise.

"I would. I will," Trevor said in the same quiet tone. "I was always a better shot than you—and I have had a good deal of practice lately."

"Alfred—say something!" the countess screeched.

"Come now, Trevor. Gerald. This wrangling is unnecessary."

"I will *not* accept that woman—nor her child—in my home." His mother was being her stubborn self, Trevor noted. "Nor will I acknowledge her in public gatherings."

"Why should you change now?" Trevor muttered under his breath. Aloud, he said, "You will not be asked to, Mother. We shall manage to contrive. Now, if you will all excuse me, I really must be off."

"I had hoped this could be handled more amicably," the earl said in a weary voice that caught Trevor's attention.

He looked at his father intently. *Why, he is not well,* Trevor thought, somewhat surprised at realization of his father's mortality. The earl stood and took his younger son's hand briefly. Trevor noted that his father's skin looked and felt like parchment. *Not well,* he told himself again. Trevor gave the others a stiff little bow in farewell. Their faces remained closed, rejecting.

As he left his family, he felt unutterable sadness at the breach. Thinking back, he relived the entire scene and made a surprising discovery. He had actually believed what he was saying. At some point recently, he had come not only to believe Caitlyn, but to believe *in* her.

Now he wanted desperately to make sense of his life. He wanted to do something worthwhile as a legacy for his child—and maybe other children to come.

But first he would have to set about the task of wooing his own wife.

Caitlyn had been jittery all day, wondering about Trevor's interview with his father and brother. When he returned, she was entertaining callers in the drawing room. Thus, it was some time before they could speak privately.

As Aunt Gertrude bade the last of the callers goodbye, Trevor and Caitlyn retreated to the small library-study on the ground floor. He leaned over her to open the door and put his hand on the small of her back to usher her in. She drank in the faint spicy smell emanating from him, and her whole being seemed concentrated where he touched her. She moved quickly away from him as a means of preserving her sanity.

Today he was wearing a dark-blue jacket, a lighter blue waistcoat, and buff-colored trousers that hugged his thighs. The blues brought out the blue depths of his eyes. The jacket had needed but little padding to sit well on his muscular frame. She thought him the handsomest man of her acquaintance. If only . . .

She hesitated a moment, then sat in a big overstuffed chair which was, in fact, a comfortable refuge where she was wont to curl up with a book. He took a place on the settee opposite.

"Did your visit with your father go well?" she asked, making nervous conversation.

"It went . . . predictably, shall we say?"

"Is that to say it went well?"

"As a matter of fact, no."

"Oh, dear." She twisted her hands together in her lap.

"I share that sentiment."

She looked up to find him smiling grimly and to find herself mesmerized, unable to avert her gaze. His eyes were friendly and reassuring.

"But," he went on, "it is not a matter we need be overly concerned about."

"You cannot mean that," she said, appalled. "This is your family. And they are important in society."

"Ah, yes. They are that. And so my mother reminded me." He gave her a speaking look which she understood immediately.

"I take it the countess will not be calling on us any time soon."

"Nor we on her."

They gave each other weak smiles, and Caitlyn thought them more in accord with each other than at any time since his return.

"Oh, Trevor, I *am* sorry to be the instrument of discord in your family." She rose, agitated, and walked to the window to gaze out unseeingly. Suddenly she felt him standing directly behind her.

He placed his hands on her shoulders and gently turned her toward him. "This discord is not of your making," he said softly.

"But family is important." She was mindful of her own profound sense of loss on the deaths of her parents, and of her intense gratitude that Aunt Gertrude had somehow contrived to fill the void for her. "And you . . . well . . . that is . . . before . . ."

He seemed to understand immediately what she was groping to say. "Yes. Five years ago, I did attend them. And I have lived to regret it."

"You—you have?" She lifted her head, unable to keep the wonder from her tone.

He raised his hand to tuck an errant curl behind her ear, allowing his fingers to slide along her jaw to her chin. She stood very still, savoring the warmth that flowed through her.

"Yes," he murmured. "I—"

But whatever he might have said was lost and the moment was gone with a knock on the door. She tore her gaze from his and called for entry.

"Lord Latham is here, madam."

"Thank you, Thompkins. I am engaged to drive in the park," she explained to Trevor.

"Of course." His tone was utter politeness, but she thought his lips had momentarily thinned in annoyance.

Had he been about to kiss her?

How would she have responded if he had?

Twelve

For the Wallenford ball, Caitlyn chose to wear a gown of light green silk embroidered with twining leaves of darker green at the low neckline and the hem. A matching cloak was lined with fabric the color of the embroidery.

"What jewelry would you like, ma'am?" her maid asked, putting finishing touches to Caitlyn's hair.

"Hmm. The pearls, I think."

A double strand of pearls and earbobs to match were secured, and Caitlyn drew on elbow-length gloves to match the dress. Never had she been so nervous about a social affair. It was not just that this was the most exalted affair to which she had ever been invited. Though she could not explain why even to herself, she desperately wanted Trevor to be proud of her.

"You look very nice, ma'am."

"Why, thank you, Polly."

With the cloak over her arm, she made her way downstairs to where Trevor waited in the library.

"Aunt Gertrude is not ready yet?" Caitlyn asked in mild surprise.

"No. Something about a torn hem that needed stitching. I must say, Caitlyn, you look quite lovely in that creation."

"You like it?" She twirled happily in front of him.

"Very much. But . . . perhaps . . . hmm. Something is not quite right."

"Oh? What? Can it be amended?" She felt a panic out of all proportion to the issue.

"I think so. Perhaps these would help." He handed her a small flat box.

"Trevor?" She opened the box to reveal a spectacular diamond and emerald necklace, bracelet, and earrings. She looked into his eyes and was held by the emotion she saw there. "Oh, Trevor, they are beautiful."

He smiled, obviously pleased with her reaction. "Would you like me to help you?"

"Yes." She replaced the pearl earrings herself, then turned her back to him to give him access to the clasps on the pearls. As he placed the diamond and emerald necklace around her neck, she trembled inwardly at the touch of his fingers at her nape. She was acutely aware of the intimacy of the moment, and she thought he was, too.

"Now the bracelet," he said.

She turned and held out her arm as he fumbled over the clasp. She felt his closeness and smelled his shaving soap. She became very still, hardly daring to breathe. He lifted his eyes to hers and slid his hands to her elbows, drawing her closer.

"Caitlyn, I—"

The door opened and Aunt Gertrude swept in. "I am so sorry to keep you waiting."

Trevor and Caitlyn jerked apart. She thought he seemed as shaken as she as they greeted Aunt Gertrude. The older woman regarded them with curiosity.

"Just see what Trevor has given me," Caitlyn said, fingering the necklace and holding out her arm.

"Lovely," Aunt Gertrude murmured. She turned to her nephew. "So this is why you taxed me so about the gown Caitlyn would wear."

Trevor's color heightened, but he said nothing as he held Caitlyn's cloak to place it over her shoulders.

Pleased by the knowledge that Trevor had gone to such

pains for a gift for her, Caitlyn felt in particular charity with him as they drove to the Wallenford townhouse. The ball was in full swing as they arrived, though the Duke of Wallenford and his duchess still received late-arriving guests.

"The Honorable Trevor Jeffries, Mrs. Trevor Jeffries, and Lady Gertrude Hermiston."

As the butler intoned their names, Caitlyn felt rather than heard a momentary quietness as dozens of eyes turned their way. She saw many of the party look from the new arrivals to a far corner of the room. There stood the countess of Wyndham with a number of other people. Caitlyn met her eyes and watched with some chagrin as the countess very deliberately turned her back and began an animated conversation with her companions.

Caitlyn looked with interest at the others around Trevor's mother. She had heard Gerald's wife described often enough to recognize her in this group. Trevor steered Caitlyn to another area of the huge ballroom and remained standing at her side.

Even before being so pointedly cut by the countess, Caitlyn had feared being ostracized at such a *ton* gathering. However—and much to her surprise—she soon found herself holding court with a group of Trevor's friends and some of her own. Besides the ever-faithful Ratcliff, Graham, and Latham, Trevor's friends Ruskin, Wilson, Moore, and Jenkins all sought her hand for dances.

Apparently overhearing a good-natured quarrel between Moore and Jenkins as to who should have which dance with Caitlyn, Trevor spoke from behind her, giving her a start.

"Just be sure you save the waltzes for *me,* my dear," he said.

She felt a blush of pure pleasure suffuse her cheeks at the request—and the endearment.

"Now, see here, Jeffries," Jenkins said in mock indignation. "You cannot save the best for yourself alone."

"I already have." Trevor's grin was smug.

There was a lull in the conversation and they clearly heard the announcement of arriving guests.

"La Contessa Dolores Oliveira and Colonel Lord Anthony de Lessup."

The former soldiers standing around Caitlyn all whipped about. There were murmurs of surprise.

"Wha-a-at?"

"Well, what do you know?"

"La Contessa."

"Dolores?" This use of the newcomer's given name came from her husband, and Caitlyn instantly wondered at his possible connection to the woman.

"Who is she?" Graham asked the question burning in Caitlyn's mind.

"The belle of Portuguese society—or what was left of it after the royals escaped to Brazil," Wilson said.

"Her husband was killed in oh-seven when the French first invaded Portugal," Jenkins added.

"Oh, how sad for her," Caitlyn murmured.

"Ah, well." Moore sounded a bit crass. "He was a good thirty years and more her senior. Mourning was not exactly a lifetime thing for our contessa."

Caitlyn watched as the foreign woman made her way into the room on the arm of a high-ranking British officer in fancy dress uniform. The contessa was a strikingly beautiful woman with raven-black hair, a light olive complexion, and a well-molded figure set off by a white and silver gown. She greeted several people before she spied the men around Caitlyn and steered her aging companion toward them.

"Ah, my friends from Lisboa," she trilled. "Lieutenants Moore and Jenkins. Captain Wilson. Major Ruskin. And, of course, dear, dear Captain Jeffries." She tapped Trevor's arm with her fan. "You were a naughty boy," she simpered, "leaving as you did without bidding poor Dolores a proper goodbye."

Trevor colored noticeably and grasped Caitlyn's elbow. "May I present my wife, Contessa?"

"Your wife?" She seemed surprised, but quickly recovered and exchanged customary pleasantries even as she gave Caitlyn a calculating look. She was introduced to the other gentlemen, whom she proceeded to charm with her flashing eyes, ready smile, and delightful accent. Then she turned back to Trevor.

"Oh, Captain Jeffries," she said with a teasing smile that included Caitlyn as well. " 'Twas very bad of you to marry before I arrived in England."

There was a moment of pregnant silence. Then the musicians swung into dance music and the hosts took the floor to lead the first set. Theo Ruskin had requested Caitlyn's company for this country dance.

"I hope you do not take the contessa's flirtatious ways to heart, Mrs. Jeffries," he said in a kindly voice. "She is really quite harmless."

I wonder? Caitlyn thought, but aloud she said, "Oh, my, no." Then to change the subject, she said, "And you really must call me Caitlyn since you are such a very close friend to Trevor."

"I am honored, Caitlyn. And I am Theo."

"Short for Theodore, I presume."

"Actually, no. My father is a student of ancient history and literature. He named me for Theocritus—an ancient Greek poet."

"And your second name is . . . ?"

He looked a little sheepish. "Euripides."

She grinned. "A poet who advocated romantic love and a dramatist who cherished women. Did your father have these traits in mind when he named his son?"

Theo looked down at her in utter surprise. "Good heavens," he said in mock horror. "The lady is a bluestocking!"

She laughed, feeling wholly at ease with him. "No. Not at all. But my father was a voracious reader. His greatest gift to me was his love of literature."

"Even so, there are precious few people in all of England who would have so casually known either of those names."

As the movements of the dance separated them, Caitlyn glanced around discreetly to see that the raven-haired beauty danced with the man named Jenkins. The two seemed to be enjoying a hearty joke. Later, Caitlyn danced through two more sets with Graham and with Moore before Trevor came to claim her for the first waltz.

She steeled herself for the feel of his arm about her, and for that surge of emotion that was sure to come. She closed her eyes briefly, savoring his nearness as they swept into the steps of the dance. She cautioned herself not to become lost in the moment. Oh, but it felt so right!

"I saw you dancing with Theo," Trevor said. "You were the prettiest woman on the floor."

"Why, thank you." This was the second time this evening he had paid her a fulsome compliment. She must not read too much into such flattery, no matter how sincere he sounded. "I like him—Theo, I mean."

"Theo?"

"We agreed on first names—but if you object—"

"Not at all. Theo is my best friend. Saved my life."

"Then I shall treasure his friendship all the more."

He did not answer, merely pulled her slightly closer.

Later, yet another dance partner had returned her to the sidelines where she joined Aunt Gertrude, sitting near one of the room's huge Greek-styled pillars.

"You seem to be enjoying yourself, my dear," Aunt Gertrude said.

"Yes. I am. And truly I did not expect to do so."

She looked out on the floor to see Trevor dance by with La Contessa as his partner. This caused a twinge of emotion. Jealousy? Surely not. Did he not have a perfect right to dance and laugh with whomever he pleased?

"Well, you know"—a voice, slightly louder than one might

have expected, came from the other side of the pillar—
"Trevor was involved with that woman in Portugal."

"Involved? How?" asked another voice.

Aunt Gertrude leaned closer to Caitlyn to whisper, "Lydia.
And Miranda, I think. Shall we move elsewhere?"

Caitlyn knew very well she should say yes, but something
held her rooted to the spot. She shook her head no. The first
voice continued.

"It is said she was my son's mistress."

"Surely not, my lady."

"I am afraid so, my dear. Colonel Lord Oglethorpe told
me so himself."

"Oh, my. I surely hope Trevor is not going to spring yet
more scandal about our heads."

"At least this one is not likely to involve a child born on
the wrong side of the blanket." Lydia's laugh held little mirth.

The voices moved on.

Aunt Gertrude patted Caitlyn's hand. "Of all the malicious,
hateful things to say! Pay them no mind, my dear."

Caitlyn made no attempt to hide her pain as she looked at
Aunt Gertrude. "But you heard them. They said Trevor—"

"They were repeating gossip. And who is to say they were
not making the whole thing up? One thing is certain—they
knew you would hear them."

"How could they know that?"

"They walked past me only a moment before you left the
dance floor."

"Then they—"

"—were being deliberately cruel. Pay them no mind."

However, try as she might, Caitlyn could not forget what
she had heard. The evening, which had started out on such
a warm, positive note, had taken a cold, bleak turn.

Fearful that someone of his family would contrive to em-
barrass or humiliate Caitlyn, Trevor had made a point of being

with her or ensuring that she was accompanied by those who would offer subtle protection all evening. Even as he danced with others, he was aware of where—and with whom—Caitlyn was to be found. He cursed his luck that he had been unable to avoid the machinations of Dolores, who had manipulated him into dancing with her.

He saw Caitlyn and Aunt Gertrude and then he spied his mother and sister-in-law standing only a few feet away. Despite the intricacies of the dance, he glanced at Caitlyn repeatedly. He saw her face take on a stricken look which she was not wholly successful in hiding, and he saw his mother and her companion walk away.

Damn! They must have said something to hurt her.

Later, though, he saw Caitlyn laughing and chatting merrily with Willard Ratcliff. When Trevor claimed her for the second waltz, she seemed herself again—or as much of such a self as he now knew. That he truly wanted to know more came as a surprise. Being aware of a woman's physical charms was one thing. This desire to know Caitlyn's emotional depths was quite another.

Finally, the ball was over. Trevor handed his wife and his aunt into the carriage and noted with an inward smile of gratitude that Aunt Gertrude had taken the seat opposite Caitlyn, leaving the space near his wife free. Caitlyn moved slightly to allow him more room than he wanted.

"Such a wonderful ball," Aunt Gertrude observed in a conversational tone. "The duchess was in alt—two crowned heads of the continent and the Prince Regent, too, among her guests."

Caitlyn chuckled. "All that royal splendor was rather dimmed by the appearance of the Spanish general with his miles of gold braid and all those medals. They kept clinking!"

"There must have been fully half of England's notable families represented tonight." Trevor was determined to uphold his part of any conversation.

"Oh, rather more than half, I should think," Caitlyn offered. "Even Lady Hedley made an appearance, and she is really quite a recluse."

"She is a distant relative—a cousin, I believe—of the duchess, who was a Spenser, you know," Aunt Gertrude explained.

"No, I did not know." Caitlyn seemed uninterested in the topic. She leaned her head back against the squabs at the back of the carriage seat and closed her eyes, effectively stopping the discussion.

Neither woman had mentioned the spectacular entrance of La Contessa Oliveira. Trevor wondered why, for the Portuguese beauty had certainly made a splash in the pool of London society.

Trevor had known Dolores well in Lisbon. She had long since come out of mourning when he met her. A vivacious flirt, she had welcomed the company of men nearer her own age than her husband had been. Reeling from the pain and scandal of his marriage, Trevor had sought to ignore his own recent past and simply enjoy the superficial and frivolous banter of Lisbon's social offerings.

His battered ego had responded eagerly when the contessa singled him out. It suited both of them to have others believe there was much more to their relationship than there was. The truth was that, beyond a quick kiss or two, there had been nothing physical between them. They simply enjoyed each other's company, and he had called often at her villa. She was invariably properly chaperoned, and more often than not there was a crowd of laughing guests, anxious to forget previous battles and forestall the prospects of new ones.

Since neither Aunt Gertrude nor Caitlyn had mentioned the Portuguese beauty, Trevor wondered if he should bring up the topic, especially given Dolores's effusive greeting to him. But he was somehow reluctant to introduce the subject himself, lest he be required to make awkward explanations.

So nothing was said, and on arrival home, the three of them bade each other good night and sought their own chambers.

Trevor spent much of the night deep in thought, prompted by the interview with his family. Given the reality of his daughter—a reality he no longer questioned in the slightest—he determined that it was past time he took a more active interest in his own estate matters.

With this in mind, he arose in the middle of the night to search for the ledgers and files Whitcomb had pressed upon him a few weeks ago. He pushed his bed pillows into a pile, lit the bedside lamp, and examined several sheets on the "desk" of his drawn-up knees. He fell asleep before he had gained more than cursory information.

The next morning after his usual outing with Ashley, he sat at a writing table in his chamber and studied the documents in earnest. And was baffled by what he saw.

Aside from the land and buildings—which were admittedly of considerable value—Atherton had had few assets when it came into his hands so fleetingly before his departure for the Peninsula. Profits from the estate had dwindled steadily since his grandfather's death some fifteen years earlier. That is, they had dwindled until about four and a half years ago. Then they had stopped altogether.

For nearly two years, there was little in the way of income from the home farm, and nothing from the tenant farms that made up the bulk of the estate. This was especially puzzling. No matter how badly things had deteriorated, there should have been *something* coming in from the rents. There it was—nothing in the way of such income.

By contrast, there were great outlays. These were not specified in great detail in the ledgers other than "buildings," "supplies," "stock," or "repairs." With no appreciable income, where on earth had the money come from for these ambitious expenditures?

Trevor knew that neither his father nor Gerald would have franked such a venture, even had he or Caitlyn had nerve enough to ask them to do so. Whitcomb had said Marcus was not involved, and Trevor remembered his brother's own cash-poor status earlier. Also, Whitcomb had openly admired Caitlyn's business acumen.

Still—where had *she* obtained adequate funding for the expenditures he was seeing? She had come to him virtually penniless, and he very much doubted the Baron Fiske would have advanced her any monies. Surely she had not contracted for vast loans—or had she gone to the cent-percenters? No. Not likely. But how . . . ?

An image of Caitlyn head-to-head, laughing gaily, with the immensely wealthy Willard Ratcliff flashed across his mind. Graham, too, was known to be a very rich man—as was Latham, though Latham, Trevor knew, had only recently inherited.

The longer he studied the books, the more agitated he became. Finally, it occurred to him that the documents he had were not up-to-date. Nor did they tell the whole story since they dealt only with Atherton and did not include household expenses in London or other investments which Whitcomb had mentioned in passing.

Whitcomb had also said Trevor's allowance had come in recent years from Atherton. Had it really come from Ratcliff or Graham? Or Latham? And if it had, what sort of "bargain" had his wife made?

He had worked himself into quite a snit of anger by the time he met Caitlyn and Aunt Gertrude in the dining room for luncheon.

"I trust your morning went well," Caitlyn said brightly to the others once they were all seated.

"Yes," Aunt Gertrude said. "Mine went very well. I finished a new book by that wonderful lady who wrote *Sense and Sensibility*. Such a delight."

"I shall have to read it," Caitlyn said. "And you, Trevor? Have you had a good morning, too?"

"I, too, have been doing some reading," he said.

"Anything of interest?" Caitlyn asked.

"Of immense interest." Trevor waited for the servant to

finish serving and leave. "I have been reading ledgers and files Mr. Whitcomb gave me."

He saw the surprise in Caitlyn's eyes before she quickly lowered her lashes. Finally, she spoke slowly and cautiously, no brightness in her tone now. "I was not aware that you had seen Mr. Whitcomb."

"I did so some weeks ago, just after my return."

"I see."

Trevor decided to plunge right in. "The information he gave me is far from current—or complete. I should like to see those ledgers you labor over so on a daily basis, if you do not mind."

He saw her blanch and swallow hard before exchanging a look with Aunt Gertrude, but her voice was steady.

"Of course, Trevor. I shall get them for you after lunch."

Thirteen

"Here you are." Caitlyn set the ledgers down and gestured to Trevor. "You will be more comfortable here at the desk, I think." She tried to sound unconcerned.

"Thank you."

"If you have questions, I shall be in the sunroom with Aunt Gertrude."

"The books will probably speak for themselves."

Caitlyn raised an eyebrow at what seemed to her to be a typical male sense of superiority in matters of business, but she said only, "I shall leave you to your study, then."

Not until she had closed the library door did she allow anxiety to gnaw at her. Aunt Gertrude lifted her head and set aside her embroidery as Caitlyn entered the sunroom.

"You seem worried, my dear."

"I am. I just gave Trevor the account books."

"Why should that be worrisome? I am sure you have recorded things accurately and honestly."

"To the best of my ability, in any event."

"Well, then . . . ?"

"Why now?" Caitlyn asked, assailed by doubts and apprehension. "He has shown no interest heretofore. While he was away, he did not correspond with Mr. Whitcomb, yet he apparently consulted the solicitor before making his presence known to us."

"But he did not know we were in town, did he?"

"And now," Caitlyn went on, consumed by her own

thoughts, "he demands to see the accounts only after he has visited his father and brother."

Aunt Gertrude's expression was genuinely confused. "What has that to say to anything?"

"Do you not understand? He must have changed his mind. They have convinced him they were right all along. You heard his mother. They have persuaded him to pursue a divorce after all." Her voice broke on this thought.

"Now, my dear. You do not know this to be true. You are anticipating trouble that may never materialize."

"How I wish you were right, but . . ."

"Think, Caitlyn. Besides the scandal attendant to divorce, it is an incredibly expensive and time-consuming affair. And *complicated* beyond all reason—what with ecclesiastical as well as civil courts—and these court proceedings are only the start. Then it takes an act of Parliament. What is more, one cannot be assured of the outcome at any stage."

"Aunt Gertrude, you know as well as I do that the wheels of law and politics—even within the church—are greased by money—and His Lordship, the Earl of Wyndham, has a ready supply of such lubricant."

"True, but—"

"And I have nothing—nothing—with which to fight them. Trevor controls all that I have—and if he behaves as he did before . . ." Her voice trailed off.

"You must not become all to pieces, dear. Why not wait to see what happens?"

"I must. I have no other option but to wait. There is simply nothing else I can do. I truly hate this—waiting on the choices others make!"

"I know, love," Aunt Gertrude consoled. "Many a woman would share that view."

"For five years I have made my own decisions. And I have loved having charge of my own life."

"You have a done a fine job of it, too. But perhaps . . ." Aunt Gertrude's voice faded.

"Perhaps what? What were you about to say?"

"Only that *sharing* responsibilities can be rewarding, too. Surely you can admit that you would have welcomed another view of many of the problems we have confronted in the last few years."

Reluctantly, Caitlyn nodded. "Yes. And I have appreciated *your* support, Aunt Gertrude. But somehow I doubt sharing is what Trevor has in mind."

"Well, you must wait to find out just what he does have in mind. Here. Here is something to take your mind off your worries." She handed Caitlyn a book—the very book she had mentioned at lunch.

"*Pride and Prejudice?* I suppose the pride is male and the prejudice is female. Am I right?"

Aunt Gertrude chuckled. "I rather think each gender has its share of both—but read it and see what you think."

Soon Caitlyn was lost in the world of Elizabeth Bennett and her Mr. Darcy.

In the library, Trevor found the account books meticulously maintained in a neat, round hand. Three years ago the home farm had started to turn a profit. The rents from tenant farms had actually increased overall, though they tended to fluctuate from one farmer to another and from one year to another. That was odd. The farms were of a size; their rents should have been a flat sum from each.

The profits had financed improvements on the estate, for the most part. He heartily approved of such a practice. But some had been invested on the 'Change. Risky business, that. One had to be knowledgeable about the market, and a host of factors could make or break the investor. His disapproval was thwarted, however, by these ventures having also turned a modest profit.

Who had been advising her? Trevor doubted the steward, Felkins, possessed such expertise. Graham? He came from an important banking family. He might have done so. Despite Trevor's reservations, one thing was clear. The financial status of the Trevor Jeffries household was, indeed, steadily improving and promised to continue on course. While he might never head one of the richest families of the realm as his father did, his situation would be decidedly comfortable.

Still—questions remained. *Where* had the initial funding come from? He remembered all too well the run-down condition of the estate and the dilapidated buildings of the tenant farms. And *where* the money had come from was not the only question. Also, from *whom?* And on what terms?

Could this newfound Jeffries wealth be based on his wife's having bargained her favors? He hated himself for such a demeaning thought, but had she not once been party to an equally nefarious scheme? If that were the case, how could he possibly carry on? The truth was, he could not.

But he could not bring himself to challenge her outright— at least not yet. He would give her ample opportunity to volunteer the information he needed. And he would visit Atherton for a firsthand view before bringing up the matter himself.

"Did you find everything in order?" Caitlyn asked later, her expression bland.

"For the most part, yes. You seem to have been very diligent."

"I try to be." She chewed on her bottom lip for a moment. "Does your sudden interest in the books mean you want to take them over?"

He stared at her, trying to discern whether she was dissembling. Finally, he shrugged. "Not yet. I shall want to see the estate first and talk with our people."

"Of course."

It would not have taken an Oxford don to recognize that the budding warmth of a few nights ago had suffered a definite chill, Trevor thought, feeling rather testy about the situation. Yet he had to admit to himself his continued attraction to her. The notion of wooing her had not lost its appeal. Occasionally, he would catch her looking at him with a vulnerable, apprehensive expression in her eyes. But as soon as she realized he had caught her out, she would quickly right herself and make some lighthearted comment.

This, too, Trevor found frustrating. What was it she feared in him? Was he not living up to their agreement? Other than discussions of Ashley's activities, their conversations again centered on polite banalities. The two of them were rarely alone together. Trevor was convinced that Caitlyn deliberately planned that fact of their lives.

Despite the coolness of the Wyndham household toward the earl's youngest son, invitations continued to pour in from others to Trevor, Caitlyn, and Aunt Gertrude. Aunt Gertrude had informed him of Caitlyn's overhearing "cutting remarks" made by his mother and Miranda at the Wallenford ball, though she had not shared the specifics. He and his aunt now tacitly joined forces to protect Caitlyn from any repeat of such embarrassment. Only when they knew that Caitlyn was involved with someone "safe" would they pursue their own interests at a ball or rout.

Trevor often took a rather jaundiced view of what he had come to view as "safe." Was he to consider it "safe" to see his wife waltzing in the arms of Ratcliff? or in obvious *tête-à-tête* in a drawing room with Graham? Or riding of a morning with the ever-persistent Latham?

One evening he chanced to overhear part of a conversation between Caitlyn and Ratcliff that gave him pause. They had attended musical presentations sponsored by the dowager countess Terwilliger. At an interval between performances, Trevor had gone to procure drinks for himself and Caitlyn. Aunt Gertrude was off with other guests elsewhere in the room. As Trevor returned, carrying two glasses of punch, he saw that Caitlyn and Ratcliff had their heads together and were unaware of his presence.

Ratcliff bent over Caitlyn's hand and was saying, "—cannot begin to express how wonderful for me our relationship has been. A most rewarding delight."

Caitlyn smiled fondly and replied, "The rewards are mutual, I am sure. After all, Will, where would Atherton Farms be without your help?"

Trevor was stunned. It was one thing to entertain vague suspicions. It was quite another to have them confirmed. He cleared his throat rather noisily, and the two jerked apart, startled.

He handed Caitlyn one of the glasses. "Your drink, my dear." He was pleased at how level his voice was.

Ratcliff jumped up. "Sorry, my friend. Just wanted a word with your lovely wife."

Was that a smile or a smirk on his face? Trevor nodded and took the vacated seat. Aunt Gertrude returned, bubbling with some tidbit she had learned. Trevor was inordinately quiet for the rest of the evening, unable to put that snippet of conversation from his mind. Will? She called him Will? He was grateful that Aunt Gertrude's presence precluded an immediate confrontation.

Caitlyn was mystified by her husband's behavior. Beyond examining the account books, he had not challenged any of her decisions. The gift of the emeralds had thrilled her—more for his search for the right gift than for the jewels themselves. There had not been another such impromptu gift, nor another moment of tenderness between them. However, she had received several bouquets of flowers which arrived with no identifying card, and she suspected they came from Trevor.

Whenever they were invited out, it seemed the Portuguese beauty was also among the guests. Caitlyn grew accustomed to seeing La Contessa dancing or conversing flirtatiously with Trevor, but she could not accustom herself to her own twinges of jealousy. The insidious poison of her mother-in-law's words worked its deviltry despite her wish to ignore them.

Seeing Trevor happily laughing and chatting with that woman was especially painful because he was rarely that way at home—except with Ashley. Gradually, Caitlyn arrived at the conclusion that her husband was miserably unhappy in his marriage and that it was only a matter of time until he took steps to free himself of a wife he detested.

Then two events occurred to distract her from these dark musings.

Caitlyn and Aunt Gertrude were sitting in the sunroom late one morning. Trevor had gone out with Ashley. Thompkins appeared in the doorway with a puzzled expression on his usually impassive face. He carried a salver with a card.

"There is a visitor, madam, asking to be presented."

"At this hour?" Caitlyn took the card. "Sheffield?" She glanced at Aunt Gertrude.

"Melanie!" the two of them cried in unison.

"Show her in immediately," Caitlyn instructed.

Suddenly there she was—fresh-faced, lively, and cheerful as ever. Melanie was dressed in a fashionable walking dress of wide stripes of brown and yellow and green and wore a pert little straw hat. The three exchanged warm, excited greetings, and Melanie was invited to sit and take a dish of tea.

"Thank you for seeing me so unexpectedly." Melanie's eager gaiety was irresistible. "Andrew has gone off to the Foreign Office this morning, but I could not wait to surprise my favorite brother! We arrived yesterday. Mother assured me Trevor is in town, too."

"Yes, he is," Caitlyn said. "He should be back momentarily."

"You are staying with Lydia and Alfred, then?" Aunt Gertrude asked conversationally.

"Oh, no. We are with Andrew's parents. Gerald and Miranda are at Wyndham House, too, you know."

"Yes, we did know," Aunt Gertrude replied, "but it is a huge house, after all."

"But not as comfortable as the Sheffield home," Melanie

said frankly. "Neither Miranda nor the countess is happy having small children around—and I am sorely afraid both of mine take after their mother in hoydenish behavior, though little Anna is not yet a year old."

"We look forward to meeting her as well as seeing Elizabeth again. And Sir Andrew, of course," Caitlyn said.

"What is more to the point," Melanie went on, barely pausing, "I wanted to be able to entertain *all* the members of my family as I wish." She gave her listeners a speaking look.

"You have heard, then—" Caitlyn murmured.

"Yes. And I think the whole situation is simply ludicrous."

She might have said more, but at that moment the door opened and Ashley skipped in, followed by her father, who stopped in surprise on the threshold.

"Melanie? Melanie!" As she rose, he enfolded her in a long, tight bear hug. "Let me look at you."

Melanie stepped back and turned in front of him. "Not bad for an old married woman, mother of two, eh?" She laughed.

"Not bad at all." He hugged her again. "I hope Drew appreciates his good fortune."

"Oh, he does. Occasionally, I remind him just to keep him alert."

"I'll just bet you do."

"Mama, who is that lady?" Ashley asked.

They all laughed and reintroduced Ashley to her aunt. Then Caitlyn suggested she and Aunt Gertrude would see Ashley up to the nursery and thus give Trevor some private time with his sister.

Later in her own room, Caitlyn thought with longing of the spontaneous warmth of Trevor's greeting to Melanie. How she envied the easy rapport between the two of them—the mutual love that neither made any effort to hide. If only . . .

In the next few days they saw much of Melanie, who brought her older daughter to play with Cousin Ashley. Melanie's little girl was a year younger than Ashley, but as

Elizabeth was rather large for her age and possessed of the same precociousness her mother must have displayed as a child, the two little girls got on amazingly well.

"Two peas in a pod," Aunt Gertrude observed with a smug note as the two little heads of blonde curls bent together over a toy.

The other major event which distracted not only Caitlyn, but all of London, was the nation's all-out welcome of its favorite hero. The object of this unprecedented public appreciation was Arthur Wellesley, Duke of Wellington, lately commander in chief of the allied forces in the Peninsula.

The Prince was determined to prove to one and all his own immense gratitude to the general—and, incidentally, to share in the nation's accolades. To this end he hosted a glorious ball at Carlton House. He apparently hoped future accounts of this grand affair would one day dazzle the grandchildren of those attending. Wellington was to be the guest of honor, but invitations—which, of course, amounted to royal summonses—went out to hundreds of the country's notables.

Caitlyn and Aunt Gertrude sat in the drawing room one evening. Trevor had gone out to his club some time before.

"As you hold a title in your own right, *Lady* Gertrude," Caitlyn said, "I fully understand your being invited to the Prince's ball. What I do not understand is how Trevor and I came to be invited."

"Perhaps because Trevor served as an officer in the army Wellington commanded."

"Or—the royal summons extended to sons of peers."

"Possibly."

In preparing for the ball, Caitlyn chose a brilliant green gown that would complement her emeralds. In nervous anticipation, she met Trevor and Aunt Gertrude in the library before they set off. Trevor's eyes lit up on seeing her, and she thought he was pleased she had worn the emeralds.

Trevor, dressed in the formal uniform of his regiment for this grandest of military balls, looked devastatingly handsome. Caitlyn thought her heart might melt away right there and then, but she was careful to hide her reaction.

"What a truly handsome pair the two of you make," Aunt Gertrude exclaimed.

"Well, then, that makes three of us," Trevor said and gallantly offered one arm to Caitlyn and the other to Aunt Gertrude.

The line of carriages seeking entry to Carlton House seemed endless, and once they were inside, the line of guests waiting to be received by the Prince and his lordly honoree stretched for some distance. Finally, Trevor and his two ladies were presented. The duke was shorter and less physically prepossessing than Caitlyn had imagined, but when he spoke, he was clearly a man used to being in command.

"Captain Jeffries. 'Tis a pleasure to see you again." The duke turned to the Prince at his side. "May I recommend Captain Jeffries to you, sire, as a man of great fortitude and courage."

Surprised at the duke's singling out her husband so, Caitlyn watched as the Prince gave Trevor a piercing look and murmured a polite greeting. Then Trevor presented his wife and his aunt and they were ushered into the crowd of guests. Caitlyn floated through much of the evening, enjoying the dancing, and trying to memorize the elaborate decorations. The Prince had spared no expense. Two orchestras were discreetly hidden by banks of flowers. Murals of military scenes, gilt statuettes, and colorful drapery all combined to create a fairy-tale effect.

The duke and the Prince, having left the reception line, circulated among the guests. By some stroke of ill luck, Caitlyn thought, she and Trevor were standing in close proximity to Lord and Lady Wyndham, though in separate groups. Melanie and Andrew, along with Captain Ruskin, were talking quietly with Caitlyn and Trevor.

"I say, Wyndham." The duke's braying voice caught the attention of everyone near. "You must be proud of this son of yours." The duke drew Trevor into the other circle, and Trevor brought Caitlyn with him.

The Earl of Wyndham colored and coughed discreetly, but Wellington seemed not to notice and continued, "Yes, sir. You have cause to be proud. Our nation owes a great debt of gratitude to two of your sons."

"Is that so?" The earl seemed merely curious, but Gerald, standing at his father's elbow, preened.

"Trevor here distinguished himself at Vitoria—was wounded even—but he came back to be a vital factor in our taking San Sebastian."

Caitlyn saw shocked surprise on the faces of all Trevor's family but Melanie's, which registered only delight. Obviously, they had known nothing of the exploits of their son and brother on the field of battle. But then, neither had his wife.

"Of course, we are very proud of our children," the countess put in, nudging Gerald to the great man's attention.

"Marcus Jeffries was invaluable to us in Paris," Wellington went on. "Still is. Too bad he could not join us tonight. Good men, both of them."

With that, the duke and his host moved on, leaving a much chagrined Gerald unable to meet his brother's eyes. He, his wife, and the countess quickly began to move away. But the earl paused.

"I should like to be presented to your wife, Trevor," the earl said.

Caitlyn saw anger flash across the countess's features as the woman distanced herself even farther from Trevor and his father. Gerald and his wife tried to conceal their shocked disgust with polite smiles pasted on their faces.

Trevor made the introduction, and Caitlyn offered the old man her hand. He held her gaze momentarily, then bent his head over the proffered hand.

"Lovely," he said to Trevor and addressed Caitlyn with "I am very pleased to meet you, madam."

Surprised and disconcerted, Caitlyn murmured what she hoped was an appropriate response. Lord Wyndham, like Wellington, was smaller than she expected; both his sons towered over him. But he was a man fully aware of his own worth, and he presented a sense of power and control. It struck Caitlyn that she had lately perceived such qualities in the man's younger son.

"Alfred." The countess's tone was insistent. The earl gave a slight grimace and followed his wife.

Trevor and Caitlyn turned to each other.

"Well, what do you know?" he asked rhetorically.

"That was certainly unexpected," she replied.

"I knew Father would come around," Melanie said. "This is a beginning, at least."

Any sense of triumph Caitlyn might have felt was quickly doused as La Contessa, with a soldier on each arm, approached their group. Dolores immediately became the focus of attention, and when Latham invited Caitlyn to dance, she eagerly accepted. Soon thereafter, she saw Trevor partnering the contessa and struggled to squelch what she recognized as rampant jealousy.

In the carriage on the way home, Aunt Gertrude said, "Trevor, you did not tell us of your exploits on the Peninsula."

"You heard, then?" He seemed slightly embarrassed.

"You must know that every word the duke uttered tonight was endlessly repeated. And there I was—with no idea my very own nephew was a famous war hero."

"Not such a hero at all," he protested.

"But you were wounded," Caitlyn put in.

"A flesh wound." He touched his jacket just below his right shoulder. "I was fortunate that it was not worse."

"Hmm." Aunt Gertrude sounded disbelieving, but said no more.

Caitlyn pondered what she had learned after Theo filled her in on Trevor's actions. Her husband was, indeed, a hero. He had repeatedly put himself in great danger to save others. The wound had been far more serious than he would have them believe, and he had suffered other, less serious wounds, as well.

She had, since his return, been struck by the contrast between the man he seemed to be now and the callow, self-centered, naive youth who had been manipulated into deserting his wife. Yet even then—five years ago—she had been attracted to some core of inner strength in him. It was a quality she had ignored in her subsequent anger and resentment.

Now, here—along with his acceptance and love of their daughter—was confirmation of her instinctive admiration for him.

She sighed.

Unfortunately, it was too late.

Fourteen

The next week saw the entire household at sixes and sevens as they prepared to remove to Atherton. Trevor's round of visits to say farewell centered on Melanie and Theo, both of whom would also be leaving town soon, Theo going to his father's primary holding in the Midlands, and Melanie to Timberly to visit her childhood home. Later, she and her young family would visit Atherton.

Trevor watched idly as two coaches drew up in front of the house. There was another vehicle for luggage. He knew that Caitlyn's mount and other cattle were stabled at nearby mews. He had taken little interest in them before now. The black was missing. Caitlyn must have sent him on ahead, or intended to have him brought later. It struck him that these teams were especially fine-looking animals.

With that observation came a familiar wave of annoyance. No need to ask where his wife had come by such excellent horseflesh. After all, the Ratcliff stables were well known. Ratcliff had certainly become a firmly rooted fixture in Caitlyn's life. Trevor wondered just when it had happened. It was an ongoing matter—of that much he was sure, judging by that bit of conversation at the Terwilligers's musicale.

At their first stop to change horses, Trevor made another discovery: The replacement teams were also their own cattle. The Jeffries household boarded its own teams at changing stations between Atherton and London! He knew this was a common practice among those who could afford it. That *he* could afford such luxury came as a surprise until he remembered the figures in those account books.

The three adults traveled in the first carriage, with Ashley and four servants in the other. There were additional servants riding on the outside of both carriages, for the weather had continued to be cooperative. Their schedule in recent days had been hectic. They were all tired, especially in the afternoon after a stop for the midday meal. In the front carriage, Aunt Gertrude was the first to nod off. She and Caitlyn had been sharing the forward-facing seat.

Apparently seeing the older woman's head bobbing up and down, Caitlyn said, "Here, Aunt Gertrude. There are some extra cushions—and if I sit across with Trevor, you may be more comfortable."

"Hmm. You are always so thoughtful," Aunt Gertrude mumbled, accepting her bonus of comfort.

Trevor made room for Caitlyn on his seat.

"You do not mind, do you?" she asked.

"No, of course not." The truth was, he quite welcomed her closeness and the subtle, tantalizing scent she wore. He rested his arm along the back of the seat behind her.

They talked quietly of inconsequential matters such as the weather and road conditions. There were also periods of silence, but these were not uncomfortable. Neither had spoken for some time when Trevor noticed Caitlyn fending off drowsiness.

"Come. Don't fight it." He gently pulled her head to his shoulder. She hesitated only a moment, then snuggled closer and was soon fast asleep.

For some time he sat savoring the experience of simple togetherness. Then he, too, nodded off, his head resting on hers. He loved the softness of her hair against his cheek. When the coach lurched to a stop at an inn for the next change of horses, all three of them were startled to wakefulness. Caitlyn seemed embarrassed at finding herself so firmly in his arms.

"I am sorry." She sat straighter. "You cannot be comfortable with me crowding you so."

"On the contrary. It felt . . . right to me." He reluctantly released her and leaned across her to open the carriage door. He heard her sharp intake of breath at this moment of further closeness. Trevor handed both ladies from the carriage.

Sometime later, the two vehicles were on their way again, with the addition of Ashley to the forward carriage. Her questions and chatter entertained them until their stop for the night. Trevor was surprised that this break in their trip came in the same town and at the same inn where he and Caitlyn had spent the first night of their marriage over five years before.

He looked at Caitlyn and knew she had only now realized the significance of this particular location.

"Oh, dear," she said softly, glancing at him, then away.

"Is something amiss?" Aunt Gertrude asked.

"No. Not at all." Caitlyn recovered quickly, but she refused to meet his gaze.

Trevor chuckled and jumped from the carriage. "I shall see to our accommodations."

He noticed an inordinate amount of activity in the inn yard. It occurred to him that traffic had become much heavier as they entered this town. A servant who had been sent ahead to secure their rooms and arrange their meals met him at the door.

"I done me best, sir, but the inn is real full. There's a mill takin' place here tomorrow."

"Are you telling me we have no rooms?" Trevor demanded.

"Oh, they's rooms all right, but only two, you see."

By now the harried landlord had joined them. He was a burly, red-faced man of middle years, wearing a once-clean apron. Trevor observed that the taproom was crowded with an eclectic group of *ton* dandies, cits, and local farmers.

"I am sorry we can't do better by you, sir," the innkeeper

said. "As I was tellin' your man here, the whole town is full up for this boxing match tomorrow."

It developed that these were, indeed, the last two rooms available in the entire town. Moreover, Trevor was informed, surrounding villages were likely to be just as crowded, for this sporting event pitted two very popular pugilists against each other.

When he explained the situation to Caitlyn and Aunt Gertrude, Caitlyn said in a matter-of-fact voice, "Well, we shall just make do. It is far too late to drive on now."

However, he thought she seemed much less complacent when it became clear that she would be sharing a room with him, while Aunt Gertrude, Ashley, and their three female servants were allotted the other, slightly larger, room. The coachman and other male servants would sleep in the stables.

The inn's only private parlor had been taken over by a group of Corinthian revelers. The Jeffries party therefore dined at a table the landlord set up in the room Trevor and Caitlyn would share. Caitlyn surveyed the fare and then shrugged.

"It is a bit cozier than we anticipated, but it will have to do," she said to Aunt Gertrude as the two of them waited for Trevor to join them.

"Beggars are not allowed to be choosers," Aunt Gertrude said.

"It never occurred to me that we should reserve rooms in advance."

"Perhaps there is a message to be had in this little twist of fate," Aunt Gertrude said archly.

"I cannot imagine what it would be."

But Caitlyn, who found it difficult to control her nervousness about sharing this room later with Trevor, knew very well what her aunt had in mind. More than once, the older woman had hinted at hoping that Caitlyn and Trevor could resolve any differences between them.

Trevor came in at this point. There was an air of boyish excitement about him. "You will never guess who is below," he said. "Jenkins and Moore. They knew all about this contest. I've promised to join them later."

Caitlyn did not know whether to be pleased or dismayed at this news. She made a polite response, as did Aunt Gertrude, and the meal progressed amicably. Then Trevor left to join his friends, and Aunt Gertrude retired to the other room.

Left alone with her own thoughts after dismissing her maid, Caitlyn was apprehensive about the forced intimacy of their shared accommodations. Would Trevor expect to assert his rights as her husband when he returned?

Did she want him to?

Facing this question honestly, she did not know. She freely admitted to her own physical attraction to him—and to being mildly surprised at this response to a man who had wronged her. She chastised herself for being "such a strumpet," though she supposed a purely physical reaction to an attractive male was a natural response.

Then an impish demon in the back of her mind suggested that she knew other men who were equally handsome. None of these caused her to experience the shortness of breath and flood of awareness that assailed her whenever her husband was near.

What kind of woman would welcome the advances of a man who had once so forcefully rejected her?

A strumpet, of course. But, God help her, she thought she might welcome Trevor's presence in her bed again.

She sat in a lacy bedgown and brushed her hair vigorously. Then she tried to pick up a book she had tucked into her portmanteau. Her mind kept drifting, her thoughts punctuated by the merriment floating up from below.

Finally, she climbed into bed, turned the lamp low, and waited for Trevor's arrival.

And waited.

And waited.

She hardly knew whether she was angry or disappointed about his continued absence. Drowsiness overcame her and she slept. It was much later when she heard a key turn in the lock. She was instantly alert, but she lay still, feigning sleep.

She heard clothing rustling and the soft thud of his boots hitting the floor. Then she felt his nearness next to the bed. She caught the scent of his shaving soap mixed with brandy. Beneath her lashes, she saw him bend over to touch her hair spread on the pillow. Then he straightened, heaved a sigh, and extinguished the light. He moved away to settle himself on a chaise longue in the corner.

Caitlyn felt a distinct sense of loss.

Trevor awoke early the next morning, hurried through his ablutions, and left the room before Caitlyn arose. She had awakened, however, to bid him a shy "good morning." When he returned shortly for breakfast, Aunt Gertrude and Ashley had joined them.

The journey started with Ashley again in her parents' coach. The conversation was limited to answering her interminable questions and sharing in her chatter with her ever-present doll.

Trevor had not slept well on the chaise longue. Even as he had conversed earlier with Jenkins and Moore, his mind had drifted to the thought of Caitlyn alone in the room above. He had wanted to go to her then, but was unsure of his welcome. Now whenever he closed his eyes or stared, unseeing, out the coach window, the same image haunted him: Caitlyn lying in bed, her hair fanned out on the pillow. The temptation to take her right then and there had been nearly overwhelming. Why had he hesitated? She was his wife. Husbands had certain rights, did they not?

Then he answered his own foolish question. Trevor Jeffries had never in his life taken a woman against her will. He certainly would not start with his wife.

It was another long day of travel. Darkness was settling in as they arrived at the familiar driveway to Atherton. Trevor could see little, but he thought the general scene was neater. There was a sense of trim, clean lines about the place. Lanterns showed the stone steps leading to the entrance swept clean, and there were pots of bright flowers on either side.

The door swung open to reveal a golden glow of light from within. Merrill seemed unsurprised to see him. Was that the customary stoicism of a well-trained butler? Or had Caitlyn sent word ahead? Both, he decided.

Inside, the transformation was astonishing. Treated to a quick tour, he found that such floors as were not covered with carpets, as well as every other noticeable piece of wood, were highly polished. The walls were clean, and the furniture showed not a speck of dust. Some familiar pieces had been refurbished. New pieces had been chosen with care and good taste.

"Very comfortable," he said, and Caitlyn seemed pleased.

"I have had your things put in here." She opened the door of what he knew to be the master bedchamber—one they had previously shared. She apparently read his unasked question, for she went on, "I shall have the room next door." She *had* sent word ahead, then.

The master chamber had been completely redone, but he was pleased to note that the style was subdued, the colors restful blues and greens. In fact, every room he entered showed subtlety and restraint in the use of style and color. Nor had modern comforts been ignored. Gaslights in the hallways and lamps in each room provided soft illumination.

The London travelers were exhausted and all retired early that night. Before seeking his own room, Trevor decided to look in on Ashley. As he opened the door to her room, he

saw the glow of a candle. Beside the bed, Caitlyn looked up
as he entered.

They stood in companionable silence gazing at the angelic
countenance of their child asleep. Trevor could not resist
reaching to touch an errant blonde curl.

"She is so beautiful," he whispered. Profoundly moved, he
turned to Caitlyn and made no effort to hide his emotions.
"Thank you. Thank you for giving me this child."

Her response was a soft, nervous laugh. "Perhaps I should
thank you. Ashley is quite simply the best thing that ever
happened to me." Her eyes shone brightly in the candlelight.

Not knowing what to say, he reached for her hand and
locked his fingers tightly with hers. They stood in quietness
for a few moments, each lost in thought; then she gently
disengaged her hand. She extinguished the candle as they left
the child's room and descended the stairs to their own chambers. Reacting to the shared moment, Trevor felt a wave of
desire, not just to possess her woman's body, but to erase her
concern, to protect and cherish.

At her door, she quickly stood on tiptoes, kissed his cheek,
and murmured, "Good night, Trevor." She put her hand on
the door latch.

Stunned, he hastily placed his hand over hers.

"Caitlyn, I—"

Her name was an anguished groan on his lips as he pulled
her into his arms and pressed his mouth to hers. She stiffened
and for a fraction of a second was very still. Then—wonder
of wonders—she was responding, her arms around his neck,
her mouth welcoming.

He drew back and gazed into her eyes. He saw confusion
and vulnerability in their depths. "I . . . I think we must
talk," he said.

"Yes." He heard the apprehension she seemed to be trying
to hide from him. "Yes. We do. Tomorrow. After you have
seen what we have done here at Atherton. Then we can discuss . . . everything."

She stepped away, opened her door, and slipped inside. Trevor stood before the closed door, confused. Angry frustration was tempered by amusement at this peculiar predicament of wanting desperately to make love with a wife he did not quite trust.

A wife who seemed willing—but was she? Did not that closed door clearly belie the passion of her kiss?

Yet what choice did she have if he wanted to assert his rights? Perhaps she had welcomed his embrace because she could not afford to reject his advances. Trevor was well aware of the sheer power every husband wielded over a wife in modern England. To keep her child, a woman would probably endure anything. Anything at all.

Deep in thought, he sought his own empty bed. But sleep was elusive.

Caitlyn had hurried into her own room and dismissed her maid as quickly as possible. Trevor's kiss upset her, but even more upsetting was her reaction to it. How could she possibly remain in charge of her own life if she could not even control her response to a simple good-night kiss?

A simple good-night kiss, was it? her inner imp challenged. *A simple good-night kiss would not convey the deep longing, the yearning for fulfillment this one had. Oh, no, my girl. You cannot fool yourself that there was anything "simple" about this kiss at all. That kiss on his cheek was "simple." What followed was something else altogether.*

Uneasy sleep that night increased her nervousness the next morning. Anxious to show Trevor what had gone on in his absence, she had ambivalent feelings on the matter. On the one hand, she wanted his approval as a validation of her work. On the other, she feared he would usurp her position and simply take over to push the estate in a different direction and leave her out. For five years she had identified her very self and measured her worth by her not inconsiderable achievements at Atherton. Was she about to lose it all?

Caitlyn was already in the breakfast room when Trevor came down. Aunt Gertrude had sent word she was having a tray in her room this morning. Caitlyn returned his cheerful "good morning" and went back to sorting through the post as he filled his plate.

"I am looking forward to the grand tour," he said as he sat down.

"Yes. Well. I have asked Mr. Felkins to join us to answer such of your questions as I cannot."

She knew she was being a coward. There was not a single question about Atherton she could not answer herself. She simply wanted a third party along as a buffer—not only to parry objections, but also to keep the situation impersonal.

Trevor seemed thoughtful for a moment; then he grinned. "I was looking forward to getting you off alone, but we probably should have him along. From what I saw in the ledgers in London, I must have underestimated Felkins in the past."

Flustered, Caitlyn looked down. She wanted to scream at him that it was not Felkins he underestimated, but if she did so, she would lose that buffer. Before she could reply, Merrill announced the arrival of Mr. Felkins, who was invited to have coffee as Trevor and Caitlyn finished their breakfast.

The meal over, they found John Coachman in front with an open carriage.

"I usually take the gig," Caitlyn said, "but as there are three of us, John will drive us."

Trevor handed her in, and Felkins joined John on the driver's seat.

"We will visit tenant farms first," Caitlyn explained, "and then return to the home farm."

"All of them?" Trevor asked.

She laughed. "No, that would take far too much time. Is there a particular farm you would like to visit?"

"No-o. I think not. Wait. Yes. The Hawkins farm. I remember that Mr. Hawkins was very kind to Terrence and me when we visited Atherton as children."

"The Hawkins farm it is." She had raised her voice slightly for the benefit of John Coachman, who flicked the reins to set the carriage in motion.

When they arrived at the Hawkins place, Caitlyn hoped Trevor saw what she saw in the neat, whitewashed buildings, the repaired thatch of the roofs, and the profusion of bright flowers. Hawkins, his wife, three half-grown sons, and two younger daughters came to greet them when the carriage approached.

Greetings over, Trevor asked, "Where are your sheep? We saw none as we drove up."

"I got no sheep now, sir. Taylor and Adams, they got sheep. Porter's got some, too. Me an' the boys are raisin' chickens now."

"Chickens?" Trevor shifted a surprised glance from Caitlyn back to the farmer.

"Doin' pretty well, too. Between us and the Watsons over t'other side o' the creek, we supply eggs for most folks hereabouts. Meat, too, for lots of 'em."

"You don't say. I see you have quite a garden, too." Trevor thus directed everyone's attention to a large plot that looked productive and well tended.

"I have fresh green beans already," Mrs. Hawkins said with obvious pride. "You must take some to Mrs. Perkins, ma'am."

"I shall do so quite happily," Caitlyn replied.

"You want I should show you around, Mr. Jeffries?" Hawkins asked. He sounded eager to display his achievements.

"Yes. Please." Trevor jumped down from the carriage and handed Caitlyn down. "Will you join us?" he asked her.

"You go ahead. I shall stay here and talk with Lena and the girls."

Half an hour later they were back in the carriage and on their way to other farms where the scene—with some variations—was repeated. Along the way, they passed through the village.

Trevor looked around him with apparent curiosity and wonder. "I remember this little hamlet as poor and run-down. It seems quite prosperous now. I assume there are sufficient customers for the goods we see in these windows?"

"Oh, yes." She signaled John to stop and explained, "I promised Aunt Gertrude I would pick up some yarn for her."

They traipsed into the mercantile shop, which sold a bit of everything.

"Ah, Mrs. Jeffries. Welcome home." White, the tall, mustachioed proprietor greeted her. "And Mr. Jeffries. We heard you had returned from the war, sir." The man's voice was more reserved, impersonal in greeting Caitlyn's companion.

"How do you do?" Trevor offered the man his hand.

Caitlyn obtained the yarn and completed the transaction as Mr. White chatted on. "Please tell Her Ladyship we have a bolt of nice blue print she might like," he said. "Oh. And here's a treat for our little miss." He tucked a peppermint stick into the package.

"Now, on to the home farm," Caitlyn said.

They arrived at the main house via the same route they had traveled the night before, but everything was clearly visible now. Instead of stopping at the entrance, the carriage swept around the house and the outbuildings beyond.

Caitlyn was proud of the now neatly landscaped home with its extensive gardens free of encroaching weeds. There was also a large vegetable and herb garden.

"What the . . ."

She heard the surprise bordering on shock in Trevor's voice. She looked at him questioningly.

"Those are all stables!" he challenged.

"Yes. They are." She did not understand this statement of the obvious.

"We cannot possibly require so many animals for our transportation needs."

Confused by his reaction, she laughed nervously. "Of course not. But we manage to supply the needs of others."

Felkins offered one of his rare observations as he turned on the driver's seat. "Our business is fairly new, sir. We are truly just getting started, but already the Jeffries Farms are gaining a good reputation." There was a note of pride in the steward's tone.

"Mighty fine cattle," John Coachman added.

"And out there . . . ?" Trevor waved his hand at a neatly fenced-off area.

"Our track for training the racing stock," Caitlyn said, beginning to feel truly apprehensive about his tone.

"Jeffries Farms. It was not Cousin Algernon at all," Trevor said to the total mystification of his wife. He turned to her. "You allowed this to happen? You turned *my* property into a horse farm?

"Well, yes. I—"

"Without consulting me? Without even bothering to find out if I wished such a thing to transpire?"

He was fairly ranting now, and his anger both surprised her and sparked her own temper. The carriage had drawn into the central stable yard, and several workers there had stopped to observe on hearing Trevor's raised voice.

"It is potentially a very profitable endeavor," she said through clenched teeth, "but I think we should discuss this elsewhere."

He jumped down and held his hand to aid her. She wanted to ignore his help, but knew she might fall on her face if she did so.

"Yes, madam, we shall most assuredly discuss this." He had never sounded so stern to her before.

Fifteen

Trevor had been alternately impressed and confused much of the day. Clearly, it had been a stroke of genius to have Atherton's tenant farmers diversify their crops and livestock. The greater variety and cooperation brought the people together in a working, profitable interdependence. But simple farmers did not have the wherewithal to initiate such changes themselves. Families who lived hand-to-mouth could not afford the capital investment needed to make such drastic changes.

Trevor congratulated himself on not being fooled for a moment about precisely who had really orchestrated the success of these new endeavors. Caitlyn might make a great show of deferring to Mr. Felkins, but it was apparent to anyone with eyes in his head where the real authority lay. That Felkins and the individual farmers knew this, too, was obvious in the way they all waited for Caitlyn's views and suggestions.

Hardworking farmers, descendants of stubborn Anglo-Saxon forbears, might harbor some misgivings about such a role for a woman, but Trevor sensed grudging admiration and pride in them for Atherton's eccentric mistress. He also observed genuine affection for her both in the men's deference and in their wives' eagerness to share their produce and pass along gossipy tidbits to the lady of the manor.

Still—how *had* she done it? The answer was clear once they drove into those elaborate stables. The alliance between Atherton and Ratcliff was obvious. Caitlyn had not only been carrying on with the man, but apparently she had agreed to allow Atherton to become an extension of Ratcliff Farms.

Now that the truth had so clearly manifested itself, Trevor was furious.

He told himself that his anger stemmed from the fact that she had pursued the one activity he would deplore: raising blooded horses for pleasure and sport. However, he was honest enough to admit that beneath this anger was a molten stream of fury that had nothing to do with the horses.

Now as he followed his wife to the house, he saw her own flare of temper in her determined pace and her tight grip on the small packet from the mercantile shop. And in the not-so-gentle sway of her skirt as she walked. Despite the seriousness of the situation and his own anger, he had to smile in appreciation of that trim female form in front of him.

"The library," she said tersely, charging through the kitchen and the hallway beyond. She put the packet on a hall table and removed her bonnet with abrupt gestures. Several servants looked surprised and wary. Trevor followed as she swept into the library. He closed the door firmly.

"All right," he demanded. "I want an explanation—and a full accounting."

She whirled around. Bright spots of anger shone on her cheeks. "And just what is it you would like explained? Why I chose to make this estate a paying proposition? *Some*one had to do so when you so willingly ignored your responsibilities."

" 'Ignored my—' You go too far, madam." He knew that any semblance of control was slipping away from him. "Having been tricked into an unsavory marriage, I could hardly be labeled irresponsible in leaving such a wife firmly established on *my* property and in control of over half my own income."

" 'Unsavory—' "

He went on, ignoring her shocked response, "The army certainly never considered me 'irresponsible.' "

"You did not desert the army!"

They both stilled, each seemingly aware of the dangerous territory these invectives opened.

"So that's it," he said in a quieter tone. "Your revenge was this horse farm."

She, too, calmed down. "Revenge? Trevor, I have no idea what you are talking about. East Anglia is horse country. Newmarket is only a few miles away. It seemed a likely endeavor for Atherton."

"Ratcliff's principal farm is also in the area—what? Five miles away?"

"Seven." She gave him a questioning look.

"I suppose that is merely a happy coincidence."

"I . . . Yes. It has been fortunate." Her voice was hesitant.

" 'Fortunate.' " He deliberately mocked her.

"Will—Sir Willard—has been most helpful to us. A good friend."

"Oh, I'll just bet he has. 'Will' says it all. You have allowed your 'friend' to turn Atherton into an extension of his own farms, have you not?"

"What are you implying?" Her tone was dangerously quiet.

"Even an ignorant soldier knows that one does not—willy-nilly—decide to raise horses without a considerable outlay of funds, dear wife. I imagine Ratcliff thought this a fine investment from his standpoint. Especially if the soldier failed to return."

" 'Imagine.' Yes. Precisely the right term." Her eyes blazed.

"The money for breeding stock—not to mention improvements on tenant farms—had to come from somewhere. I know my family did not support this project. And I seriously doubt that your loving Uncle Fiske parted with any of the ready."

"And you assume it came from Sir Willard Ratcliff." Her voice held a note of curiosity along with barely controlled rage.

He shrugged. "Latham had no access to his fortune yet.

Of course, there is always Graham. Lord knows *he* has been equally attentive."

"What you are suggesting is entirely despicable."

"Isn't it just? Adds a nice touch to your revenge—for surely you cannot expect me to believe you truly thought I would approve establishing a horse farm."

She turned to give the bellpull a hard jerk. When she turned back to him, her voice sounded bleak, defeated. "Trevor, I no longer harbor *any* expectations or hope of your believing in me."

With a knock, Merrill came in answer to her summons.

"Please ask Lady Hermiston to come in here," Caitlyn said to the butler.

"Why are you dragging Aunt Gertrude into this?"

"You shall see."

A few minutes later Aunt Gertrude entered. She apparently sensed that something was terribly wrong, for she kept glancing nervously from one to the other.

"You wanted something?" she asked Caitlyn.

"Trevor is quite concerned about where I obtained financing for our breeding stock," Caitlyn explained.

Aunt Gertrude perched on the edge of a settee. "Did you not tell him?"

"I thought it would be better if he heard it from you."

Trevor began to get a sick feeling about what Aunt Gertrude would say.

The older woman looked up, her face reflecting concern. "I sold my townhouse and some other properties to invest in this venture."

"You allowed her to involve *you* in this risky business?"

"I persuaded Caitlyn to allow me to invest in it. It was all very legal and very formal. And I am beginning to realize a return on my investment, so it has not proved so very risky."

"But—" Trevor began.

Ignoring his attempt to speak, Aunt Gertrude continued, "I had—and still have—great faith in Caitlyn."

Caitlyn went to the huge oaken desk that dominated one wall of the library. Late afternoon sun from a window behind it glinted off a brass lamp and desk accessories. She pulled open a drawer and slammed a ledger on the desk.

"Here is your detailed accounting for Atherton," she said coldly. "You will find Aunt Gertrude's investment fully documented there—along with measures for repayment."

She gestured to the book and the chair behind the desk. He felt compelled to see the physical reality, but he also dreaded having to face his own misconceptions in front of her and his aunt.

Caitlyn, whose pacing seemed dictated by her emotions, made several circles of the room as she gave him the full accounting he had demanded. Her voice was clipped, formal, and impersonal.

"You see there precisely where the funding was spent. Several of our mares we purchased from Ratcliff Farms where they were bred. You will also see that Sir Willard has continued to offer such services of his farm in exchange for our training certain of his carriage teams, for he is much more interested in purely racing stock."

She pulled a folder from a drawer in another cabinet and thrust it at Trevor. He took it silently.

"Here is the document formalizing the *business* relationship between Atherton and Ratcliff Farms."

"I think you had best tell him about the first years of rents on the tenant farms," Aunt Gertrude said.

"Oh, yes. Thank you, Aunt Gertrude. For the first two years, we—I—did not collect rents at all, with the understanding that each of our farmers would use that money to make improvements on his own holding. At the end of the two years, they would resume their rents as a percentage of their profits."

"And . . . ?" he prompted.

"It was hard at first. We missed that income. But, as you can see, almost all of them are paying a smaller *share* of their own earnings in rent, but our revenue is greater than it was before."

"In other words—" He looked up from the document he held, but she refused to meet his gaze.

"In other words," she finished, "almost all our tenant farmers are on a more profitable footing than in the past."

Trevor sat staring, unseeing, at the documentation laid out before him. "Caitlyn—Aunt Gertrude—I . . . I hardly know what to say."

"An apology would be a nice way to start," Aunt Gertrude said, but her voice was gentle.

"Of course. And I do most sincerely extend my apologies. Forgive me, Caitlyn."

But he knew he did not deserve her forgiveness. Not since Terrence and Jason had died had he been so thoroughly filled with disgust at himself.

Still refusing to meet his gaze, Caitlyn said only, "I accept your apology."

However, he suspected it was not going to be that easy to reestablish rapport between them. His suspicion was confirmed when she politely but coldly excused herself and left the room.

Trevor gazed at his aunt, who gave him a look filled with both exasperation and sympathy. He ran his hand through his hair in nervous distraction.

"Oh, Lord! I have fairly done it now, have I not?"

"Yes, you have." Her tone was matter-of-fact, but it softened as she added, "But Caitlyn is a very giving and forgiving person—although right now she is very hurt."

"I know." He sighed. "I should never have—"

She rose to leave. "But you did. And you deserve to stew in your own juices for a bit." Her smile took the sting out of this rebuke. "Give her time, Trevor. She will come around."

* * *

Several days later, Trevor was sure Aunt Gertrude's customary insight had failed her this time, for Caitlyn had not "come around." She avoided being alone with him as much as possible. She was scrupulous about ensuring that he was informed on all matters of the estate, but these sessions always took place with Felkins in attendance. Caitlyn even made a point of deferring to her husband on many matters, especially if others—servants or tenants—were present.

When he met with Caitlyn and Aunt Gertrude for meals, the conversation was likely to be formal, reserved—and meaningless. Only when they were with Ashley did Caitlyn allow him a glimpse of the warm woman behind the demeanor of cool formality.

Caitlyn continued to ride every morning, though the black gelding, he learned, had been sold before they left London. In fact, he was told, the black had been sold several weeks before, but Caitlyn insisted on refining its training. He thought she often drove her mounts too rashly.

Trevor tramped miles over the lands belonging to Atherton, sometimes carrying his lunch with him in a haversack. He discovered the lake—an artificially devised body of water, to be sure, but large enough to afford great sport in swimming or fishing. It was fed by the same creek that ran between certain tenant farms. Local boys could be found splashing around in it in the afternoons, but Trevor found he had it all to himself in the mornings.

Frequently as he returned from an invigorating swim, he would see Caitlyn with a groom returning from her morning ride. He thought nostalgically of such rides he once enjoyed with Terrence, Jason, and Melanie. Well, those days were over.

Still, he was drawn to the stables. On his first visit, the men working there greeted him with reservation and even suspicion. Obviously, word of his antipathy to horses had traveled rapidly along that mysteriously efficient route of communication among servants.

He watched with interest but without comment as trainers

put young horses through their paces. He walked through the stables and noticed they were clean and smelled of fresh hay. A large chestnut with a white blaze on its head gazed at him over the half-door of a stall. A young groom worked nearby putting fresh straw in empty stalls.

Trevor approached the horse, allowing it to smell his hand, then caressed its nose. "So what did you do, my fine fellow, that you are being punished by having to stay in your room whilst everyone else is working or playing?"

The young groom—who could not have had more than twelve years—came over and patted the horse's cheek.

"This here's Chief," the boy said. "Actually, the mistress named him Warrior Chieftain of Araby, but we calls him Chief on account of his bein' so proud, you see."

"Aha," Trevor responded in a musing tone.

"An' he ain't being punished."

"No?"

"Nah. Jimmy—he's the head groom, you know—Jimmy said he got Chief all prettied up an not to let 'im get mussed 'cause some lord was comin' for 'im today."

"Ah, I see. A gentleman must not offend his valet." Trevor gave the horse another pat and turned to the boy and asked conversationally, "What is your name, young man?"

"Jackie . . . uh, that is . . . Jack." The boy squared his shoulders. "Me pa's Clarence Tanner, the head trainer here at Jeffries Farms." There was a note of pride in the boy's voice.

"I am pleased to meet you, Jack Tanner." Trevor solemnly offered the boy his hand, which Jack took after first wiping his own hand on his pants leg.

"Likewise, Mr. Jeffries, sir."

Trevor felt the boy's gaze follow him from the stable. He hung around the stables and paddocks for some time, observing and occasionally asking a question. Gradually, he felt the reservations of the stable employees melt away.

He overheard one of them say, "The man knows horses."

"Wonder why he don't ride," another asked, but Trevor did not listen for the response.

Thereafter, he was often to be seen in and around the stables, though he put himself in the saddle only on rare occasions—to visit a distant farm or perform a similar duty. Even for these errands, he usually took the gig or had John Coachman drive him in a carriage. He often took Ashley along on such excursions.

Caitlyn knew Trevor visited the stables, though the two of them were rarely there at the same time. At first she had feared that, in his anger, Trevor would insist on their selling all the horses and returning the home farm to what it once was. He had not done so. Though he did not take an active role in management of the animals, he had gained a favorable reputation among Atherton's stable hands and trainers for his expertise.

Feeling that both she and the horse farm were in a state of limbo, Caitlyn tried to carry on as usual with training schedules and sales of blooded stock.

"I do wish I knew what Trevor intended to do," she complained to Aunt Gertrude. They sat in the drawing room one afternoon after the vicar and his wife, among others, had departed.

"You could ask him."

Caitlyn emitted an unamused little laugh. "I learned some time ago not to ask questions to which the answer might be unpalatable."

"I should think that not knowing would be quite . . . well, painful. I must admit *I* find the situation between the two of you rather disconcerting."

Caitlyn shrugged. "It is that." Then she posed a question she had actually wanted to ask Trevor. "Have you any idea why Trevor holds this attitude he has toward horses?"

Aunt Gertrude gave her a surprised look. "He did not tell you? I assumed you knew."

"Knew what?" Caitlyn felt a tingling of apprehension feather through her.

"Caitlyn, darling, I was so sure you did know."

"Know what?" Caitlyn's voice rose slightly.

"About Terrence and Jason."

"I know they died in some sort of carriage accident a few months before our marriage, but no one has ever spoken of the details."

So Aunt Gertrude told her—to Caitlyn's growing wonder and chagrin. She told of the young Trevor and his love of horses and the young man who eagerly embraced life's adventures. She also related what she knew of his devastation and guilt over that accident.

"I honestly thought he would get over forswearing the pleasure he once got from just being around and working with horses."

"He forswore it? Why did I not know? No wonder he was so very angry."

"Oh, my. This is my fault." Aunt Gertrude was clearly distressed. "I assumed this was something you and Trevor planned together before . . . that is, before he went to the Peninsula."

"No. It was not." Caitlyn leaned forward to pat the older woman's hand. "However, you must not burden yourself with such. The fact that Trevor and I have never communicated well is certainly not *your* fault."

"But I was so sure. Sure you knew. And sure it did not matter so much anymore to Trevor."

"Well, now we both know." Caitlyn sighed. "I am not sure, given my anger when he left, that his wishes—had I even known them—would have been of major concern to me."

"Oh, dear."

"However, this does explain his comment about revenge."

"Revenge?"

"Trevor accused me of using the horses as revenge. It must look that way to him."

"Revenge?" Aunt Gertrude repeated with a ladylike snort. "What a preposterous idea."

"Not so very preposterous. I freely admit that a great deal of pride was the basis of wanting to make Atherton a success."

"Understandable, my dear."

"And we all know 'pride goeth before a fall.' "

"Actually, the line is 'before destruction,' and you are not destroyed, love."

"I hope not," Caitlyn said, but privately she thought that perhaps the fragile relationship between her and Trevor had been damaged beyond hope.

"Now—about Melanie's visit . . ." Aunt Gertrude said brightly, shifting the subject.

It had long been planned that Melanie would bring her husband and children to visit Atherton after she had paid a brief visit to her father's chief estate.

Earlier, Caitlyn and Aunt Gertrude had planned to use the occasion of Melanie's visit to host their most ambitious social affair yet, a ball in Melanie's honor to which half the notable families in East Anglia would be invited. It was to be a very grand undertaking with a house party of some duration for faraway guests.

It was late afternoon when Melanie's carriages arrived. By the time she and Andrew had been properly welcomed and the children settled into the nursery, it was growing dark and the visitors barely had time to change for dinner.

Trevor had looked forward with eager anticipation to his sister's arrival. Perhaps Melanie's ebullient cheerfulness—along with the presence of additional guests at an extended house party—would ease the subtle tension that was a constant at Atherton these days. He may have cringed inwardly at seeing Latham's, Graham's, and Ratcliff's names on invitations, but their presence would be offset by the company of Theo, Moore, and Jenkins.

The next morning, Melanie and Andrew joined Caitlyn, Aunt Gertrude, and Trevor in the breakfast room. Melanie had come in from a walk in the gardens, unconcerned in the least about her wet shoes and damp hem.

"Caitlyn, those roses are marvelous. You must tell me your secret, for as soon as this business in Vienna is over, Drew promises me we will settle on his property in Kent, and I want roses as lovely as yours."

"I shall happily share my limited expertise," Caitlyn replied.

"I spied those stables, Trevor. I *do* want to see them up close. From the little I could see from this distance, there are some fine animals out there."

Trevor swallowed uncomfortably. "That is Caitlyn's concern," he mumbled.

"I beg your pardon?" Melanie said.

"The horses are Caitlyn's project." Trevor hoped his tone was dismissive enough to divert his sister's attention.

He should have known better.

"Caitlyn's? And you have nothing to do with it? My brother, the consummate horseman, has a marvelous stable and numerous animals and dismisses his association with them?"

"Umm . . . Mel," her husband interjected, apparently attuned to Trevor's discomfort, "perhaps we should discuss this later, my dear."

She readily agreed. "Of course, Drew. We shall save it till Caitlyn and Trevor give us a proper tour of their facility."

Andrew sighed aloud and shrugged his shoulders in a helpless gesture. Trevor groaned inwardly. Aunt Gertrude redirected the breakfast table conversation, but Trevor knew very well that his misgivings about the morning were not misplaced.

Nor were they.

Aunt Gertrude begged off, but the two couples made their way to the stables. Caitlyn and Melanie had stopped in the kitchen to fortify themselves with apples, carrots, and chunks of sugar for the horses. Trevor smiled on seeing their bulging pockets. Watching indulgently as the two women eagerly greeted the animals and the stable hands, he nevertheless felt some apprehension about his own presence here. It occurred to him that he did not feel such discomfort when he came on his own.

The four of them found few animals in the stalls, for most of them were roaming freely in the pastures or being put through training paces. They watched a harness race in progress as Clarence Tanner explained the merits of the horses involved.

Caught up in the trainer's comments, Trevor asked some penetrating questions. Tanner took these queries as a matter of course from the master of Atherton, but Trevor observed that the discussion brought a speculative gaze from Caitlyn. However, she made no comment.

"Oh, Trevor," Melanie said later, impulsively taking his arm and thus leaving Andrew to offer Caitlyn a supporting arm. The four of them were alone in the middle of the stableyard. "This is so wonderful! I am so happy to see you at home among horses again. I have worried about you so much."

Distinctly uncomfortable, he stopped short to face his sister. The other two were forced to be onlookers.

"Melanie," he said, "you do not understand. I had nothing to do with these stables."

"But these are such splendid animals . . ." Melanie replied with a sweeping gesture.

Trevor gave an equally sweeping wave of his hand. "This is all Caitlyn's doing. None of mine." His voice held a note of bitter regret which he tried to hide. Melanie caught it nonetheless.

"Are you telling me you will have nothing to do with this splendid horse farm?"

"Nothing."

"Unbelievable." She turned to Caitlyn. "Can this be true?"

"More or less," Caitlyn said, sounding rather hesitant.

"But *why?*" Melanie demanded of Trevor.

"Melanie," her diplomat husband admonished, "perhaps this is a subject best left to Trevor and Caitlyn?"

"No! He is my brother, and I want to know precisely why he is taking such an idiotic course!"

Andrew gave Trevor a shrug as much as to say "I tried." Knowing Melanie to be as persevering as the proverbial dog with a bone, Trevor grimaced at him sympathetically.

"Why, Trevor?" Melanie demanded again.

"You know why, Mel," he said in a sad voice. "These are fine animals, but they are bred to race and show. It was my pursuit of such that killed Terrence and Jason."

"Oh, for heaven's sake, Trevor! That was—what?—six years ago. And you are still wallowing in self-pity?"

Caitlyn and Andrew gasped. Trevor felt himself blanching.

"Mel—" her husband started.

"I don't care," Melanie said. "That is what it is. Terrence and Jason died in an unfortunate accident." She turned to Trevor. "An accident, you hear?"

"Yes, but—" he began.

She rushed on. "And if Terrence could see what you have done to yourself over an *accident,* he would be for taking you behind that stable and thrashing some sense into you." She gestured to a nearby structure. "As for Jason, he is probably laughing himself silly over your self-absorbed behavior."

"I think you have said quite enough." Trevor's words sounded tight, forced.

"Oh, Trevor," Melanie cried, tears in her eyes and in her voice, "do you not realize how they loved you? I love you. Terrence and Jason never would have made such an untoward demand of you. Why? Why must you do this to yourself?"

Too shocked by her words to make a coherent reply, he simply stared at her, unbelieving, for a moment. Then he turned on his heel and walked away.

"What have I done?" Melanie cried, slumping against her husband.

He patted her shoulder. "Ah, Melanie. My sweet, wonderful, impetuous Melanie. How could I help loving you?" He kissed the top of her head.

"Well, I doubt Trevor is feeling very loving toward me at the moment." Melanie sniffed rather indecorously.

"No, but perhaps he is thinking," Caitlyn said.

Sixteen

Trevor deliberately absented himself from luncheon. Perhaps he *was* being a bit childish, he mused, but he could not bring himself to face family members yet. He wandered into a wooded area, roaming around aimlessly until he finally found a fallen tree on which he sat, lost in thought, until the elongated shadows around him caught his attention.

Later, when he entered the drawing room before dinner, he found the rest of the family already assembled.

"Hello, everyone."

They all turned to him with concerned expressions. Melanie looked particularly distraught.

"Oh, Trevor, I am so sorry," she cried as she sprang from her chair and threw her arms around his neck. "I should never have opened my big mouth. Please forgive me."

He hugged her rather awkwardly and patted her shoulder. "It is all right, Melanie." His voice husky, he raised his gaze to meet those of others in the room, for his next words were intended for them as well as Melanie. "You were right, Mel. I . . . I guess I was pretty self-absorbed."

She stepped back and gave him an arch look. "Yes, you were. But that did not give me leave to berate you so."

His grin was a little shaky. "When have you ever waited for permission to rip up at me?" She gave her head a saucy flip as he went on, his arm still around her waist. "And this time I guess I needed it. You were right about what Terrence and Jason would think."

He released his sister and looked at Caitlyn. His eyes held hers for a long moment. "And you were right, too, Caitlyn. This *is* horse country. I shall endeavor to be more supportive from now on."

"Thank you, Trevor." Her eyes seemed inordinately bright.

There was a heavy pause. No one seemed to know what to say. Then Andrew cleared his throat.

"May I get you a sherry, too?" he asked Trevor with a gesture at others' glasses.

"Yes, please."

The tension eased as Melanie and Trevor began to regale the others with stories of their shared childhood adventures with horses. The easy atmosphere continued over dinner. With only the five of them present, the table was set with all the places at one end and the conversation was a free-wheeling continuation of what had started earlier.

Trevor was pleased to note the easy camaraderie between his wife and his sister. He was already well aware of the motherly concern Aunt Gertrude extended to Caitlyn. It struck him that this—the teasing, the bickering, the caring, and the protectiveness—*this* was what a family was all about. He also realized in a flash of insight that so long as he and Caitlyn were at odds, *their* family would be incomplete. He glanced at his wife and caught her looking at him. He thought he saw questioning vulnerability in her eyes before she quickly lowered her gaze.

Forgoing the usual male ritual of port and cigars after dinner, Trevor and Andrew joined the ladies immediately for tea in the drawing room. When an impromptu game of whist was suggested, Aunt Gertrude excused herself and, taking up her embroidery, was content to offer pertinent comments now and then.

The two couples recombined after each game. It was the men versus the women the first time. The women won handily. In the second game, Trevor partnered Melanie against Caitlyn and Andrew.

"As much as we have played together in the past, dear sister," Trevor said in a great pretense of disgust, "we should have won that game."

"Mayhap Drew and Caitlyn concentrated more. Next time *we* shall cheat."

"Oh, no. I can win without cheating. And I will prove it—but with a new partner."

"Hmmph." Melanie sniffed. "Well, Caitlyn, that means you are stuck with him this time."

The four players paused as Aunt Gertrude bade them good night, then resumed their play with a continuation of the light-hearted banter that had marked the earlier games.

"There!" Trevor said with a laugh as he and Caitlyn took the winning hand. "You see? All I needed was the right partner."

Melanie gave him a solemn look. "The right partner. Truly, that is all any of us needs." She yawned rather indecorously. "And I am taking *my* partner to bed."

When Melanie and Andrew had left the room, Trevor turned to Caitlyn and asked in a deliberately flirtatious tone, "Do you intend to leave me all by lonesome self?"

"Not . . . not if you do not wish it."

He thought she seemed a bit nervous at being alone with him. He went to the sideboard and brought a wine decanter and two glasses to a low table before a settee near the fire-place.

"Join me?" he invited.

She nodded and took the glass he offered, sipped, and set it on the table. She sat on the settee rather stiffly, he thought as he sank down beside her. He was rather nervous himself. He set his own glass on the table and half turned toward her, his arm on the upholstery behind her.

"Caitlyn." He waited for her to look at him and then held her gaze. "I meant what I said earlier."

"What you said earlier . . . ?"

"About supporting you in establishing a horse farm."

She closed her eyes briefly and sighed. "Thank you. Thank you, Trevor."

She impulsively squeezed the hand lying across his lap. When she would have released her grip, he refused the separation, intertwining his fingers firmly with hers. Intensely aware of their physical contact, he wanted only to extend it. He lowered his other arm to her shoulder and pulled her closer. She looked up at him with a clear question in her gaze.

"Trev—?"

But her question was lost as his lips captured hers in a kiss that was at first tentative, exploring. He felt her stiffen; then her lips softened and returned the pressure of his. With a low groan, he gathered her closer, his tongue seeking entry, which she readily granted. He felt her hand along his jawline, then kneading the back of his neck. The kiss deepened. His hand moved up to cup her breast. She murmured softly and seemed to move into him. His desire soaring like a balloon, he was torn between wanting this moment to continue and wanting to extend their lovemaking to the next level.

Suddenly she seemed to come to her senses and pushed against him. "Trevor, no. I cannot. Please."

There was a panicky note in her voice. He leaned back, the ache in his loins a manifestation of his yearning. He held her quietly for a moment.

"It's all right, Caitlyn. I will not pressure you." He rose and extended his hand. "Come. Let us go up."

She took his hand and allowed him to keep his hold on her until they were at her door.

"Good night, Trevor."

"Sleep well, my dear." He brushed his lips against hers in the merest whisper of a kiss before turning to his own door.

Caitlyn lay awake staring at the canopy over her bed. The dim light from the fireplace bounced off the ridges and crevices of the familiar brocade design. She wallowed in a pool of self-recrimination. Why had she stopped him? She might even now be languishing in his arms but for her own . . . her own-what? Fears. Fear of Trevor? No-o-o. Then the answer hit her. No. Fear of herself. Fear of her reaction to him. Fear that the wild desire in her own heart would bring only more pain, more rejection.

If only—

If only, she thought.

Finally she slept.

The next morning, Caitlyn reported to the stables early. This was the time she usually met with the head groom to check on training progress and other matters of concern with a growing herd of fine, blooded stock.

She was surprised to see Trevor there before her. He was in the office conferring with Tanner and the head groom. Well, she told herself, he certainly wasted little time.

"Good morning," she called, and all three men turned with welcoming smiles and answering greetings. As her eyes met Trevor's, she wished, incongruously, that she had donned the more attractive blue riding habit rather than her old, faded gray one. "You started without me?" She kept the question light.

"Uh . . . not really, ma'am," Tanner said. He was a rather squat, barrel-chested man with a florid complexion and friendly black eyes. He walked with a limp, for a horse had rolled over on him several years ago.

"Clarence and Jimmy were showing me the books on our newest acquisitions while I waited for you," Trevor said.

She noted his use of the word *our* even as the rest of his statement captured her attention. "Waited for me?"

"To go riding. I shall accompany you this morning, if I may." He gave her a disarming smile that had her heart imitating a flutterby.

"Of course." She nodded in acquiescence, but she wondered at this sudden transition in her non-riding husband. However, she had no intention of questioning him in front of their employees.

There was some more small talk about various animals and routine discussion of training problems.

"I am thinking of taking the grays to Newmarket for the show and races along with Sheik's Queen and those other teams," Caitlyn said to Mr. Tanner. "Can they be ready by then?"

"Oh, I'm sure they can," Tanner replied. "Fact is, they're ready now."

"Really?" She was surprised.

"Yes, ma'am. Don't you agree, sir?" Tanner's asking for Trevor's opinion caused her eyebrows to rise in further surprise. Tanner never needed confirmation of his judgments about horses. The trainer apparently noted her reaction, for he added to her, "Mr. Jeffries has been watching us work the grays."

"I see." She was thoughtful for a moment. "Hmm. When our houseguests arrive in a few days, I think it would be best if we did not show off the grays overly much."

"Ri-i-ght." Jimmy grinned in approval.

Tanner nodded. "No sense showing the competition what they're up against."

"The competition?" Trevor asked.

"Harrison and Bowles," Jimmy said.

"Especially Harrison." Tanner's tone had taken on a stony quality.

"I am not sure I understand." Trevor's brow wrinkled in consternation.

Caitlyn answered. "This particular show will draw a great deal of attention among buyers. It was already being talked about in London during the season."

"I thought every horse show did."

"Yes. But this one has a number of new farms—or ones not long established—pitted against each other."

"Ah, I think I see. Bowles and Harrison are trying to establish a good name for their farms."

"As are we," she said.

"Harrison thinks he has an edge with those chestnuts of his." Tanner sounded skeptical.

"We'll just see about that," Jimmy put in.

Trevor looked at Caitlyn, then shifted his attention back to Tanner. "What about the Ratcliff Farms? Will they not be at the meet?"

"He'll be there—don't you doubt it! But he concentrates on stock for riding and racing, not those trained for harness," Tanner explained.

"And Ratcliff Farms already have an established niche in the market for good horses," Caitlyn said. "The stakes are higher for the rest of us."

"So why did you invite the enemy into your own territory?" Trevor demanded. "I saw both Harrison and Bowles on your guest list."

"I could hardly leave them off. They would be miffed, and probably suspicious as well. And they are neighbors. It just would not be the thing to do."

"No. I suppose not," Trevor agreed.

"Still, we need not reveal all our secrets to them." Her smile included all three men in her conspiracy.

A few minutes later, Trevor boosted her into her sidesaddle and they set off. Very aware of his presence, she noted with some irony that Jimmy, who usually accompanied her on morning rides, never commanded so much of her attention as Trevor did. She also noted that Tanner's and Jimmy's respect for Trevor's horsemanship was not misplaced. The man was a superb rider, handling a spirited animal with ease and quickly attuning himself to the large black horse he had chosen.

He apparently noticed her surreptitious glances at him, for

he pulled his mount alongside hers and said with a laugh, "Surprised you, eh?"

"Well . . . yes."

"Riding is like . . . well, like many other physical activities—one never forgets how, once the skill is mastered."

She looked at him, caught a teasing twinkle in his eyes, and felt herself blushing furiously.

He chuckled and pointed. "Race you to the top of that hill."

She gave him a speaking look and he added, "All right—you can have a lead as far as that boulder."

He pointed again, and she immediately urged her mare forward. She pushed the mare hard and felt her respond to the competition. The black and his rider came up beside them just as they arrived at the top of the designated hill. Both Trevor and Caitlyn were out of breath, and as they reached the goal, both were laughing. He dismounted and came round to help her dismount.

"You cheated," he challenged as his hands reached for her waist.

"I did not." Her grin belied her words as she looked down at him.

"You did so. You were supposed to await my signal."

"Well, why did you not say so?" she asked in a pure mockery of innocence. She placed her hands on his shoulders for balance and slid into his arms.

"Stupid me," he murmured as his arms tightened around her and he lowered his mouth to hers.

Fleetingly, she wondered if he referred only to the banter over the race. Then she lost herself to the ecstasy of his lips on her own. Her arms around his neck, she clung to him, leaning her body into his. She had wanted him to kiss her again, but the vehemence of her desire surprised her. She pulled away slightly.

"T-Trevor?"

"S-shh." He recaptured her lips, and she welcomed his exploration. Finally she pushed back from him. She felt his hands still locked behind her waist.

"Trevor, stop. We need to talk."

"I rather liked this other means of communication."

"Do be serious." She smiled in spite of herself.

"All right. We shall talk." He tied the horses to a nearby bush and pulled her down to sit very close to him on a grassy slope of the hill. "So? Talk," he commanded gently.

"I . . . I . . . hardly know where to begin. I feel so . . . so out of control."

"Good. I like you out of control." He slipped his arm around her and kissed her again.

She responded—out of control for a moment—then abruptly pulled away. "No. Stop. You know very well I can neither think nor talk while you are kissing me!"

He chuckled and relaxed his hold on her, but she was pleased he did not break the contact.

"Well?" he prompted.

"I—you seem to have taken such a turnabout."

He sat silent for moment, looking out over the green valley at their feet. "I know it must seem that way. But in truth, it probably started when I left for the Peninsula."

"Wh-when you left?"

He turned to face her and took her hand, lacing his fingers loosely with hers. "I do not want to sound as though I am making excuses to justify my behavior, but I was so young when we married."

"We both were."

"Yes, but I was immature and irresponsible as well." He closed his eyes. "I made so many mistakes in pursuit of a good time."

"All young men sow wild oats, do they not?"

"Perhaps. But few with such disastrous results. That race and the wager with your uncle were beyond the pale. Look what happened. Terrence and Jason dead, the lives of others ruined—yours, mine—perhaps Melanie's, too."

"Altered, yes, but not necessarily 'ruined.' Melanie is very happy with Andrew."

"Still—"

"And another thing," she went on, "did it never occur to you that Terrence and Jason shared your youthful recklessness? Melanie tells me the three of you were inseparable—and a pretty rackety lot, at that."

He smiled faintly in apparent reminiscence. "That we were."

Her clasp of his hand tightened. "That race and the wager that prompted it were mistakes. But Terrence and Jason could have refused to participate, could they not?"

"Ye-es," he admitted.

"There seems to have been plenty of blame to be *shared* in that accident."

"Perhaps. . . . Perhaps. But you cannot explain away my subsequent behavior."

"Probably not. But I think I have a better understanding of it now than I once did."

"How can you be so generous when I ruined our lives so?"

"Altered. Changed. Not necessarily ruined," she repeated.

Both were silent. Caitlyn noticed the sounds of buzzing insects and twittering birds around them. So. Trevor felt his life was ruined.

Finally he spoke. "I learned a great deal in the Peninsula. One has a great deal of time to think on long, boring marches between battles."

"And . . . ?" It was her turn to prompt.

"I came home thinking to free us both from an untenable situation."

She drew in a sharp breath and felt herself go very still. He still wanted to be rid of her! Well, she had expected this, had she not?

"That was, of course, before I knew about Ashley," he

continued. "That is simply not an option for us now—if, indeed, it ever was."

"What are you saying, Trevor?"

"I am trying to say I want us to make this work—together."

"Make *what* work?"

"Well . . . Atherton—though you seem to have done quite well without me so far." He sounded rueful. "And . . . and the—our—marriage."

"The marriage." Her voice sounded dull to her own ears.

"Our marriage—and our family." He squeezed her hand, and his gaze held hers. "Others have succeeded with less reason to go on than we have. At least we seem able to tolerate each other."

"Tolerate. I see." She turned away to look across the valley, willing the tears she felt not to fall. Well, what had she expected? She had known from the moment Aunt Sylvia announced this "grand match" that any dream of love and real friendship in marriage was just that—a dream. She knew that. So why had she allowed the dream to resurface in these last weeks? Why did she feel so cheated in settling for lust and tolerance as substitutes? She glanced at Trevor, and quickly away on discovering his gaze still fixed on her.

"Caitlyn?" He gently pulled her head around. He had removed his riding gloves, and his bare fingers on her cheek sent a tingly feeling coursing through her. "Can we do this?"

"Do what?" she asked dully, her mind sunk in despair.

"Make the marriage work." He looked at her oddly, not seeming to understand her reaction.

She felt herself blushing. "You . . . mean totally?"

"If you are asking me if I want you in my bed—yes. I do. I want that very much."

Searching his eyes, she perceived a certain vulnerability and raw yearning.

"Do you not want more children?" he asked softly.

She nodded.

He hugged her more closely and bent his head to kiss her again. But this time, she thought, it was different.

The hope was gone.

Trevor sensed a subtle, subdued change in her, but as he deepened the kiss, her response awakened and she returned his ardor in kind. He leaned back, drawing her with him. He planted little kisses on her eyelids, her jawline, the tender spots just below her ears, and on her neck as far as the neckline of her riding habit allowed. He ran his hand down her shoulder and over her body and felt her tremble at his touch.

"Caitlyn?"

"Yes, Trevor. Yes."

Trevor stifled an inward groan at seeing Melanie and Andrew in the stableyard as he and Caitlyn returned. He had not anticipated such an abrupt end to his private time with his wife.

"You two were certainly off early this morning," Melanie said. "Do you always keep such hours, Caitlyn?"

"Usually."

Trevor reached to help Caitlyn dismount and let his hands settle on her waist slightly longer than necessary. Her back to Melanie, she looked at Trevor with a secret, teasing delight. Disconcerted, Trevor looked at his sister to see her in a near paroxysm of silent giggles, and Andrew wore a broad grin.

"Thank you, Trevor," Caitlyn said. "I enjoyed the ride."

As she turned to go to the house, he saw it. Caitlyn's soft gray riding habit was covered with grass stains in the back from her shoulders to her thighs. He felt the color flooding his face as Melanie and Andrew caught his eye. Melanie gave him a wink and a smile.

Seventeen

During the next few days, Caitlyn came to realize—if she ever doubted it—that there were few secrets in a large household such as hers. Both family members and servants seemed to know and to approve of the change in the relationship between Atherton's master and mistress.

Caitlyn found that she, too, definitely approved the change. The mature Trevor was proving to be a considerate, caring lover—solicitous of her desires, taking care to ensure that she derive genuine pleasure from their encounters. Despite his affinity for "this other means of communication," Trevor readily discussed and shared ideas about every aspect of running the huge enterprise that was Atherton.

Nor had he rushed in to usurp her authority. In fact, he frequently deferred to her. Where another man might have barged in to assert himself as the chief decision-maker, Trevor had not done so. Caitlyn smiled at remembering the surprised looks on certain male faces when Trevor responded to a question or concern with "You must consult Mrs. Jeffries on that" or "I shall ask my wife."

She appreciated the fact that he took time to acquaint himself thoroughly on a matter before asserting his own ideas or opinions. His approach not only commanded approval from male servants, tradesmen, and tenant farmers, it also elicited growing respect from his wife.

It was not a marriage made in heaven. They were developing a partnership based on mutual respect and shared goals.

That was a good deal more than many women had from the institution of marriage. She was, in truth, inordinately lucky.

So why did she feel this vague dissatisfaction?

Preparations for the house party went ahead at a furious pace. While Harrison, Bowles, and Ratcliff—along with several other prospective guests—lived near enough to ride or drive in for all activities, a number of guests would be staying over. Rooms had to be prepared for them and accommodations provided for their servants. Aunt Gertrude supervised much of this activity, but Caitlyn found herself dealing with a multitude of details.

In the midst of it all, an accident in the stables unnerved her. Tom, one of the grooms, was injured when he was crushed between a big roan and the side of a stall.

"I don't know what spooked him," the wiry little man said through painful breaths as soon as Caitlyn had rushed to his side. "He ain't never got out o' hand before."

"Ssh. Never mind right now," she soothed. "We must get the doctor for you."

Trevor arrived then and was quickly apprised of the situation. He organized two other stable hands to take Tom to his quarters and await the doctor's arrival; then he questioned others.

"Wasn't anybody in here but Tom an' me an' that new feller, Mason," the youthful Jack told him.

"And where were you? Could you see what happened?"

"No, sir. I was clear down t' other end. But Mason, he was in the stall next to where Tom and Sun's Fire was." Jack gestured to Mason, who stood in the background.

"Mason?" Trevor questioned.

"I didn't see nothin'," Mason said. "Heard the commotion, an' when I come around, Tom was already down."

Jimmy and Clarence stepped out of the stall in which Tom had been working.

"Anything?" Caitlyn asked.

"Not really. He's still skittish, though. Seems to have some tenderness on his left hind quarter," Clarence answered.

"Perhaps he was stung by a bee," Caitlyn suggested. This seemed a reasonable theory to the rest, who nodded or murmured their agreement.

Living quarters for several stable hands were located above the stables along with the office. Reluctant to invade their strictly masculine domain, Caitlyn waited in the office while Trevor accompanied the doctor to examine the injured Tom.

"How is he?" she asked the moment they returned.

The doctor responded, "He has some broken ribs. I've wrapped him tightly to hold them in place. He's in a good deal of pain. I assume you have laudanum on hand?"

Caitlyn nodded.

"He probably won't be able to work as usual for two or three weeks."

"Oh, no-o-o." Caitlyn heard herself in a near wail as the consequences of this information hit her.

"Caitlyn?" Trevor's voice held surprise at what he must have seen as her insensitivity. "We surely have enough hands to take over Tom's duties as he recuperates."

"Of course we do." She felt embarrassed at the way the doctor and Trevor were regarding her. "You misunderstand. You see, Tom is our best harness man."

"So?"

"He was to show the grays at Newmarket."

"That does pose a problem. But we shall work it out. Come." He motioned to her and the doctor. Saying he had another patient to see to, the doctor refused their offer of refreshment.

Caitlyn was lost in thought as she and Trevor made their way to the house. Once there, she immediately dispatched a servant with the painkiller and a tray of food for the injured Tom.

Later that day, the first of their guests began to arrive and her life assumed a whirlwind atmosphere.

* * *

Taking on the role of host at even such a modest gathering was a vastly new experience for Trevor. He found he quite enjoyed it. He was even able to greet Latham and Graham as resident guests with true equanimity. Theo, of course, he welcomed enthusiastically, and he looked forward to enjoying the company of Moore and Jenkins as well.

The highlights of the party—which would last for a fortnight and more—were to be a ball and, two days later, the horse show at Newmarket. To fill out the rest of the time, Caitlyn had planned a busy schedule, but one that allowed guests to participate or not at their own paces. Outdoor activities included riding, fishing, and lawn bowling. Some of the more intrepid of the men joined Trevor for his morning swims. Guests were encouraged to enjoy the gardens at their leisure. Evening found them playing cards or charades or listening to music as provided by one or the other of the ladies in the group.

Everything had gone smoothly, Trevor thought, until the ball. He knew Caitlyn had gone riding or driving with Latham and Graham on occasion, but always properly accompanied. At an *alfresco* picnic, she had spent an inordinate length of time in deep conversation with Ratcliff, but the discussion had occurred, after all, out there in front of the whole company. And, he recalled with an enormous degree of male smugness, it was his own bed she readily shared every night.

The ball—ostensibly to introduce Melanie and Andrew—was a rather large affair. Local guests swelled the attendees to well over a hundred people. Prior to the ball, there was a dinner party to which many of the "horse set" had been invited. In the drawing room, after the gentlemen had rejoined the ladies, much of the talk was in anticipation of the Newmarket show.

Trevor stood at the side of the room talking with Theo.

He observed Bowles and Harrison approach Caitlyn as she stood speaking with their wives.

"I say, Mrs. Jeffries," Harrison boomed, thus capturing the attention of nearly everyone in the room. "I just heard your driver for the team race was injured."

"Yes, he was," she said, but did not elaborate.

"How unfortunate." Harrison's tone held a distinctly false note of sympathy, Trevor thought. "I expect this means you will decline to participate, then."

"Not at all." Caitlyn's voice was casual. Too casual. Trevor waited. In the flurry of activity in the last few days, he and Caitlyn had not discussed the horse show, though he was aware that everyone at Atherton was looking forward to the meet as a means of displaying the best that Jeffries Farms had to offer.

"Oh, you have found a new driver, have you?" Bowles asked. "On such short notice?"

"We had a second driver all along," Caitlyn paused and glanced at Trevor, then back to Harrison and Bowles. Trevor felt a premonition slither through him. "I shall drive the team myself."

Stunned silence greeted this announcement. Trevor felt as though he had turned to stone. Good God! What *was* she thinking of? Handling the reins of a spirited team under ordinary driving conditions was difficult for a man—and this little slip of a woman proposed taking on such a task—in the heat of a race, yet? Impossible. Not if her husband had any say in it—not while he still drew breath!

"I beg your pardon!" Harrison sounded blustery.

"*Un*heard of," Bowles said.

"Surely you do not doubt my horsemanship?" Caitlyn's tone was silky.

"Mrs. Jeffries." Harrison apparently intended this as a fatherly reprimand. "I have the greatest respect for your ability. For a woman, you do exceedingly well."

"For a woman?"

Trevor wondered why the others did not seem to notice the steel in her voice. "Excuse me," Trevor said to Theo and moved to stand next to his wife.

Harrison continued, oblivious. "Females simply do not race teams. Good heavens, woman, they are rarely even capable as ordinary riders."

"Mrs. Jeffries is a *very* capable rider." Ratcliff joined the group as though he were leaping to Caitlyn's defense.

"That, however, does not make her a capable *driver.*" Bowles sounded testy.

"Have you seen me drive a team?" Caitlyn's tone was very reasonable.

"Well, no, but—"

Harrison interrupted. "I am not racing my team against a woman."

"Nor am I," Bowles concurred.

"May I ask why?" Caitlyn asked in that same reasonable tone.

"My dear lady." Harrison was definitely condescending now. "It would not show to our advantage to win out over a woman."

"Assuming you would, indeed, win," she responded.

"The alternative would be *most* unlikely, my dear." Harrison shrugged. "In any event, it is a moot question. I seriously doubt that any of the gentlemen showing their stock at Newmarket will agree to race against a woman."

Trevor moved closer to Caitlyn and gripped her elbow. His voice was hard. "Well, then, Harrison, you will have to settle for being bested by one of Atherton's second-rate drivers."

"And who would that be?"

"Me."

"You? Everyone knows you have not driven competitively in years."

"True. It is, however, a skill that one does not forget once it is mastered." He grinned at Caitlyn and was warmed by her blush and the appreciative twinkle in her eyes.

"Well, in that case . . ." Harrison grumbled.

"Shall we adjourn to the ballroom, my friends?" Caitlyn's voice was bright, but Trevor sensed the undertone of tension.

The ball itself proceeded without incident, for which Caitlyn was grateful. Trevor led his sister out for the first dance, and Andrew partnered Caitlyn. Soon other couples joined them. As hostess, Caitlyn had not expected to have such a good time, but she danced every dance and enjoyed the laughter and repartee with her various partners.

She thought she might have shocked any high sticklers present by dancing three times with her own husband. Although she had come to expect the intense awareness she felt when he was near, that reaction had not lessened with their increased intimacy.

She dutifully danced with her male houseguests, including Latham and Graham. Bertie had made his annoyance quite clear when Caitlyn refused a second dance with him in favor of a third with Trevor. Graham had been kindness itself since his arrival. Tall, dignified, and with an air of bearing great problems, Graham had reformist interests that paralleled her own. She simply appreciated his friendship.

As she did Sir Willard Ratcliff's. After dancing with Ratcliff, she stood on the sidelines with him, sipping a glass of lemonade.

"You were wise to let Trevor take over as driver, you know," Willard observed.

"*Let* him? You may have noticed that I had little say in the matter."

"Still, it was a good idea. Harrison does carry some weight in certain circles, as you well know. He could have made things very difficult."

"And he cannot do so now?" she asked with disbelief.

"Let me just say he is less likely to now. Besides, it truly is better for Trevor to do the driving."

"Oh? You think he is that much more skilled at handling the reins than I?"

"Well, he *is* stronger, and that is important. But it is also quite beside the point."

"And the point is . . . ?"

"Just this. I assume you mean to show your team to best advantage."

"Of course."

"How much attention do you think the animals would get when the spectators faced the unusual phenomenon of a *woman* as the driver?"

"I suppose that *is* a consideration," she said, grudgingly accepting this argument.

Ratcliff chuckled. "Harrison actually did himself a disservice."

"What do you mean?"

"I know your cattle and their lineage very well—remember? I doubt his will show to better advantage than those from Jeffries Farms. He would have done better to let potential buyers be distracted by a woman as whipster."

She laughed. "All right. You have convinced me. I shall stop feeling so put upon."

"Good." They stood in companionable silence for a moment, then Willard cleared his throat. "I . . . uh . . . I wonder if you are fully aware of how much importance is being attached to this . . . competition . . . especially between your cattle and Harrison's?"

"No more than is customary, I assume."

"But it is. I have an idea your husband is not fully aware, either."

She felt herself coloring up. She did not want to discuss—even with Willard—the fact that Trevor had only recently learned of Willard's close association with Jeffries Farms. "Why is this particular meet so extraordinary?"

"Perhaps it happened after you left the city—but there was a—*discussion*, shall we say?—in one of the clubs. White's, I think. I was not there, but it seems Lord Carstairs was bragging rather forcefully about the merits of a mount he recently purchased."

"Black Knight. A wonderful horse."

"Harrison was there, and when Carstairs made known where he had obtained this splendid animal, Harrison made a slighting remark."

"Did he now?" She could feel her hackles rising.

"Then someone else said that Jeffries Farms was producing some right smart looking carriage teams as well. Harrison took singular exception to this. One thing led to another, and the upshot of it all was a number of bets placed in the books."

"Wagers? On what?"

"Harrison's stock versus yours. To be decided at the New-market meet."

Caitlyn closed her eyes briefly. "Good heavens."

"I thought you and Trevor should know. There will be a goodly number of people in the crowd at Newmarket who have a vested interest in the outcome."

"I suppose you mean to say half the *ton's* male element will be there."

He chuckled. "Perhaps not *half,* but a goodly number. Newmarket is drawing as much interest as Brighton this year."

"Oh, good heavens," she said again. The races at Brighton were the premier competition for race horses, with the Prince himself keenly involved. "No wonder Mr. Harrison seems so self-confident."

"Smug, you mean." He was thoughtful for a moment. "Changing the subject—"

"Please do."

"I hope I am not out of line in saying this, but you seem happier—more content—now than when we were in town."

"I am always happier here at Atherton."

He took her hand and brought it to his lips. "I think it is

more than that, my dear." He laughed. "And judging by that scowl your husband is directing my way, I am sure of it."

Startled, Caitlyn looked at Trevor who stood several feet away and was, indeed, scowling. She smiled at him and withdrew her hand from Willard's grasp. Did Trevor's scowl indicate genuine feeling for her alone? Or was this merely a male creature asserting territorial rights? She hoped it was the former.

"In any event, Caitlyn, I am glad to see you happy."

"Thank you, Will. I have always valued your friendship."

"Mutual, my dear." He looked around the room. "What do you think of the Brentley chit?"

"Belinda? She seems a tolerable sort. I do not know her well. Why?"

"My mother is pushing her as a candidate to become the next Mrs. Ratcliff."

"Oh. Well, then, I shall have to become better acquainted with her."

"There is no hurry."

They were joined then by two other couples, and the talk became more general.

Later that night, she and Trevor lay together in his big four-poster bed, his arm around her, her head tucked into his shoulder. They sleepily congratulated themselves on the success of the ball. She told him of the heightened interest of the *ton* in the Newmarket meet.

"Hmm. That puts a slightly different light on things, does it not?" he observed.

"I should think so. Uh—Trevor?"

"Hmm?"

"I know that racing is not something you truly *want* to do. . . . We might be able to find a replacement for Tom."

"Other than you, you mean?"

"Yes." She told him of Ratcliff's reasoning about a woman driver.

"Ratcliff's right, of course. But it would be most difficult to replace Tom at this point with someone unfamiliar with our stock."

"Then you truly do not mind racing them yourself?"

"No, of course not."

But she thought his answer was a bit too glib.

"Let us get some sleep," he said, pulling her closer and kissing her tenderly.

She snuggled into the warm protectiveness of his embrace and was soon asleep.

Trevor lay awake for some while thinking about what had transpired and contemplating the coming race.

Caitlyn's announcement that *she* would drive the Jeffries team had struck sheer terror into his heart. Instantly, he had seen the wreckage and broken bodies of the accident that had claimed Terrence and Jason. A flashing image of Caitlyn lying sprawled, injured and unconscious, had sent a wave of nausea through him. There was no way in this world he could stand by and watch her engage in such a madcap scheme, though he readily admitted that she was assuredly the most skilled horsewoman of his acquaintance.

No! He could not run the risk of losing her, too. Not now. He kissed the top of his sleeping wife's head and drew in the faintly flowery scent of her hair.

Yes, he was doing the right thing in rescuing the reputation of the farms that bore his name—farms for which Caitlyn had worked so hard. But he could not shake a profound sense of guilt and betrayal. Had he not sworn never to do again precisely what he had just agreed to do? What kind of hypocrite was he, anyway?

With this question gnawing at him, he seemed to see Terrence and Jason as they sat across from him arguing that they should take his place in that long-ago race. Only now Terrence was saying, "This is different, Trev. This is not just a sporting event—a mindless competition of boys trying so hard to prove themselves as men that they ignore the dangers of an open road. The purpose here is to display the results of the work of many people at Atherton and to ensure proper reward for their efforts."

Jason nodded agreement.

And Caitlyn deserves this chance, Trevor thought, before drifting off to sleep himself.

Eighteen

Most of the Atherton household arose rather later than usual the next day. The morning post brought several items that had been forwarded for Melanie and Andrew and a few for other guests as well. Caitlyn was pleased to see that their guests were casual, comfortably reading their mail or newspapers, occasionally sharing tidbits of gossip.

"I see the Princess of Wales has not curbed her behavior at all," one matron noted.

"That quarrel between the Prince and the Beau seems to be taking on the proportions of a feud," grumbled a gentleman.

"One has to admire the sheer nerve of Brummel," another expounded. "Even after his ill-timed remark about Alvanley's 'fat friend,' he continues to place himself in situations where he might encounter the Prince."

"Who never acknowledges his *former* friend."

"Brummel does seem to inspire a greater degree of friendship and loyalty than does George, Prince of Wales."

This bit of desultory conversation was interrupted by a little squeal of delight from Melanie. Caitlyn lifted her eyes and waited for Melanie to explain. Trevor was less patient.

"Are you planning to share, Mel?"

"Marcus is coming home!"

"Really?" Trevor seemed as delighted as Melanie. "When?"

"It says a month here—but this was written a fortnight

ago. He will be in London and then proceed to Timberly. That means he will be there for the Harvest Festival. Oh, Trevor, do say you will be there, too. It will be a marvelous reunion."

Trevor demurred. "We shall discuss that prospect later."

Undaunted by his lack of a clear response, Melanie began to regale others of the company about her fabulous diplomat brother whose exploits were apparently second only to those of her fabulous diplomat husband.

Later in the day, she did manage to corner Trevor and drag him into the library, where Caitlyn was stealing a moment to catch up on accounts.

"I have persuaded Drew to keep the gentlemen occupied in the billiards room, and Aunt Gertrude is instructing the ladies on the particulars of raising prize roses," Melanie announced. "So now we can talk."

"About what?" Trevor asked with brotherly suspicion.

"About your visiting Timberly for the Harvest Festival."

"Visit Timberly?" Caitlyn's voice was weak as a distinct feeling of trepidation overtook her.

"The Harvest Festival is a Jeffries family tradition that goes back nearly two centuries," Melanie said. She turned to Trevor. "Have you not told her about it?"

He shrugged. "It just never came up."

"Well, it has now."

Caitlyn looked at Trevor, then at his sister. "Umm . . . Melanie, dear, has it escaped your notice that we—that is—Trevor and I—are not precisely on the best of terms with *all* of the Jeffries?"

"Yes, and it is beyond time that that situation was changed."

"And you plan to change it unilaterally, do you?" Trevor asked.

"Not exactly. I spoke with Father about it, and he truly wants to mend the breach, Trevor."

"Really? You could have fooled me."

"You may recall," Melanie said with an ultra-patient tone, "that it was Father who asked to be presented to your wife at the Prince's ball."

"And it was *his* wife and *his* heir who made a point of cutting her." Trevor's anger was evident. "Why are you urging this now, anyway?"

"I suppose the fact that Marcus is coming home pushed me over the top. However, I fully intended to broach this topic with you before I left."

"Why?"

"Trevor! It has been six years since we were all able to attend the festival. It is important that we do this."

Caitlyn could see how very important it was to Melanie, and despite her own reluctance to put herself in the path of Lydia's and Miranda's contempt, she felt sympathetic toward the distraught Melanie.

"I do not see why it is so crucial," Trevor said. "As you say, the family has missed the last six to one degree or another."

Melanie sighed, and her voice was solemn. "Because this may be the last chance we get to celebrate together."

Trevor seemed startled. "What do you mean?"

"Surely you noticed that our father is not as robust as he once was?"

"Are you saying the earl is ill?" Caitlyn asked.

"He is *very* ill," Melanie answered. "Not even the countess knows how truly serious it is."

"How did you learn of it?" her brother asked, seemingly stunned by the news.

"Well, I noticed little things, and I kept nagging at him until he told me."

"You always could get 'round him," Trevor said with a hint of long-standing sibling rivalry.

Melanie went on. "He has the wasting sickness. The physicians give him a year—perhaps more, perhaps less."

"My God!" Trevor ran his hand through his hair. "I knew something was amiss. . . ."

"Had you been able to have the longer visit I had, I am sure you would have seen it, too."

"You say the countess does not know?"

"Not yet."

"Gerald?"

"He knows, but in his blustery way he ignores the reality of it." Melanie's tone became embittered. "However, Miranda is already planning changes she will make in Timberly."

They all sat in silence for a moment as Trevor and Caitlyn digested this news. Then Melanie spoke again.

"Father wants to try to put things right with you, Trevor. He truly is sorry about how things were handled after the accident and . . . and with your marriage. I know he would very much like you to be there this year."

Caitlyn could see how affected Trevor was by this news. She spoke softly, but firmly. "I think you must go, Trevor."

"And leave you and Ashley here in East Anglia? Not for an instant."

"No. Father was very clear. He wants Caitlyn there, too. And Ashley. He even insisted on Aunt Gertrude's presence—if she will come."

"I will not have the countess—nor Gerald and Miranda—belittling my wife and pretending my daughter does not exist."

Caitlyn was heartened by this affirmation, but would treasure it later.

"I rather think they can be brought around." Melanie did not explain this enigmatic statement, but went on, "Besides, Marcus and I and Drew—*and* you, I assume—will be able to forestall and protect as necessary. No one—not even the countess—would dare insult a guest to whom Father had extended a particular invitation."

"Caitlyn?" Trevor's gaze clearly told her he would support

her view. He was leaving it to her to decide whether she should subject herself to possible censure.

"I think this is something we must do, Trevor. You would never forgive yourself for rejecting such an overture."

"We shall think on it and discuss it later and let you know," he said to Melanie, but Caitlyn thought the decision to go had, in truth, been made.

The Jeffries Farms planned to show a number of horses at Newmarket, though attention focused on the grays. The cattle were taken to Newmarket the previous day and installed under canvas awnings that served as temporary stables.

When Trevor and Caitlyn arrived with their entourage of houseguests, they found the normally sleepy little town to be the proverbial "beehive of activity." On the show grounds there were kiosks offering food and drink and a few souvenirs. Grooms stood around with particular animals, ready to describe their merits to prospective buyers.

Would-be buyers mingled with a multitude of people who seemed to be searching, not for an improved means of transportation, but for adventure and amusement. Trevor noticed many who sported the garb of well-dressed members of the *ton*. All of the serious buyers and most of the spectators were men, but there was a generous sprinkling of females in the gathering. Trevor had attended only one other such event in his entire life, but he would have known—even if Caitlyn had not passed on her information—that this was an unusual crowd for a country fair.

Small groups of men collected here and there, talking and gesticulating excitedly. Trevor surmised that they were laying bets on various races. He was pleased to see that the track on which the races were to be held was laid in a grassy field. The harness horses were on display in a separate location, and he nervously checked on his, noting that Mason and the boy, Jack, had been assigned to watch out for the grays. Jack, especially, was highly excited to be here.

Trevor examined each of the horses carefully and watched as Mason and Jack hitched them to the vehicle he would drive. It would be some minutes before their race was called.

"Trevor!"

He turned to see Theo approaching.

"Thought you might need some moral support about now."

"You know me too well, my friend."

"Nervous?"

Trevor leaned closer to Theo and said in an exaggerated stage whisper, "Very." Then in a normal tone, he added, "I took them out yesterday before they were brought here. Just to get used to them. They really *are* a fine team."

"Seem to be."

Trevor's attention was distracted by Jack's voice. "What are you doin'?"

"Just checkin' their feet and legs," Mason responded.

"Mr. Jeffries already done that."

"Did he now? Well, never hurts to double check. You wanta remember that, boy."

"Good luck, Trev." Theo held out his hand. "I shall make myself available to hold your wife's hand through this ordeal."

Trevor grinned. "Better you than Latham or Ratcliff."

"I am not at all sure you have not just cast aspersions on my reputation as a ladies' man."

Trevor grinned even wider at this. Theo was a fine man, a courageous soldier, but hardly the Don Juan type. Theo liked women well enough, and Trevor knew his friend was more sought after than even Theo himself was aware.

"I shall see you after the race." Trevor climbed into the driver's seat and took the reins and whip that Jack and Mason offered. "Here we go." He flicked the whip to urge the team to take their position on the course.

* * *

Standing with Melanie, Andrew, and others of her guests, Caitlyn watched nervously as Theo approached.

"Is everything all right?" she asked.

"Looks fine."

"Is Trevor all right?"

"He is fine, too. You must not worry about Trevor. Any man who can hold off seven or eight Frenchies single-handedly can surely manage a team of fine carriage horses."

She felt herself relaxing at this sally.

Melanie cut in with, "Seven or eight? Single-handedly? Is that true?"

"Actually, it is, but I doubt Trevor would thank me for bandying it about."

"Oh. They are starting," Melanie cried.

With Theo's and Andrew's help, the two women moved closer to the rope meant to hold back spectators. Caitlyn saw Harrison standing with some of his cronies several people down the line from her.

"Ah, Mrs. Jeffries." He tipped his hat to her. "May the best team win."

She nodded acknowledgment and turned her attention to the race. While there were three teams involved in this race, Caitlyn knew the crowd to be truly interested in only two of them—Harrison's and Atherton's. The race would consist of three laps around the track.

Harrison's blacks were off the mark first, but gradually Trevor maneuvered his vehicle even with theirs. At the beginning of the second lap, the grays shot ahead and there was an excited reaction from the crowd. As some cheered and others groaned, they all watched eagerly as Atherton's grays established a commanding lead over the other two teams.

Then, as the leading grays rounded the curve ending the second lap, the crowd noise took on a more subdued tone.

"What's he doing?"

"What's wrong?"

"Is he forfeiting?" This was a burst of surprised outrage.

Craning her head to see beyond the much larger men who also strained for a view, Caitlyn saw Trevor pulling hard on the reins. Despite his efforts, sheer momentum kept the team going at a furious pace. However, the grays responded to the driver's commands, and as they approached the area where Caitlyn stood, she saw with a sinking heart both Harrison's and the other team pass the team from Jeffries Farms.

"What's going on here?" Harrison sounded both curious and angry. He shot a baleful look at Caitlyn.

She shrugged helplessly even as she tried vainly to see what *was* going on. Then other snippets of comments registered.

"Look. The left horse."

"Yea. His front leg."

" 'e's a' favorin' it."

"Something is definitely wrong with that horse's foreleg." This word made its way through the crowd as Caitlyn watched Trevor guide the team off the track.

"Come." She tugged at Theo's arm only vaguely aware of the race continuing behind her. Melanie and Andrew followed closely.

When they reached Trevor and the team, they found a number of people had already gathered. Trevor jumped down from the driver's seat. Jack and Clarence Tanner stood holding the harness at the team's heads, calming the animals. Trevor was running his hand over the front legs of the left horse. The horse was skittish, obviously distrustful. Clarence crooned comforting works to it as Trevor continued the examination. Caitlyn moved closer.

When he lifted the horse's right foreleg to examine the hoof, Caitlyn saw it even as Trevor said, "Aha. Here's the problem." With his finger, he tried to dislodge the stone they all saw.

"Here." Someone thrust a small, dull hook into his hand. He popped the stone out with the hook.

Trevor picked up the stone, looked at it, and handed it to

Caitlyn. It was small and sharp and must have hurt like the very devil, she thought. She handed it to Clarence, who drew in a long whistling breath. The horse put its foot down gingerly and looked around as though to say "thank you."

Trevor patted him on the neck. "You are all right now, boy." Then he turned pain-filled eyes to Caitlyn. "I'm sorry, Caitlyn. I am so very sorry. I wanted to do this for you." He lifted his arms in a helpless gesture.

Without an instant of hesitation and without consciously considering her actions or their audience—seeing only his need and her need to answer it—she walked into his arms and felt them enfold her tightly.

"Never mind, darling, never mind." Her arms around his neck, she held his head close, the endearment had come unplanned, unbidden. "You did the right thing in stopping. It would have been unconscionable to do otherwise."

Suddenly aware of others, she stepped back, but Trevor kept one arm around her waist, as though he were reluctant to break the contact.

Clarence held up the stone for others to see. "Thing like this could do real damage to a horse. Maybe even cripple him permanently. Good job you stopped, sir."

The horsemen in the crowd agreed.

Trevor's brow wrinkled in consternation. "I'm wondering where this stone came from. All we see here are smooth round pebbles."

"That's right," someone said in surprise.

" 'Twas a good race," someone else said. "Shame it had to be stopped."

"Couldn't be helped, though," another replied.

A large, middle-aged man with a distinguished air about him shouldered his way through the crowd. He handed Trevor a card.

"My name is Nelson, sir. I represent the Duke and Duchess of Blasingstoke." The man's tone was authoritative but hearty.

"Yes?" Trevor responded.

"Those are damned fine looking animals. Begging your pardon, ma'am." Nelson lifted his hat in Caitlyn's direction. "I like a man who protects his cattle. I am interested in buying this team right now, and I would like to discuss others you may have available now or later."

Caitlyn listened quietly as Trevor invited Nelson to Atherton to look over other carriage horses. She caught the eye of Ratcliff, who gave her an encouraging grin. Blasingstoke was known to keep one of the finest stables in the realm.

Later, Caitlyn and Trevor shared their carriage with Melanie and Andrew on the return to Atherton.

"I must say," Melanie observed, "you two seem to have turned a possible disaster into a triumph!"

"That we have," Trevor replied, but it was Caitlyn's gaze he held as he turned to her on the seat next him. "Disaster to triumph," he said softly as he brought his lips soundly down upon hers. She knew he meant far more than the horse race.

"Drew, darling," Melanie asked in an ultra-casual tone, "do you feel we are perhaps a trifle *de trop* at the moment?"

The next few days were among the happiest of Caitlyn's life. Soon all of their guests had departed except for Melanie and her family. Caitlyn and Trevor were rarely out of each other's sight, though they shared a great many of their daylight hours with the rest of the family.

Perhaps, Caitlyn mused, she had not captured her husband's heart as Juliet had Romeo's. Perhaps that kind of love existed only in stories and never—or rarely—in real life. The truth was, he had made a great personal sacrifice in agreeing to run that race for her and for Jeffries Farms. She could not but be grateful to him. She could not help loving him for the man he was.

The work schedules and routine training in the stables continued as before—with one exception. The groom Mason had disappeared. In discussing this strange occurrence, Trevor and Caitlyn recalled that, not only was Mason the last person to examine the grays, he had also been working in the next stall when Tom was injured.

"Do you suppose he deliberately tried to undermine our success?" Caitlyn asked Trevor.

"He had opportunity and he is gone now, but that hardly constitutes proof."

"So—we may never know the truth." Wanting the matter brought to a neat, tidy conclusion, Caitlyn was mildly frustrated by their lack of answers.

"Who hired him?" Trevor asked. "Jack said he was new. How new?"

"He came to Atherton after we went to town for the season."

"But who actually hired him?"

"I suppose Felkins did, but he would have consulted with Jimmy or Mr. Tanner, I am certain."

"Do we know where he came from? Did he have references we could check?" Trevor persisted.

"References can be forged. I honestly do not know where he came from. Perhaps Mr. Felkins can tell us."

When Mr. Felkins presented himself, the steward seemed agitated and embarrassed when asked if he knew anything of Mason.

"I think I know more now than I did when he arrived. You know what the sages say of hindsight."

"I do not understand," Caitlyn said.

"He came with proper recommendations and all. Seemed good with the stock, though he kept to himself a lot, the others tell me. After he disappeared, it hit me. Don't know why it did not occur to me earlier."

"What? *What* hit you?" Caitlyn's patience was wearing thin.

"Mason was Mrs. Bassett's maiden name."

"They were related?" Trevor asked. Caitlyn had explained

earlier about dismissing the housekeeper and the woman's
seemingly idle threats.

"Perhaps her threats were not so idle, after all," Trevor
noted. "We could ask the magistrate to question her—for all
the good it might do."

"That would be difficult," Felkins said. "She's gone. Left
the area—along with Mason, it seems. Some say she is living
with a sister in Sussex. Word is she had a fierce quarrel with
her son-in-law. Looks like she will be gone a good long
while."

"As I said, we may never know the truth," Caitlyn said.

"Perhaps we learned *something*, though," Trevor said.
When Caitlyn and Mr. Felkins stared at him with curiosity,
he continued, "We know now to keep a closer watch on new
people until they prove themselves."

With that, the matter was closed, and Caitlyn concentrated
on enjoying the interlude before the journey to Timberly.

She knew she would remember these days as an idyllic
time. The two sets of young parents decided to teach their
daughters to ride. Trevor found two small ponies on a neighboring farm, and squeals of delight from the little girls mingled with laughter and advice from their parents.

Aunt Gertrude joined them on some of their outings and
for most meals. Several times, Caitlyn caught the older
woman eyeing her nephew and his wife with a satisfied
look. One morning as Caitlyn sat in the sun room idly
catching up on gossipy items in the newspaper, Aunt Gertrude came in.

"Caitlyn, my dear, might I have a serious word with you?"

Caitlyn immediately set aside the newspaper. "What is it?"

"Nothing to be alarmed about, I assure you."

Caitlyn relaxed, but waited with anticipation.

"You may remember that when I first came to Atherton,
I told you I would stay as long as you needed me?"

"Y-yes . . ." Caitlyn was fearful of where this was leading.

"Well, it occurs to me that you no longer have need of a

chaperon—or a companion. It would appear that you and Trevor have resolved the differences between you. In fact, I would wager that you are quite content now."

"Yes. I am. But while I may have little need of a chaperon, I still very much welcome your company."

"I know you do, my dear. And I am ever so grateful for that. But I think I should like to spend more time in town."

"You would leave us?" Caitlyn could not help the wailing note of despair in her tone.

"Not permanently, dear. I know you have little interest in spending more time in the city, but I should like to be there for the little season."

"You *will* come back then?"

"But of course."

Caitlyn rose from her chair to sit next to the older woman on a settee and put her arm around her shoulder. "Aunt Gertrude, you must know that you are precious to me. I went without a mother for so many years—and then there *you* were."

"Thank you, love." Aunt Gertrude had tears in her eyes.

"Very well," Caitlyn said in a parody of granting permission. "You may go to town, if you must, but you will promise to come back and I will keep your room always ready for you. You must join us for Christmas, though."

"I should love to. Thank you for understanding, Caitlyn dear."

"Oh! And you *will* go to Timberly with us, will you not? I really do not think I could face Trevor's mother without you by my side."

Caitlyn and Trevor had agreed to accompany Melanie and Andrew back to Timberly for the all-important Harvest Festival. Caitlyn dreaded the encounter, but she knew it was important for Trevor to make this visit. There was, of course, the matter of his father's health. But Caitlyn thought he needed this meeting to achieve a sense of completion to a particularly painful aspect of his life. Now she was begging Aunt Gertrude to see her through yet another crisis.

"I would not miss it for the world," the intrepid Lady Gertrude Hermiston said.

Nineteen

A caravan of carriages—five in all—set off for Timberly in the southwest section of England. The Jeffries and Sheffield families had two vehicles each, and since Aunt Gertrude planned to proceed to London from Timberly, she traveled in her own coach.

It was a long, tiring journey, though they planned a leisurely pace with comfortable stops at inns along the way. To relieve the boredom, the occupants of the carriages switched places periodically. They also read aloud from books—mostly novels—they had chosen for the trip.

Still, there was a good deal of time for conversation, and Caitlyn learned all about the Timberly Harvest Festival one afternoon as she sat comfortably leaning against Trevor across from Melanie and Andrew.

"It began," Melanie explained, "as a religious gathering to offer thanks for good crops and it just grew from that."

"Needless to say, there is a great deal of tradition about it, too," Trevor said. "For instance, the earl is expected to bring a sack of his own grain to the mill to be ground."

Melanie gave a little laugh. "In former times, it was a huge sack that he was expected to hoist to his shoulders. Nowadays, it is largely symbolic—weighing about ten pounds—a stone or two at most."

Trevor went on. "The resulting flour—or some of it—is baked into a loaf that is shared at a huge dinner for the entire estate."

"That must be quite a loaf," Caitlyn observed.

Melanie smiled. "Oh, it is. But it is merely a symbol for all the other loaves that arrive."

Caitlyn could not resist asking, "And does Lord Wyndham provide fishes as well?"

The others were momentarily puzzled, then hooted with laughter. Trevor gave her a gentle pinch on the arm.

"Do not be sacrilegious, my dear."

She ignored this. "Is there anything else I should know about this grand affair?"

"Hmm. Well," Trevor said, "it goes on for three days. It is really like a country fair or market."

Melanie added, "There are jugglers and clowns, Gypsy fortune tellers, and acrobats. It truly is great fun." "And the beer flows freely," the usually quiet Andrew put in.

"It culminates with a grand ball in the great hall." Melanie smiled in anticipatory delight.

"The great hall?" Caitlyn asked.

Melanie shot her brother an exasperated look. "Honestly, Trevor, have you told her nothing of your youth, your boyhood home? What *do* the two of you talk about?—Whoops! Never mind answering that."

"Honestly, Melanie," her brother imitated her tone, "do you ever *think* before you speak? And you married to a diplomat!"

Melanie gave him a saucy look, stuck out her tongue quickly, and then focused on Caitlyn. "Timberly was once a castle."

"A castle?"

Trevor explained. "A rather modest castle even in its heyday. The moat is long since gone, and the wall that once surrounded the keep and other buildings was used as a quarry for houses and barns on tenant farms."

"Sounds fascinating."

"As children we loved the place with its strange rooms

and passageways." Melanie leaned forward with childlike excitement. "There is even a ghost in the tower."

"Melanie, you know very well it is the wind that makes that strange noise."

Melanie ignored Trevor's interruption. "But it is a friendly ghost. She was a beautiful daughter of the third earl who pined away when her father refused to allow her to wed the man she loved. He died in battle and she never married. Now she wanders the battlements calling her lover's name."

Trevor snorted. " 'Tis the wind. And there are no battlements."

"There once were. Besides, my tale is far more romantic than ' 'tis the wind.' Do you not agree, Caitlyn?"

"Oh, of course."

Caitlyn was grateful for this lighthearted banter. Not only was she learning about what to expect when they arrived, she was gaining further insight into the life experiences that had shaped the man she willingly admitted—if only to herself—that she loved. The discussion also diverted her from worrying about the reception she herself might receive at Timberly. Could she endure for the planned three weeks?

In the event, the earl received her cordially. His second son, Marcus, was warm but initially somewhat reserved in greeting this sister-in-law he had not met before. However, there was no reservation at all in the greeting between Marcus and Trevor. Although Marcus was some years older, Caitlyn sensed genuine affection between these two brothers—the same regard for each other that characterized Trevor's friendship with Theo and, to a certain extent, with Andrew.

If one were to judge another by the respect he or she commanded, Caitlyn thought, then her husband was a very worthy man indeed.

Gerald was aloof but carefully polite to her. Miranda and the countess were cool in acknowledging her. Melanie had assured her that the earl would ensure a guest's comfort, and now Caitlyn surmised that the countess and Miranda had had strict orders to behave themselves. Nevertheless, it was clear to Caitlyn that these two women found her presence distasteful.

Caitlyn, however, was determined to see this thing through—for Trevor's sake. Had he not taken over that race for *her*? She could do this much for him.

By the second day of the visit, Caitlyn was aware of the "protection" that others were according her. When the whole family gathered, Trevor never left her side. If the ladies met separately, Melanie or Aunt Gertrude always maneuvered to place themselves as buffers between Caitlyn and her mother-in-law and the mother-in-law's favorite daughter-in-law.

A few days after the arrival of the Atherton visitors, the castle began to fill with other guests. These were largely members of the *ton*—leaders of society and important members of political and financial circles. The women seemed to take their cue from the countess, according Caitlyn cool, grudging admission to their circle.

One afternoon as the gentlemen were off on a shooting expedition, the ladies met for tea in the drawing room. Caitlyn felt Miranda gaze at her in a calculated manner. When Caitlyn caught her eye, Miranda looked away with a haughty shrug.

"Such a shame," Miranda said to the room at large, "that La Contessa Oliveira could not come to the Harvest Festival."

"I did invite her," the countess assured her audience. "She was such a dear in making Trevor comfortable in her homeland, I felt it incumbent upon his family to return the favor."

Caitlyn knew very well this bit of dialogue was designed for her. She tried not to let it hurt or irritate her. But it did both. She glanced at Aunt Gertrude, who rolled her eyes in disgust.

It was Melanie who responded. "Oh, I imagine Colonel de Lessup is managing to make her welcome enough without our help. After all, it was Trevor who persuaded the rather shy Anthony de Lessup that Dolores was truly interested in him."

This brought an immediate buzz of response in the room. Melanie leaned over to say quietly to Caitlyn, "That is absolutely true, in case you wondered. Theo told me."

Caitlyn was pleased by this information—and grateful to Melanie for diverting the spite intended by Miranda and Lydia.

"Trust our Melanie," Aunt Gertrude murmured approvingly as the general conversation turned to other topics.

Caitlyn, Melanie, and Aunt Gertrude continued to spend a good deal of time with the children. They took Ashley and Elizabeth on walks in the elaborate gardens. They played hide-and-seek and other childhood games with the girls. Occasionally their fathers joined in the fun.

Although neither the countess nor Miranda was especially fond of children, both seemed to try to be tolerant. They tended to be effusive in singing the praises of "darling Elizabeth," hugging Melanie's child and readily holding her hand on walks. It infuriated Caitlyn, Aunt Gertrude—and Melanie—to see grown women thus exclude an innocent child. Caitlyn tried to compensate by showering more affection on Ashley, but she knew Ashley sensed her grandmother's antipathy.

After two days of this subtle exclusion, Aunt Gertrude had had enough. "I am going to speak to Lydia. This is ridiculous—and hurtful."

"Do you really think you should?" Caitlyn questioned.

"*Someone* should! And the men rarely have opportunity to see such despicable behavior."

Sometime later, Caitlyn saw Aunt Gertrude in another section of the garden in earnest conversation with the countess. Lydia sported two bright spots of color and raised her voice, though Caitlyn could not distinguish her words. Soon, the countess cast a malevolent look in Caitlyn's direction and stalked back to the house with an angry flounce.

"Oh, dear," Caitlyn murmured to herself.

A furious Aunt Gertrude immediately sought Caitlyn to say, "That woman drives me mad. It is hard to believe she was related to the man I loved."

"What happened?"

"You cannot want to hear her exact words."

"The gist of them, then."

"She says her husband and Marcus may be willing to accept a cuckoo in the nest, but she and Miranda and Gerald never will."

Saddened but not surprised by this comment, Caitlyn felt tears stinging her eyes. "She simply refuses to believe. And frankly, I am not at all sure the earl and Marcus truly believe Ashley is Trevor's child. I think they *accept* her because they know Trevor wants them to do so."

Aunt Gertrude patted her hand. "At least Trevor believes it—and that is what is truly important."

"Yes. Trevor believes it. But I think it hurts him—as it hurts me—for our daughter to suffer any degree of rejection. And what happens when Ashley is grown? Will her own grandmother continue to view her as an interloper? The *ton* is likely to take its cue from a socially prominent countess. Will Lydia and Miranda spoil my daughter's chances in life?"

"You must not fret about it, dear. In truth, the *ton* will not care. Many an elevated matron in society has borne children who were not fathered by her husband."

"*Not* in my family. Nor yours. And, apparently, not in Trevor's. I hate that such a label is so unfairly attached to Ashley—and to me. I hate it!" She clutched her fists helplessly in her lap.

Aunt Gertrude put her arm around Caitlyn and held her close. The older woman's voice had tears in it as she said, "I know, dear, I know. Perhaps in time . . ."

"Perhaps." But Caitlyn did not believe time would influence the cold heart of the countess.

She did not want to burden Trevor with her worries, but these days it was not easy to keep anything from him. He had become extraordinarily sensitive to even the slightest changes in her mood. That night, he lay in bed watching as she brushed her hair thoroughly and began to pin it up.

"No. Leave it loose," he said. "I like to see it down." He gazed at her, the beginnings of desire clear in his eyes. She looked away. Immediately, he rose on one elbow. "What is the matter, Caitlyn? Is something wrong?"

"No, nothing. Nothing at all."

"Come here." He scooted over and threw back the covers to welcome her. When she was firmly ensconced in his arms, he put his lips against her temple. "Tell me. Let us have no secrets between us."

"Oh, Trevor, I did not want to burden you."

His response was a tender growl. "Out with it, wife."

And so she told him—everything, including her thoughts about the attitudes of the earl and Marcus. He was quiet for such a long time that she feared his reaction. She twisted slightly to look at him, the light from a bedside lamp revealing his grim expression. He tightened his embrace, and there was a certain sadness in his voice.

"My mother is one of the most arrogant, unfeeling females who ever existed. And Miranda is of the same ilk. What's more, she—the countess—was likely guilty at one time of what she suspects of you—and of me."

"Oh, Trevor—no!"

"I do not know that for a certainty—and I do not *want* to know—but I am sure my father knows—or suspects it."

"How sad for him."

Pulling back, Trevor stared at her. "Caitlyn, you are a wonder! Instead of anger at her, your first reaction is sympathy for him."

She did not know what to say.

He drew her closer again. "You are right about how Father and Marcus feel. They have said nothing to me, but I believe they are both willing to take their cue from me. And neither of them would knowingly hurt a child. Or anyone else, for that matter."

"And Gerald?"

"The heir apparent is as arrogant and pigheaded as our

mother. And as shallow. Sometimes I truly believe he has room to let upstairs, for he must be hit over the head before an idea sinks in."

"I suppose there are a good many people like that in the world."

"Unfortunately."

"Perhaps they *will* all come around eventually," she said, but even she knew she did not sound very convincing.

When he did not respond for a long period, she wondered if he had fallen asleep.

"Caitlyn?"

"Hmm?"

"Would you rather we left? We can return to Atherton tomorrow, if you wish. I will not have you hurt."

She felt a delicious warmth at these words. Actually, he offered precisely what she *wanted* to do—go home to Atherton with her own little family.

"No. I—we—cannot do that, Trev. Your father would be very hurt. He wants this time with his children around him. And . . . and I am sure he deserves this much. I can endure. And Ashley is too young to comprehend."

"Oh, God, Caitlyn, I love you." The words seemed wrenched out of him. "You are so good and kind and true—"

She thought her heart would explode with its fullness. She stopped his words with a fierce kiss.

"And I love you," she said, "but I never dared hope—"

It was his turn to stop her words as she had his. "I don't deserve you, Caitlyn, my love."

She took his face in her hands and held his gaze. "Love is not to be 'deserved.' It just *is*. It is a gift from heaven, and one we have only to accept."

"Oh, I do accept." The pledge in his eyes was a reflection of that in her own. "I accept with humility and gratitude." He kissed her deeply.

"And with just a touch of passion?" she teased.

"And with an everlasting reserve of passion," he said—and

proceeded to spend much of the night establishing the truth of that assertion.

Sometime during the night, Caitlyn and Trevor had agreed that they would return to Atherton soon after the grand ball that was to be the climax of the Harvest Festival. Three more days, Caitlyn told herself. Meanwhile, she set out to enjoy as much of the company as she found congenial and to spend time with Melanie, whom she had come to love dearly. Melanie and Andrew would stay at Timberly until the Congress was truly convened in Vienna to deal with Bonaparte's now defunct empire.

Caitlyn appeared at the ball in an ivory gown of shimmering silk. The dress was designed on classical Greek lines, and her hair was arranged in a classical style as well. She also wore the diamonds and emeralds Trevor had given her in London. She knew the two of them made a striking pair this night. In his dark, stylish evening wear, he quite took her breath away.

Melanie had taken her on a tour of the castle when they arrived, so she was not surprised by either the size or decor of the great hall, which soared upward two stories and contained armor and armaments, some dating back to the Middle Ages. An enormous fireplace dominated one long wall of the spectacular room.

On the walls at either end were hung tapestries that must have been especially commissioned for this room. One depicted a scene from the Battle of Agincourt, in which a Jeffries ancestor had distinguished himself. The other showed a highly stylized and symbolic hunting scene, complete with unicorn.

Light from two massive chandeliers of brass and crystal, with dozens of candles each, bounced off the pieces of armor. Chairs and settees arranged strategically around the room seemed dwarfed by the scale of the room itself. The focal

point of Timberly's great hall was the fireplace on one wall—
or, rather, the painting that hung over it.

The work—of such dimensions that the figures in it were
life-sized—was a portrait of the current earl and his family,
made when the older children were young adolescents, the
twins six or seven, and Melanie four or five years of age.
They were an incredibly handsome family, Caitlyn thought.
She noticed that the countess—still a strikingly lovely
woman—tonight wore a gown that, though modern in style,
had obviously been designed with the gown in the portrait in
mind.

In the portrait, the earl and his four sons were all dressed
in formal wear, while the child Melanie was attired in a beautiful dress of royal blue trimmed in silver. The artist had captured handily her golden curls and sparkling eyes, and the
sense of closeness between the twins and their little sister.

"What a beautiful family," Caitlyn said softly to Trevor.

"I suppose we were," he agreed, "but you see how the
family was divided even then. Notice that Father is off to the
side slightly—above it all, aloof. Gerald and the countess
were quite a team even then."

"And you three younger ones seem to have made a pact
against the world.

He laughed. "Well, against the rest of the family, anyway.
Though we quite liked Marcus—see how he sort of hovers
protectively there?"

"And did he? Protect you, I mean?"

"Always."

Caitlyn looked around the crowded room. "Have you seen
Melanie?"

"Not yet. Andrew is here, though. Melanie is always late.
I guess some things never change."

The Earl of Wyndham and his countess, along with Gerald
and Miranda, were holding court, as it were, in front of the
fireplace, beneath that spectacular portrait. The room was
abuzz with dozens of conversations, and musicians played

softly in the background. In a few moments the dancing would begin.

Then quite suddenly it began to grow quiet in the room. The silence swept in a wave from the entrance. Even the musicians faltered and stopped as a path was cleared between the group at the fireplace and the vision at the door.

Caitlyn drew a long, deep breath.

"Good God!" Trevor murmured in wonder.

There stood Melanie arrayed in a grown-up version of the royal blue dress that the child Melanie wore in the portrait. In each hand she held the hand of a modern duplicate of the little girl with golden curls and sparkling eyes. Ashley and Elizabeth were wearing identical replicas of the gown the girl child wore in the portrait.

A wide smile broke across Trevor's face, and soon he was laughing aloud. "Trust Melanie to make her statement in a most dramatic way."

Still gripping a child's hand in each of hers, Melanie strode the path that had been spontaneously cleared for her toward the stunned tableau at the fireplace. Just as she reached it, Andrew and Marcus joined her.

"Come, my darling," Trevor whispered with a touch of irony. "We must not be left out of this family picture. Melanie needs our support."

They arrived in time to hear the countess hiss at Melanie, "Have you completely lost possession of your senses?"

But the earl was smiling broadly. Despite his precarious health and sallow color, his voice was strong as he announced, "Ladies and gentlemen, may I present my granddaughters— Ashley and Elizabeth." He patted each child on the head, then laughed. "Or is it Elizabeth and Ashley? You know, my twins were ten years old before I could tell them apart."

With that, the guests let out a collectively held breath and the room erupted in murmurs of wonder and approval. Someone motioned the musicians to resume playing. Caitlyn heard snatches of conversation.

"Exactly like that portrait."

"Darling children."

"Which one is which?"

And "Lydia will never be able to deny that child now."

Ashley, seeing her father, said, "Auntie Mel told me and 'Liz'beth we could come to the ball. It was to be a s'prise. Are you s'prised, Papa?"

Trevor bent to swing her into his arms. "Yes, poppet, I am 's'prised.' " He kissed her cheek. "You may have one dance and then it's off to bed with you."

"*Both* of them," Melanie said.

Ashley put a small hand on his cheek to turn his face to hers. "May we each have one of those lemon tarts Cook was making, too?"

Trevor's response was a laugh that was at once carefree and loving. The musicians swung into a waltz, and Trevor and Andrew charmed everyone in the room by taking the floor with their small daughters.

Alfred, Lord Wyndham, then asked Caitlyn to dance, and Marcus joined them with his sister. Soon, others caught the spirit of the dancing pairs already on the floor. Caitlyn and her father-in-law moved closer to Trevor and Ashley.

"How about we trade partners, son?" the earl asked.

Then Caitlyn was in Trevor's arms, and as the two of them watched fondly, the earl lifted Ashley into his arms and whirled her around the floor.

"My father knows how to make a statement, too," Trevor said, pride overcoming a catch in his voice.

Epilogue

Trevor settled at his desk to deal with a modest pile of correspondence that had arrived with the midmorning post. As was his custom, he saved the best till last. Thus, it was some time before he actually read the letter from his brother Marcus.

Marcus was now the Earl of Wyndham. Trevor thought with sadness of his father who had died only weeks before Napoleon escaped from Elba. At least he was spared the terror that event posed for England, Trevor thought. But he also missed knowing his newest grandchildren by only a few weeks.

Trevor's heart filled as he thought of his family—Caitlyn, Ashley, and the twins, Terrence and Jason. He smiled at the memory of the surprise Jason had been. The midwife had warned them that she suspected there might be *two* babies, but Caitlyn had dismissed the idea and so he had as well. Later, he thought his wife had dissembled a trifle in that—to spare *him* the worry she sensed in him.

He remembered the sheer joy he and Caitlyn had shared with her pregnancy. If anything, she had seemed even more beautiful to him then. There had been a special glow or aura about her. And now she had it again, though it was early yet. They were both hoping for another girl this time.

Ashley had initially greeted the advent of baby brothers

with special glee. She had warm, living dolls to play with! However, as the babies became pesky little brothers who refused to cooperate at her miniature tea table, she was less enchanted with them. Still, she tended to "mother" them—with a protective attitude that clearly imitated their mama.

He picked up the letter again. Seeing the earl's coat of arms on the seal in connection with Marcus still caught him by surprise. Though it was not an especially *welcomed* idea, the entire family had fully expected Gerald to hold the title for several decades. Such was not to be. Within a matter of months, Gerald, too, was dead of a virulent fever, leaving no direct issue. Miranda's tenure had been blessedly short, considering her grandiose plans for changing both Timberly and Wyndham House in London.

Taking the missive with him, Trevor went in search of his wife. He found her in the garden playing hide and seek with all three children and their nursemaid. Caitlyn strolled toward him, leaving the children at play under the watchful eye of the maid.

Seeing the paper he held, she said, "Is something amiss, love?"

"No, not at all." He frowned. "Should you be running about like this?"

"Now, Trevor, you know very well I need to exercise."

"Hmmph."

She laughed and waved at his paper. "What have you there?"

"A letter from Marcus. He has invited us to this year's Harvest Festival at Timberly."

"He plans to renew the family tradition, then?"

"Yes. Proper mourning for first father, then Gerald, effectively eliminated the festival the last two years."

"And you wish to go." She smiled indulgently.

"Well—yes. It would afford opportunity to see Melanie and Andrew as well. And," he could hear his own eagerness mounting, "Marcus is also inviting one of my comrades from the Peninsula days—Captain Berwyn. He is now a baronet."

"How did Marcus come to know him?" Her voice showed casual curiosity.

"Hmm. I am not sure." He consulted the letter again. "Apparently something to do with this ward Marcus inherited along with the earldom. Small world, what?"

"It would be nice to see Melanie again."

"Aunt Gertrude will be there, too."

"Wonderful! And the countess?"

"I doubt Miranda will be there," he said, deliberately misunderstanding her.

She swatted him playfully on the shoulder. "You know very well I was referring to the *dowager* countess—my inimitable mama-in-law."

"We are spared. My mother is still in Italy."

Caitlyn did not say so, but Trevor knew his mother's absence would make the proposed visit more attractive to his wife.

"I assume the invitation includes the children," she said.

"Of course. The Harvest Festival would not be the same without multitudes of children."

She laughed. "I see—they are part of the 'harvest'—is that it?"

"You might say that." He gave her a smug grin, then turned serious. "My only concern is whether you should travel such a distance." He slid his arm around her waist and steered her to a more secluded area of the garden.

She gave him a quick kiss on the cheek. "You must not worry. It is very early yet. I hardly show—even when I have few clothes on," she said with a blush and a teasing smile.

"True." He allowed his hand to rest on the barely perceptible swelling of her abdomen. He nuzzled her neck just below her ear. "And even with all these clothes on, you are a very enticing bit, my wife." His voice was husky.

"Trevor! It is the middle of the afternoon!"

"So?" He laughed.

"So. Save your enticement—*your* children are demanding attention."

And sure enough, insistent calls of "Mama!" and "Papa!" penetrated his consciousness.

He gave an exaggerated sigh and kissed her deeply. "Tonight, my sweet."

"Tonight," she murmured, her lips lingering on his, her promise a symbol of happiness that he might once never have imagined.

ABOUT THE AUTHOR

Wilma Counts lives in Nevada. She is currently working on her fifth Zebra regency romance, THE TROUBLE WITH HARRIET, the story of Marcus, his precocious ward and the troublesome woman with whom he shares guardianship. Look for THE TROUBLE WITH HARRIET in July 2001. Wilma loves hearing from readers and you may write to her c/o Zebra Books. Please include a self-addressed stamped envelope if you wish a response, or you may e-mail her: *wilma@ableweb.net*

BOOK YOUR PLACE ON OUR WEBSITE AND MAKE THE READING CONNECTION!

We've created a customized website just for our very special readers, where you can get the inside scoop on everything that's going on with Zebra, Pinnacle and Kensington books.

When you come online, you'll have the exciting opportunity to:

- View covers of upcoming books
- Read sample chapters
- Learn about our future publishing schedule (listed by publication month *and author*)
- Find out when your favorite authors will be visiting a city near you
- Search for and order backlist books from our online catalog
- Check out author bios and background information
- Send e-mail to your favorite authors
- Meet the Kensington staff online
- Join us in weekly chats with authors, readers and other guests
- Get writing guidelines
- AND MUCH MORE!

**Visit our website at
http://www.zebrabooks.com**

More Zebra Regency Romances